NO PRECEDE

John Uttley was born in Lancashire just as the war was ending. Grammar school educated there, he read Physics at Oxford before embarking on a long career with the CEGB and National Grid Group. He was Finance Director at the time of the miners' strike, the Sizewell Inquiry and privatisation, receiving on OBE in 1991. Shortly afterwards, he suffered his fifteen minutes of fame when he publicly gave a dividend to charity in the middle of the fat cat furore. Following this, he took an external London degree in Divinity while acting as chairman of numerous smaller companies, both UK and US based. He is married to Janet, living just north of London. This is his second novel. Since writing the first, he has undergone several of the rites of passage of later life; in particular, he has given up up his residual business interests, his three grown children have flown the nest, and the old family dog has died.

NO PRECEDENT

John Uttley

For the means of grace, and for the hope of glory.

Book One

CHAPTER ONE
March 2015

I'd better introduce myself, in case anybody ever gets to read this. You never know, maybe I'll die before I've decided it's best thrown away. It's going to be as near factual as I can manage, as I'm losing my taste for fiction. Truth's meant to be stranger than that. I've always wanted to write, and something's happened today which might just end up as interesting. To me that is, probably not to you. I've often wondered if telling a real story can reveal a hidden meaning. Maybe this is a chance to see.

I'm Bob Swarbrick, born and bred in the Lancashire village of St Chad's. It's at the west end of the Fylde, only a few miles outside Blackpool. I don't live there now, having moved away for the second time a few years ago. My daughter does though, in my old house. I'm often back with my new partner, Wendy. The other folk I visit when I'm home, my mother, father and four grandparents, are all resident in the one place, just a few plots from each other, pushing up daisies in the cemetery at the edge of the village. I've a fair number of other relations and a few too many friends in there too. Decades ago, after my divorce and before Wendy and I got it together, I booked a plot for myself, near enough to the gate for me to look for an escape if I'm sent to the wrong place. Behind the funeral chapel, which serves both the quick and the dead, is a lavatory, only for the first category as far as I can tell. I sometimes have to be very quick in getting there nowadays. I'm past my three score and ten, and not too long ago I had a big heart attack, so it may not be long before I'm six feet under.

And there, from the very spot where the grave digger will be digging one day soon, is where I saw him. As I walked the familiar path from my parents to my grandparents, we were nearly close enough to each other for recognition to become possible. He was wearing an unnecessarily heavy black overcoat. In silhouette, he could have been the grim reaper if only he'd been carrying a sickle. The air was actually quite warm and there was enough blue in the sky to give the hope that the Lancashire rain would miss us, but in the distance, behind a fluffy cumulus, I could see a heavily-laden nimbus slowly and darkly plodding its weary way in our direction, like a bladder about to pass its load through an enlarged prostate. He was standing silently by a grave with a shiny headstone.

"Grand day," I said, although it wasn't really, hoping for some further spur to recognition. And that's what I got.

"You've got to be Bob Swarbrick, still seeing the bright side. And that's after a life more than fully lived, judging by the wrinkles on your face. Am I right or am I right?" he asked. There could only be one answer.

"As you always were, you're right, and after all this time you can still only be Paul Eckersley," I replied.

That wasn't a totally inspired guess as his surname was inscribed twice on the grave, that of his parents, which, despite a tricky reflection caused by the sun, I'd just managed to read without needing to get my glasses out. A light glaze on my gravestone will be enough, I decided. I don't go for ostentation. I hadn't seen Paul or given a moment's thought about him for fifty-odd years. I looked him in the eyes, up for a scrap I didn't expect to win. "Is there a knighthood to go with that now? Or a hereditary earldom?"

"Neither, Bob. I ended up as a humble housemaster at a minor public school."

I backed off, feeling guilty. If the headstone was a shade too showy for my taste, it couldn't be said to represent a wider vanity. Paul's parents had chosen to come back to Lancashire to be buried. The stone would have been chosen by Paul's mother anyway, who'd died after her husband, with the lettering amended later to include her. And Paul had followed his father's footsteps as a schoolteacher. That all felt right and proper. The CBE that I was about to parade was put out of mind.

"I bet you were good at that," I ventured. "Stimulating young minds must be the most satisfying thing you can do. They'd learn bucketloads from you being, should we say, intellectually perverse. And it beats running power stations, which is what I did for a living."

"I know what you did, Bob. You were often on the box or in the papers. You were CEO at Atomic Futures when it was privatised. Until you got fired."

As he said that, the glint in his eye could have been out of malice or humour. After my false start, I decided to assume the latter, or otherwise the conversation would have been terminated, a bit like I'd been, only this time without the legal agreement never to talk about it to friends or strangers.

In my year at school, Paul had headed for Cambridge to read English, hoping fervently to sit at the feet of Leavis, rather as his sainted namesake, the writer of the epistles, claimed to have done with Gamaliel, the foremost scholar of his day. My Jewish friends say that if St Paul did indeed so sit, he didn't learn that much.

"Enough," I answer them, although Pauline theology isn't always to my taste.

Or maybe Paul wanted to do what Bob Dylan did after visiting Woody Guthrie and become the disciple who eclipses the master. Paul's bad luck meant that he didn't get the chance to do either.

Leavis left Downing College for pastures new as Paul arrived.

Neither of those comparisons work well. I remember the sixth-form Paul riding a bike with straight handlebars and with three-speed Sturmey-Archer fixed gears. Mine had drop handlebars and a five-speed Derailleur. So, unlike me, Paul didn't spend the Upper Sixth year freewheelin' with Dylan. And, even back then, he thought religion was finished. On that, he's been more with the zeitgeist than me. As an engineer, I'd gone to Imperial, coming home every holiday from the delights and temptations of the Great Wen, as my older sister, already married and with children, would call it. She was too old to be allowed into the sixties. Paul kept on at school for a third year in the sixth so he could apply to Cambridge. Once there, he stayed through most vacations, eventually forcing his parents to move their home to be close to their precious only child.

Paul and I had been at odds with each other at school. With me being on the science side and him the humanities, we mainly met in the prefects' room. He wasn't a sportsman, nor did he show up at the Church youth club, where most of us went to meet the girls. That he didn't fancy the youth club was itself unusual. Only Catholics and Methodists didn't come. They had their own places. But atheists and agnostics weren't going to pass up the best offer in the village. The way he'd describe religion's passing with a studied indifference at the school debating society would make me too furious to make a rational response. He would also pour Leavisite scorn on C.P. Snow, who'd suggested that humanity students needed to understand physics, and physicists the humanities. I found Snow's novels turgid, and I knew he wasn't considered much cop as a scientist, but his view that renaissance man should try to embrace both was for me beyond challenge. Not so for Paul. Science was for lesser beings. He'd professed to be a Tory at the point when Harold MacMillan was passing over to the fourteenth Earl of Home, just before the white-hot fourteenth Mr Wilson took over Labour. So maybe 1962 was Paul's Year Zero, although I do suspect that Lord Salisbury would have been his real preference for prime minister.

In other words, I'd always thought Paul was a rum bugger. But then my granddaughter Charlotte, in reality the most conventional of girls, is always saying that our family is far too normal, me included. I don't think it's meant to be a compliment. She'd like a more entertaining personal back story to tell.

With my long hair, jeans and love of early rock, I'd thought myself then as with it and Paul as definitely without. It's only with the benefit of hindsight that I can see it could have been t'other way round. The winter of 1962 lasted well into the next year and was far and away the most ferocious in living memory. We were in the Lower Sixth, starting on our 'A' level courses. Coming out of that winter, the very late spring seemed like the first one ever on Planet Earth. In the middle of weather bad enough to be considered heavy even on the border line, a little-known Bob Dylan came to London to appear as a hobo folk singer in an oddball BBC play, *Madhouse on Castle Street*, singing the newly-written 'Blowin' in the Wind' over the final credits. I didn't know anything about it at the time; in our house we were watching Frank Ifield yodelling on *Sunday Night at the London Palladium*. Later in 1963 though, the year *Freewheelin'* was released, my independent world of thought kicked off, just at the point where Harold Wilson was elected Labour leader. I bought the album after a recommendation by John Lennon to the listening public on the Light Programme's *Saturday Club*. I couldn't believe how good it was. I'd constantly replay *Hard Rain* and was word perfect. I still am. Philip Larkin has duly celebrated the end of censorship, the arrival of the Beatles and the discovery of sex by the end of that cold winter, though the girls of St Chad's were only ready for the second of those. I was already enjoying the teasing delights of female company at the point I was introduced to Dylan. It was a feverishly exciting time.

My older grandchildren, born in the late nineties and so apparently post-millennial, are presently stuck, not for long I suspect, with a Labour leader nobody will ever remember, Ed Miliband, the son of a Hampstead Marxist, who's as lame as he sounds. Rather than taking any notice of him, they're usually online playing pretend politics, waiting for an offline world to begin.

At school, Paul would affect to like jazz. That had been for my sister's generation, not ours; she even knew how to ballroom-dance. I loved Victorian hymns though, to me rock's natural bedfellow as the people's music. My grandchildren would probably see Paul as more to today's taste. Like the rest of the country, they've given up on religion, despite our best efforts when they were younger. Seeing the few of us still going each Sunday, forlornly clinging on to our none-too-solid rock, isn't likely to change their mind. Yet I was brought up in a parochial faith, based on the synthesis of the Wesleys and the Oxford movement, of the Victorian Anglican revival, which still survived in the youth club during my time there. I'm not letting that go. It may be a small part of Christendom, built on shaky foundations, hopelessly split into different factions, marginalised in society, but it's my Church. In retrospect, I find it surprising, after two shattering world wars containing real existentialist threats to the nation, occupying a quarter of the time between Queen Victoria's death and my birth, that so little had changed by my childhood. So, by my teens, I assumed it was a culture that would endure eternally. But then, with peace and relative prosperity, things changed quickly. Well-read as she is,

Wendy sometimes looks at me in puzzlement at things which seem commonplace to me. She humours me in matters religious, without quite ever exposing her own beliefs to the full glare of ridicule in the way that I do.

I'll be writing this as a story as it goes along, but I doubt that Paul will be the main character, although seeing him has made me uneasy. I hope he doesn't figure hugely. When I knew him, he usually meant trouble for others and always for himself. As a prophet and not the messiah, maybe he could serve as some sort of John the Baptist figure, a pre-cursor to anything which might follow, though most certainly not one proclaiming the way of the Lord. I'm partly writing this to keep my brain active by the way, as I move into the geriatric phase of life, as well as it possibly forming the notes for a novel I doubt I'll ever get round to writing. My biggest problem isn't remembering details, although I guess I could be struggling with that by the time I finish. The problem is sciatica, which is excruciating when I sit down for too long, So, if the prose sometimes reads a little jerkily, then that's my excuse. And that I studied no English beyond 'O' level.

Standing there in the cemetery, my problem in moving on to what custom demanded should be discussed next was that Paul had not been that butch a guy, and age had made him sound a shade more camp.

"Any family to report, or haven't you been blessed, if that's the right word," I ventured.

He knew what I was thinking. His face permitted itself a small smile, before he turned his head so that he was at right angles to me. I could manage to make out that he looked rueful.

"No, no wife or children. The fates weren't kind. Or maybe my critical faculties became over-developed. I was engaged once, and fell in love once, not with the same woman, but both to women, since that's what you were wondering," he answered, at first softly but rising to the vehemence I remembered only too well.

I wasn't brave enough to take the issue, or lack of, any further. He hadn't asked about my family situation. I suppose he knew it already. But since you shower don't, I'd better tell you. I've got two middle-aged children from my marriage to Jane, and two much younger with Wendy. I met Wendy not long after my demise at Atomic Futures, when as a consolation prize I chaired a green energy company that she and another banker, my best friend Richard Shackleton, helped float on the Stock Exchange. She's saved me from an old age of regret. Nowadays, she's in big demand to teach on archaeology courses at the local college in Worcestershire, where we live. I can't marry her as she is still legally married to her first husband, with whom she had no family, entrapped in himself and a nursing home with early onset Alzheimer's. Alice is aged six and Richie not yet four. They've taken her surname, Smith, which I'm very happy about as Alice Smith was my Grannie's maiden name. As well as the dead of St Chad's, I'm also visiting the living, my daughter Ruth and her many children, my grandchildren. Wendy is looking after our own kids back in the village of Nether Piddle. Sadly, Ruth has not that long ago been abandoned by her husband for his childhood sweetheart. They've divorced. The purpose of the visit is to transfer my old house into her name, now it's safe to do so without her ex getting his hands on it. I'm also giving my slightly younger son Robert an equivalent sum of money in cash on the grounds of equity with Ruth. It isn't that he needs the dosh as a top city lawyer. He's told me to give it all to Ruth, but I can't do that. Equity must be equitable unless a statute applies, if I've remembered the law right.

I asked Paul instead how long he was up in St Chad's for, assuming that he, like me, was on a flying visit. I was surprised to learn that he'd just bought a house in the quite posh Little St Chad's Lane at the edge of the village. Those who succeeded in the post-war meritocracy even at relatively modest levels haven't been left short of funds. He told me that he'd always liked a circular narrative, and he was coming back to die. Without issue, he added. Part of me would like my story to end where it started too, but the other part is comfortably and firmly ensconced with my second family, including aging dog and cat, in our village, Nether Piddle. (I can't see that place name surviving much longer without challenge.)

It's always been a thought of mine that maybe the end of time and the beginning are the same place, making a circular narrative tidier. Otherwise, like on a holiday which doesn't end where it starts, there's that difficult post-trip stage of going to pick up the car at a different airport. And, if it's truly circular, all that happens must have been at some level there at the start. I suggested this concept to Paul.

"May my death be soon," he snorted. "Fifty years on and you still come out with the most preposterous notions. And you've probably invented some spurious physics to back it up. Eliot nearly had it right. If we contrive at the end of our exploring to arrive back where we started, it will be to know the place for the first time, but only because you can't view things from the inside."

"That's part of what I was saying," I replied.

He didn't take up the cudgels. Surprisingly, he asked if I'd time for a drink. I was due back at Ruth's for lunch with her family in half an hour, and had been out a while, so I asked if he could manage an hour in the pub sometime in the next day or two.

"I've nothing else to do, so that would be good," he replied.

"Would you like to meet Ruth? I'm sure Ethel next door could babysit for her," I offered, thinking I might need Ruth's conflict-management skills.

"I'd prefer not. You've managed two lots of children. I've none. Just us, if you don't mind, Bob."

It was presumptuous of me to have offered Ruth without asking her anyway. We arranged to meet at half past eight the next night in The Old Tithe Barn, a short walk from Ruth's. Paul's new home is a little bit further away, but not much more than ten minutes' walk. As we each climbed into our cars, spots of rain gently fell on the windscreens, a slow release of pent-up tension from above. As I drove off, the sound of the windscreen wipers drowned out the silent melancholy of the cemetery.

CHAPTER TWO

The Next Evening

Paul was already finishing a glass of white wine when I arrived at The Barn, despite me being early. He too no doubt finds that, at this stage of his life, drinking beer necessitates too many overnight lavatory trips. I doubt if he's ever been a five-pint-a-night man, although he has a slight paunch. I casually looked him over as I waited to be served. Slightly built, he must be five inches shorter than my just over six feet. I'd forgotten that. It's sometimes said that people's faces fall into only two categories, horses and buttons. Despite my heavy frame and ample conk, I'm a button. He's a small-nosed horse, like me thinning on top. I bought him another large Pinot Grigio and myself a similarly sized Cabernet Sauvignon.

"How'd you like being back in the old village?" I asked him.

"It's a small town now," he replied. "You can never get back all the way. Beginning and end aren't the same place, whatever you think, so I'm in for another disappointment. But once I'd retired from school, there was nothing left for me in Cambridge. Life was empty. The place is too full of genuine smart Alecs, not pretend ones like you. Here should be better for my self-confidence."

"It might surprise you to know that I've never noticed you lacking that."

"Maybe coming back is already working then," he grinned. "It's a bit quiet though. When I was surrounded by the hubbub of the school, I yearned for quiet, for stillness, interrupted only by clear ideas that I was sure would come to me in the silence. Now, I don't want that. It seems like my mind's so well-ordered that it can't create its own noise. I need some to invent patterns in what's happening."

That's not quite the way I remember him. I can recall him having temper tantrums in the prefects' room when picked on by the jocks. I'd try and act as peacemaker, usually unsuccessfully and unnecessarily. Now he's here, he'll doubtless create plenty of noise without having to try too hard.

"Don't you mean so that you can detect the patterns?" I asked.

"No, I mean invent. They're not there beforehand."

He didn't elaborate, so I did. I reckoned that none of what happens is noise: that, just as less than ten per cent of human DNA is now functional yet it was all used at some stage in evolution for us to get here, so it was with all thoughts and events. When we looked back on life, there were many things we'd regret, but they'd all served to make us the person we'd become, all of which in my grand theory had always been in us. There have been patterns, inexplicable patterns, in life which have kept me thinking there is a purpose, or at the very least a meaning.

Paul wasn't impressed. "That wasn't so much noise as an atonal cacophony, like a dripping tap or a buzzing bluebottle," he countered. "There's no meaning, apart from what we create for ourselves to keep sane, in a time that goes one way only, to death."

So, if this story isn't going to have any purpose or meaning, you might as well stop reading now. It's not likely to be entertaining. It seems as if Paul is convinced that he hasn't made enough of his life and is determined to make me feel the same about mine. I couldn't let that stand unchallenged.

"I can like both the quiet and the loud. I'll accept that rational thought gives no meaning. Words and imagination can though," I said. "As you might remember, I was hooked on Dylan's music from very early on. Still am. I also really enjoy the mannered works of Leonard Cohen, spokesperson for that still, small voice of calm, the Holy Dove. He'll sometimes use Christian imagery in his despair, but the Buddhist in him points him to a deeper order, and his Jewish roots to favouring a Messiah who doesn't see defeat as a victory. That's not me."

"Go on, let's hear you make the same idiotic arguments that you used to. I could always give you enough rope for you to hang yourself. Only the simple-minded in the prefects' room would listen to you, but that was because they didn't like me."

I ignored that, as it was probably true.

"Everybody's life ends in the defeat of death," I continued. "It's the chaotic imagery of the archetypes that emerge from Dylan's subconscious to the pounding rock beat that's been my pulse throughout: a world with the Father, a great bear of a creator, bursting out of a dinner jacket he hasn't chosen to wear, with a raging sense of irrational justice that his suffering Son struggles to tame and the Spirit flees from; a world with the devil living as a lodger in their house, ruling the physical realm of sword-swallowers and one-eyed midgets, finding, capturing and selling the Dove to the highest bidder. In the time we're living in, the family isn't fully one yet. It's still in parts. Divine omnipotence is like a UN Security Council resolution, only sticking sometimes. The world makes sense, but not a consistent sense. It's only when time's up that God will be all in all."

"I prefer my poetry without music, a category which Leonard Cohen is undeniably close to," Paul replied. "You've summed up exactly why I don't like Dylan. He's too damned Messianic. I still detest religion. Mind you, humanism's even worse. All people are best described as evil sods, and unforgiveable. I'd be a Buddhist, but they insist on being reborn, and I just want to die the once. I've told you; that's why I'm back here. To die."

Has he set up his critical faculties to exclude all hope, or is it just a façade? Perhaps he's always done that, which is why he settled for a low-key life. I don't think the temper tantrums back that up though.

We were interrupted by the clatter of a woman coming in through the door, a teacher delivering posters for the local primary school Summer Fayre, accompanied by a handsome Labrador. To accept these was beyond the delegated responsibility of the barman. The landlord, Bill Hardisty, was summoned from his private quarters with the shout that Lucy wanted to see him. Recently made a widower by a wife who'd drunk most of the profits, and with his only child living in Australia, Bill is the traditionally cantankerous landlord that's sadly gone out of fashion. But out he came from his back parlour with a smile as broad as his stomach was round. Lucy was obviously an attraction that he didn't want to miss.

He quickly agreed to take three posters from her, as she flirted with him shamelessly in the interest of her worthy cause. Probably just into her forties but looking younger, she was wearing a short, tight skirt and a revealing blouse. She spoke at nineteen to the dozen in what I detected as a gentle Prestonian burr, ill-suited to her pace of delivery. Above the compelling delights of her body, I could see a cheerful yet determined face that looked as if it would be slow to anger and very swift to bless. Her deep brown eyes, as big as her dog's, sparkled under chaotically long auburn hair that was swinging in disharmony with all her other moving parts. She was noisy. She's not a beauty but, hey, she's alright, I thought. If Springsteen's character had ever taken her on that putative trip down Thunder Road, I doubt it would have ended in anti-climax back in the porch.

She didn't fit into any stereotype of a primary school mistress

I could imagine, past or present. Nowadays, the older ones bristle with confidence and competence; the younger ones dress modestly and speak in educational jargonese. This latter group fortunately transmutes into the former well before they've reached forty. Back when I was at school, they were all older and very proper. Maybe, for one brief moment in the late sixties, a schoolteacher could look as Lucy did. And she'd captured that moment, despite not having been born by then.

I whispered to Paul: "It's a shame we didn't have teachers like that in our day."

"I don't think she'd have been my type," he replied. "Her grammar is all over the place and the poster's a mess. She's misspelt doughnuts."

But he did have a broad, almost lecherous grin on his face as he said this. I could see that Lucy's attributes had stirred him as much as they had woken Bill from his curmudgeonly slumbers. Bill offered her a free drink, which she accepted, brazenly opting for a whisky mac. Bill pulled himself a pint. They settled down at the table next to ours. I'd recognised that the primary school was the one Ruth's third child, Rachel, had just left and where fourth child, Ben, was ensconced; indeed, it's the one I attended a lifetime ago. It was called Wheat Street back then, but now it's St Chad's Church of England Primary School.

Lucy paused from talking to look our way with her face breaking into a self-conscious smile. She knew we were both watching her. I had a great chat-up line at the ready. I asked if she knew my grandson Ben Jackson.

"Know him well. Why've I not seen you before? He's as bright as a button. I'm looking forward to him being in my class again next year," she said. "They're giving me Year 4 at last. I've been doing

Year 2 for a zillion years and the Head's finally letting me have a bash with older children. Ben's already ahead of me in Maths. He'll be telling you how useless I am."

I could remember the name that Ben had been full of the previous year. "So, you're the famous Miss Fishwick? He thought you were the greatest thing since sliced bread."

"Trouble is, they all buy their cottage loaves from Booths and slice them as needed round here. I'm infamous, not famous. I've heard them call me Lucy Fishwife. And it's not fair. I'm from Preston, not Fleetwood."

"I hope Ruth wasn't in that camp," I said. My older daughter can be a bit proper.

"She's always been lovely," Lucy assured me.

Then Paul found his voice, one both Lucy and I would also have described as proper, as in proper Lytham St Annes, the type heard from the northern correspondent on BBC national news, treacherously ambivalent between the short and long 'a'.

"I was nicknamed Ecky Thump in Cambridge," he said.

"Not for long," I thought, but didn't say out loud.

Lucy's eyes lit up at his calm delivery, the antithesis of her frantic chase for words that couldn't keep up with her thoughts. I could tell that both had found their calling in their careers, something us businessmen can never fully claim. They exchanged their different teaching experiences for so long that Bill retreated behind the bar, disappointed that he'd again missed out on the main chance. Lucy and Paul joshed each other about state versus private, but they had enough similar experiences too. They joked about the half-truths they said to parents on Open Evenings. Bill gave a final scowl as he retreated back into his parlour.

"I once had to give a reference to a potential employer for

an indolent pupil. 'Anyone who gets X to work for them will be extremely fortunate,' is what I penned," continued Paul.

Lucy cackled so much in delight that her chair kecked up, revealing for a tantalising, unblushing moment the smooth, white flesh of her thigh. I think the last time I'd heard that one was from our Careers Master in our last year at school. You can usually tell when you re-tread a joke if the younger person hasn't heard it before or is just being polite. I wasn't sure this time. Perhaps Lucy hadn't heard this one, but I doubt it. Those chairs in the pub are heavy enough to stay grounded. I think she knew which role to play, the one of wannabe groupie to the rock band lead singer. Of course, Paul didn't behave as a rock star. He was playing the part of the maestro conductor of the nation's leading orchestra on its tour of the provinces.

The Labrador, whose name was Toffee, lay quietly. He'd no doubt seen Lucy's mating rituals before. I don't know if the remaining posters were ever delivered. Fed up of playing gooseberry, I left the pub after two drinks as they decided on a third. Paul paused briefly to give me his mobile number as I was leaving. I promised to call the next time we were up in St Chad's.

I described my evening once back in the house. Prudish Ruth said: "Paul had better watch out, that Lucy Fishwife has a reputation as a man-eater of all ages and sizes."

"That's just what he needs," I reckoned.

As I tried to sleep, I couldn't make sense of why Paul had wanted us to meet again. It must either be masochism or sadism.

CHAPTER THREE
July 2015

It's summer. It sometimes is in July. To my chagrin, Lancashire cricket team are ignominiously playing in the second division, having been relegated last year, only two years after being Champions. It's hard for them to compete with the southern counties when cricket isn't being played in state schools any longer. Maybe that's the best argument I can come up with in favour of grammar schools.

And this is on top of me having to stop watching football at Blackpool. I've always been a keen fan, but for a quarter of a century now we've had the most outrageous Chairman, who's treated the club with disdain. The fans have at last organised a permanent boycott, which I've joined. My friend Richard's side, Bolton Wanderers, are also in a bad financial way and aren't doing much better than us. For both Richard and me, the successes and failures of our teams are signs of whether or not we are in favour in the courts of heaven. It appears that we're not. We've had our time. At least Lancashire are winning some games this season though, so maybe things are about to look up.

Cameron and the Tories have just sneaked home in the general election with a small majority. I wasn't sure who to vote for. A lifetime after the white-hot second industrial revolution failed to ignite fully, I've developed a healthy scepticism for them all. Cameron is a dreaded Old Etonian with the swagger in his walk that goes with that territory. The stupid pillock also doesn't seem to understand how parliamentary democracy is meant to work, having promised a referendum on the EU. He's only promised that in a vain attempt to keep his party together, and on the basis that after the election he'd probably be out of office one way or another. But having won the election outright, he's probably stuck with having one. The nasty wing of his party still berates him for failing to get all the concessions they wanted on Europe. He didn't do that badly, keeping us out of the Schengen Agreement, which would have permitted free movement of immigrants without passports across the EU, and obtaining an opt-out for us on monetary union. He tried but got nothing else on immigration. EU citizens can still move here freely. That suits me fine. He never could have got more, and he shouldn't have suggested he could. Like many from the west coast, I'm naturally a bit of an Atlanticist, but the EU does us more good than harm, as far as I can see.

This referendum has all the potential to bite him, and us, in the bum. Mind you, Harold Wilson had a similar one back in 1975, and for the same reasons, that he couldn't fix his party any other way. Wilson was a canny bugger though and knew how to win. He also concluded his relatively trivial re-negotiation before calling the referendum. The fundamental rule to be taken from that experience is not to call one unless you as prime minister can be certain of the outcome. I'm pretty sure Cameron isn't. The public mood is more volatile this time round. MPs are almost universally disliked after the banking crisis, the expenses scandal and because so many of them come across as prats.

Labour's present leader may well be the wrong Miliband, not that I'm suggesting there's a right one. His brother is possibly the more talented, but I wouldn't want to be stuck in a room with either of them, a feeling I suspect would be mutual. Would it be constitutionally possible to ban anyone from North London from becoming a Labour Party member, I wonder? They make better communists or social democrats.

In my Chief Executive days, I met Blair and Brown. Tony, spiritually based in Islington, is definitely not my cup of tea. His Government was arguably a decent one, if you can ignore Iraq and Alastair Campbell. Both of those are difficult to forget in a hurry though. I like Gordon, he who saved the world in the financial crisis. The nation doesn't, unfortunately. They've no regard for depth in personality any longer. The thing I'd have liked best this time out is for Gordon's old oppo Ed Balls to have been leader after him. He at least looks like he's enjoying himself and seems like he's got a brain. Not only have we got the wrong Miliband, we've got the wrong Ed. But Balls' own constituents have just dumped him. My taste doesn't seem to be universal. It would be nice if just occasionally I was with the crowd. I never seem to be. I ended up voting for Clegg's mob, the so-called Liberal Democrats, consisting of the most judgmental people on earth, although he's quite possibly the guy who irritates me the most. The fact that he preferred coalition with the Tories to Labour says all you need to know about him. He's got his comeuppance too and has been kicked out. I can comfort myself that my conscience is clear, and a Tory victory is still in my personal economic interest, if not many other people's.

In the genteel respectability of Nether Piddle, where our circle of friends is as hidebound as we are, perhaps more so, we receive a twice-weekly running commentary on the phone from Ruth in St Chad's as to how the new scandalous liaison is going. Little St Chad's Lane is a dead end but does have a pretence of a track at the bottom which crosses a field. Then, after the traversal of a main road at a point where pedestrians are abandoned to the goodwill of motorists or an alternative fate, a much better path wends its way to Skippool

Creek and eventually to the solitude of the wide mudbanks of the River Wyre. Early morning dog-walkers have therefore been able to check which cars are parked outside which house, and which curtains are drawn, information they can share with the joint intelligence liaison committee meeting, providing they return alive from crossing the road. The committee meets twice daily outside the school gate. Initial observations suggest that Lucy and Toffee are spending Friday and Saturday nights at Paul's, returning to their small house down the Breck for the rest of the week. Fresh information has also added Tuesday on to the list of joint occupation. Curtains have only ever been seen drawn in one bedroom. Not only that, but Paul has been proved, beyond any reasonable doubt, to have baked some cakes for Lucy to sell at the school Summer Fayre. Greater love hath no man than this. Ruth said they could have done with less sugar. That's a first; someone's found Paul too sweet.

Alice and Richie have broken up for summer from school and pre-school and we've come en famille to visit Ruth and her lot for a few days. Hattie, my 12-year-old dog, a Lancashire heeler of course, is with us while a next-door neighbour is feeding Wendy's old moggy Sheba. It was Richie's birthday in the last week of term and we've first had the delight of a children's party to contend with on Saturday before travelling north. He's off to Reception Class at big school next term. I regained my respect for primary school teachers that afternoon, Lucy included. If the party had been much longer, I'm pretty sure I'd have strangled at least one of them.

With Ruth's two older children, the early Post-Millennials, also at home as well as school attendees Rachel and Ben, it's too much of a squeeze for us all to fit in the one house. Wendy and I are sleeping next door in Ethel's spare room. An old widow we know well, she's delighted to have our company.

I'd promised to ring Paul on arrival and did so earlyish on Monday morning, hoping he would have other things on during the week. He hadn't and hasn't. I asked if he'd like to meet up with Wendy as well as me, and if there was anybody he'd like to bring along. He didn't want to bring anyone, making me wonder if things with Lucy had stalled. He wanted us to meet alone, as he had last time. I've never been prepared to leave Wendy cooped up with the children for an evening while I go down the pub. So, to avoid that, I suggested a walk down the footpath from his house one morning. He wanted to know if I could manage this morning. I hesitated. Wendy was listening to my end of the conversation. She told me to get it done with, loud enough that he probably heard. I wonder if that was what she intended? She'd not even met the guy yet. I must have passed my aversion on subliminally. The smaller kids were playing happily together, despite uncle and aunt being younger than their nephew and niece. Ruth was out getting groceries. Consequently, less than half an hour later, Paul, Hattie and I were walking across the overgrown track on the way to Skippool Creek. I guess I could call the field a meadow, but it isn't really one. I gather that meadows are now referred to in legislation as unimproved grasslands. This field has been improved sufficiently to leave precious few wildflowers growing in it. They've been relegated to the hedgerows at the edge, the outcome of no spring grazing and only annual mowing for the hay. There isn't much birdsong to be heard either. At least there's no anticipation of surprise gunshot and the subsequent fluttering of feathers that we hear too often in Worcestershire.

I'd been expecting Paul to be upset about something given the urgency with which he'd wanted to meet, but he was relaxed and his usual suave self. I planned to be back at Ruth's for lunch where the shopping expedition, among many other delights, would hopefully have produced what I'd requested, a pork pie salad, with blackcurrant tart and cream to follow, high up the list of the delights available from a Lancashire cake shop. I cut to the chase as soon as I could.

"School gate gossip has it that you've been seeing a bit of Lucy," I suggested tentatively, trying to sound casual.

"And for once it's an under-exaggeration," he smirked. "I've seen all of Lucy. And she's absolutely gorgeous, tip to toe. I saw you ogling her too. There's just been one minor problem."

He stopped talking abruptly to examine a wild rose in the hedgerow. I waited for him to continue. When he did, it wasn't to tell me the problem I thought it was likely to be.

"She's writing a play for radio. A guy at Granada she called has promised to consider it. She writes a bit like that chap Peter Tinniswood used to write, a sort of northern surrealism. She's not got a bad ear for dialogue, you know, despite her dreadful grammar and even worse spelling. And that's where I come in."

"*I didn't know you cared* for that sort of stuff," I laughed.

"Your jokes are even worse than I remember them. And they were gross then."

"That's a lorra, lorra laughs I gave you then. I hope Lucy isn't dallying with you just for your editorial skills"

He chuckled at that. "She might be. It's all I'm good for. I can't even say I'm her editor, because she won't take any advice on plot or structure. Not that there's much of that in the first place. It's about a group from a British Legion club, or whatever they call themselves, on a day trip to Windermere."

He then looked straight at me before adding: "She would allow me to make a few penetrating insertions though, if only I could manage to."

I felt as if I was Sid James being told the tale by Kenneth

Williams, after a less than successful attempt at a liaison with Liz Fraser.

"Not that I've yet felt the need, but aren't there little blue pills nowadays to help would-be writers with that sort of block?" I asked, perhaps a little too smugly.

"I believe so, Bob. I haven't tried them yet. I wondered if you had. Myself, I wouldn't know them from blue Smarties."

"Sorry, I've never used them. If it's all in the head, maybe the Smarties would work just as well. But, if Lucy's happy to, why don't you give the real pills a go?"

"What if they won't work? Or they work too quickly?" he asked.

I couldn't stop myself. "Then you'll either have a story without a climax or one which happens early in the first chapter."

He grimaced ruefully. "It might save me from a coronary from over-exertion," he said.

We moved on to discussing Lucy's life story without me being sure if it was a follow-on from the previous conversation or a new one. As a teenager, she'd been a tearaway and had inevitably given birth young, after a shotgun wedding, to a daughter, Maddie. No surprise there, I thought. He showed me a photograph of Maddie he had on his phone. I put my glasses on. She was prettier than her mother, while having the same expressive face, yet with a smile that was far more knowing. A fisherman, her father had disappeared from the scene a few years after she was born. Rumour had it that he'd had mental problems and had killed himself, but the story Lucy told Paul was of an undetected slip off the trawler deck.

Paul described how Maddie had been brought up by an impoverished Lucy, who'd scraped to make ends meet in a variety of jobs while living at home with her mother. It was only when Maddie was at secondary school (on the occasions when she could be bothered to turn up) that Lucy studied to become a primary school teacher, first on the kitchen table for 'A' levels and then on an Education course. Maddie has turned out pretty well after being a tomboy tearaway as a younger teenager, screwing around from thirteen onwards, constantly in trouble with school and even the police, with girls' football the only healthy outlet for her energies. Being fit had mattered to her enough that she'd mainly stayed away from drugs. Lucy is, as customary for a Prestonian, a lapsed catholic. At eighteen, never being one to stay with the crowd and in reaction both to what she had been and to her mother's superstitious form of Catholicism, Maddie had resolved to change. She'd hitched up with a free, charismatic Church. As a result, she'd studied for a philosophy and religion degree and is presently in training for the Methodist youth ministry in Sheffield, which strikes me as about as uncharismatic as life can get. She's been over to St Chad's just the once to give Paul the once-over and has so far blessed their arrangement.

"She's bursting out of the clothes she wears," Paul said. "She walks round the house in a skimpy nightdress right in front of me. Below that provocative face, she has a body straight out of a health magazine, toned firm from exercise classes and playing sport. Her sanctimony won't be lifelong. The rebel tomboy will come out again all guns blazing, and I do mean all guns."

Whether or not he was saying she could be bisexual wasn't clear. I don't know if he's that savvy, or if I am. It was Lucy he wanted to talk about. Somewhat arrogantly, he claimed that he was beginning to predict her unpredictability. My wife Jane was highly unpredictable too, but in a way that I never saw coming. I wasn't even sure what had hit me afterwards. While Lucy had been flirting with him in the pub, he claimed to have seen that she'd been sizing him up at the same time and guessed what she was after. She'd confirmed this to him. Into her forties, she's broody for another child before the biological egg-timer's sands have fully passed. She's needing a change, and pregnancy would be a good one. She's hoping that my daughter's child in Year 4 will be her last teaching challenge for a while, indeed for good if her plays are accepted. She'd picked up quickly that he (Paul) was stimulated, at least mentally, by her and she'd somehow found his oddness arousing. She'd understood at some point during the three whisky macs that he's also someone who would like a child, in his case before the biological bell tolls midnight. He admitted to me that she's probably thinking that he will soon be dead, the easiest way for an affair to end without recrimination and remorse, unless the death is by foul means. But regrettably her judgement has been flawed. She's been over-optimistic in the ability of a 69-year-old Englishman to perform.

"Frenchmen at soixante-neuf still don't know which way is up," he quipped. "I'll soon need a bath chair. If I can't fulfil my side of the bargain, she'll soon be moving on to firmer pastures. And if she does, I don't know how I'll cope without all the lovely noise she makes."

"Well, take the bloody pills, man, and find out," I said, having been listening for longer than I found good for me. "Otherwise, you're riding for a fall, not a jump."

"I'd rather stand up for myself. It might mean something that way, though only to me. I just don't want to feel beholden to you bloody scientists."

At last, I understood why he was hesitating. His dislike of what he thought I stood for was lifelong. He was certainly a suitable case for some sort of treatment. It was time to parade my ignorance for him to feel superior again.

"But if you can't, you can't." I said. "It's nothing to apologise for at any age, and certainly not for us geriatrics. Now that we live so long, death of the libido is bound to precede actual death. It's nature's way of telling us our time is nearly up. It's the signifier before the signified."

"I had to put up with all that semiotic post-modern crap at Cambridge. The signifier is my pensioner's droop, the signified my unhappiness. There's never a precedent."

I'd once lost a woman through pretending I understood something about post-modernism. An engineer should know his limitations and stick with the empirical. I told him that, to me, it was obvious that his unhappiness was caused by, and not signified by, him not rising to the occasion. That, however, had required Lucy to be interested in him as a potential father, which certainly struck me as without any precedent. "In the beginning was the Word," I said. "In creation, the signifier came first. Lucy wanting a child is the start point. You do too. So, try the pills."

"And lose my dignity. It's all I've got left. The main drama isn't me not getting it up, it's what Lucy thinks of me afterwards when I've failed."

"No, it's not. It's what you both make of it beforehand. Then you can live with whatever happens. It will have either meaning if you fail or purpose if you succeed. So, take the pills. Or else, get down on your knees and pray."

"God, no," he snapped quickly. "What a choice, science or religion, the devil and the deep blue sea! I'm sticking with no God, no precedent, no meaning, no purpose and it looks like no sex. I've moved on from Leavis too. There's no morality."

I don't believe him. None of us can ever move on, only off. With a mix of bluster and stubbornness, I replied: "I'm sticking with my world view, even if it's bollocks. Time is circular. We're part-authors of our own misfortune, and what that makes us, all of which is in us from the start. Take the pills and change what you are into what you've always been."

"That's illogical claptrap dressed up as wisdom, Bob," Paul replied.

"No, it's not. You're confusing temporal and logical causality," I said. "Just like your head's confused your willy."

"It's Lucy that's done the confusing," he replied. "What does how the world started matter anyway? We'll never know. It probably didn't."

"It did start, either as a law of science, a random freak in the nature of nothingness, or a purposeful thought. Science reduces to nothing but Maths, so good old Gödel's shown that I can reject the first of those if I want. And I do want. I'd hate to think the universe is totally deterministic. There'd be no fun in that. And even if you try to put the Maths into language, hasn't Wittgenstein shown that no more can be said in language beyond a point? That's more your bag than mine. I just know that science can't explain the fundamental."

"The whole show is a random freak," Paul said dismissively.

"That's no explanation at all. The world starting with an act of will, a whisper of a word, makes the most sense. You're the literature man. You must want that. Don't you want the meaning to come from the story and not the equations? You're the primary mover, us bloody science-siders are just the arse end of the pantomime horse."

"Hark at you, quoting Wittgenstein. Quite the polyglot nowadays!" he replied. "In retrospect, I see no meaning in the novels I've read, nor in my life, A story can be full of sound and fury, but it signifies nothing. I think you'll find that in the literary canon. In fact, I seem to remember you read the Macbeth part in class. I was

Lady Macbeth." There was a slightly rueful smirk on Paul's face as he recalled the customary treatment given in an all-boy's school to someone whose voice broke late. "I also had to be Mistress Quickly when you were Falstaff. No wonder I can't get it up with those humiliations flying round my head. It's all your fault. And you were a terrible actor. You never wanted a part in the school play."

I grinned too at the relevance of the memory.

"I still am. All these years later, and those memories have found a reason to be replayed. That's put time back in its box. Paul, I've lived my life with people I don't want ever to see die. I guess by separating the mental and the physical that, even for a miserable bugger like you, I'm trying to find something that can survive death and can sneak into eternity."

Paul donned a deliberately nonplussed look. His range of patronising expressions was extensive. I can't think of one he didn't use in this conversation.

"The mental needs a physical brain to play on. The body can't be resurrected. That's just laughable. Nobody can be spared from death. There's nobody I'd save if I could. We're all better off dead," he said.

"I don't believe you think that," I replied. "I've not known the others, but there's Lucy. And your parents. You were their world."

We were on our return journey, having re-crossed over the main road without either of us becoming a fatality. I carried Hattie across as the only safe way for her. We walked back down the footpath that led to Flowerless Meadow. As if summoned, walking towards us were Lucy and Toffee. I could see that she was livid. Her face wasn't that slow to anger after all. Her big eyes had become slits through which diffraction patterns would have been formed if only she'd been emitting any light.

"You're an ungrateful shit," she spat out. "You're trying to keep me just for yourself. You knew I wanted to hear what Bob had to say."

I gathered from that she'd wanted to come with us on the walk and he'd either refused or had misled her as to when we were meeting. Her anger had grown over the intervening period, not subsided. Hattie and Toffee, who'd started introducing themselves when none of us humans had the manners to do so, both looked concerned. Paul tried to calm Lucy down, putting an arm around her, which coming from him was a touching gesture. She could be vengeful as a she-devil. Did I see red flash through the slits as she pushed him away so hard that he over-balanced? Or maybe there were rays from well outside the visible spectrum that caused him to fall.

Whichever the reason, it afforded a practical test of something I'd worried about before when walking with the children. Would the dense shrubbery on the bank stop someone slipping into the Main Dyke below? Fortunately, the answer is 'Yes'. There was silence as Lucy saw what she'd done before she burst out laughing, dragged Paul up from the brambles by his hands, threw her arms round his neck and kissed him. I doubt if she'd had any thought but anger before firing the venom at him. She both was and wasn't the agent. Hattie and Toffee resumed their introductions.

Lucy then turned to me: "Has he asked you about the pills?"

"He has. I've encouraged him."

"Do you take them?"

"Not yet. It probably won't be much longer that I can say that."

She turned to Paul and said: "If you won't, I'd be better off bonking him." Then she added with a nervous giggle, "Only joking, of course."

I'm not totally sure she was, but that could just be my male vanity. I'm certainly not volunteering. She kissed him again.

38

"I love you, plonker that you are."

That must have been nice for him to hear, if he was listening. Wendy has said similar things to me, although substituting 'plonker that' with 'infuriating as', before also giving me a kiss.

I guess that younger folk will see us as just another couple, fond of each other, with the occasional grumble, if they notice us at all. They don't know that it's special. My love life with Wendy is just right for my age, occasional and relaxed. It isn't a kind of loving, it's kind and loving.

And so was this moment between Lucy and Paul, I suppose.

CHAPTER FOUR

A Week Later

On the last evening of our stay, Ruth insisted that we ask Lucy and Paul round for a farewell drink, despite my many misgivings. You're better not asking a man round for cocktails who's been in the wilderness living on locusts and wild honey, even if he's now baking cakes for charity. The weather was fortunately warm enough to sit in the garden, which made keeping the children entertained while the adults talked somewhat easier.

By this time of year, Ruth's lovely garden has lost its spring freshness, with green leaves now predominating. The dahlias are just starting to bloom, with salvias and penstemon providing a decent supporting act. We've reached high summer. The blossoms on the wisteria, the apple trees and the lilacs are long gone. The apple crop won't be ready for another month though, much to the four children's disappointment. The roses are at their most prickly while in their second flush of flowering.

Ruth is an actuary working from home since her office at Lytham St Annes has been rationalised out of real existence. My ribbing of her about a date she'd been on with a client the previous night similarly produced both a flush and a prickly response. Yet again, she'd found a substantial deficit from what she'd hoped for. His liabilities far exceeded his assets, she'd quickly decided. She meant the personal baggage he was carrying, not his finances.

"We're all in the same boat at this age. We can neither forgive nor forget our own pasts, let alone someone else's," she said.

"Bob and I managed it," Wendy replied. "There'll be someone, some day. No need to rush it."

Our two guests arrived, slightly overdressed. I didn't blame them for that, as that's what I usually do when facing the unknown. To ensure that the children avoided the roses, while ducking in and out of the adult conversation, I'd been nominated by Wendy to supervise a game of Hide and Seek, the foliage providing some excellent cover. I'd already scratched myself twice in doing that. The kids had no such problems. I continued with the game while the other grown-ups sipped the mandatory chilled Prosecco as they nibbled posh crisps and nuts. I think I'd have preferred the locusts and certainly the wild honey.

Our two guests hadn't started in character. Lucy greeted Ruth warily; although usually a kind and welcoming woman, my daughter is fiercely intelligent. 'Head Girl' is stamped on her forehead in a bold, underlined and large font. Lucy listened carefully, using her best telephone voice in reply. Paul was unusually chatty, while playing down his intellectual credentials.

The false harmonies couldn't be sustained. Lucy was the first to go slightly out of tune, but only by cackling excessively at Ruth's commonplace that an actuary was an accountant without a personality. She was clearly nervous and wasn't trying to pretend anything different today, and possibly as with Paul's character reference hadn't heard the joke before. We move in different circles. She might even not have known what an actuary actually does. Wendy, a former banker and more the Form Captain as elected by the other class members than Head Girl chosen by the Headmistress, joined in the self-deprecation by suggesting that most accountants and actuaries were honest, unlike certain other finance professions she knew too well.

In the game, it was Richie's and Alice's turn to search, working together. I was hiding behind bushes right at the bottom of the garden with Hattie. Paul wasn't nervous enough. He never has been nor will be. Instead, he was bristling into a pompous tirade, loud enough for me to hear, with one of his rants straight from the prefects' room, updated for today's prejudices.

"Bankers are the worst of all and that's saying something. Society needs a moral fabric in the better-off to avoid the perils of collectivism and socialism," he declaimed. "Instead, it's a casino where the winner takes a large fortune and the loser a small one. It's all those of us outside who are the losers."

He seemed to have forgotten that he'd no time for morality earlier in the week. And that Wendy had been a banker. Mind you, I agreed with his analysis, and would have said so if I'd been a bit nearer. Wendy smiled sweetly, saying, "I'm not sure about moral fabric, but certainly we should try to behave responsibly and shouldn't exploit our good fortune. I was an investment banker and have never been part of the trading casino."

"You just made your money by arranging unnecessary transactions, with your fees paid by all the staff who lost their jobs," Paul snapped.

I hadn't realised that he knew so much about banking. I wouldn't have pleaded guilty as charged in the transactions Wendy or I'd been involved with, but there was more than an element of truth to what he said. Wendy kept her sweet smile.

"None of us pick our careers, Paul, and not always our clients. I always tried to broker deals that were worth doing," she replied. I can vouch for that. She hated a deal that was just for the sake of it.

He wasn't finished. "Worth doing for you and yours, no doubt. I chose to be a teacher," he said proudly.

At this, I couldn't help but have the unworthy thought that this was probably because no-one else would employ the pompous pillock. Both Form Captain and Head Girl moved together to pour more tea to provide a distraction. In the bushes, Hattie had just told Alice where I was hiding. Alice pointed me out to Richie, so that he could find me. I allowed him to 'tig' me straight away, so that I could go and defend Wendy's honour.

Wendy moved to change the subject.

"We're thinking of taking the kids and Hattie for a walk to Beacon Fell tomorrow. Do you know it, Lucy? It's not that far from Preston?"

"I once stood as a Labour Councillor in the ward that it's in. I lost by a country mile." She giggled pleasantly at the memory. "The only ones who listened to me were those lovely black and white cows in the fields outside the villages."

Paul's face contorted into a contemptuously wild grin, which had no other source than malice.

"That's the Labour Party. Making everyone in the country line up in a queue to be milked dry. No originality allowed," he snarled.

"That's not right, Paul," said Lucy, sticking up for herself. "Look at where you and Bob went to grammar school, not a mile from here, and where that took you. They wanted everyone to have a fair chance. And you've had it."

"You're as bad as one of those stupid cows if you think that. The school was here well before the 1944 Education Act, and even that was down to Rab Butler, a Tory," quivered Paul.

I felt I needed to cool things down, and to defend Lucy's as well as Wendy's honour too, not recognising that they were doing a perfectly good job themselves, nor that I was the definition of the wrong person for the task.

"The Tories were probably prepared for a few of us joining the ranks of their middle-class so that they could keep their own lifestyle," I said, as I re-joined the group carrying Richie. "Not that I'd blame them for that. It's a very pleasant world when the sun shines."

I was the red rag to what now became a raging bull. Paul actually stamped his foot like a toddler in a tantrum as a prelude to his charge at this pathetically unarmed matador in front of him, carrying no weapon but his worried young son.

"You're the real phoney, all things to all men. You pretend to agree with Lucy when I know better. You've set your family up in this Dingley Dell house and gardens on the back of your immoral earnings. You've just asked us along today to show off to us. It's like a 1930's vicarage tea party, without the tea and cucumber sandwiches, but with a buffoon who thinks he's the vicar."

He hesitated, I think to swallow his bile, while he framed his next insult. I put Richie down, I hope so that I could suggest that people living in the smart surroundings of Little St Chad's Lane, where prosecco was also compulsory fare in the garden, shouldn't be throwing stones at other glass houses. It could have been as a prelude to clocking him one though. I'd somehow always managed to resist that temptation at school, even protecting him from others that didn't. Just in case that's what I had in mind Lucy stepped in between us quickly.

Facing him with tears in her eyes, she hissed, "How could you do that in front of the children? And these lovely people in this beautiful garden? You can spoil anything, Paul. You're sick in the head. You've no feelings for anyone but yourself."

Then she turned calmly to the others. "Thank you for the drink, Ruth. I'll try to make sure your Ben has a fantastic year. Lovely to meet you, Wendy." She then patted Hatts before shaking my hairy mitt with her small hand, adding sadly, "Sorry, Bob, neither of us can help him. Enjoy Beacon Fell. It's really nice up there."

With that, she made to leave through the side gate. Paul was slumped in his chair. I knew the bolt was jammed, so hurried to open it for her. Once at the front, she held me by both shoulders, looked me in the eyes with tears in her own, before turning away to walk slowly down the pavement.

"You're a great lass," I yelled after her. "Look after yourself. You're worth ten of him."

"Don't you under-estimate me too. I'm worth a hundred of him," she shouted back.

I watched her to the corner, where she turned left, unbowed, towards her small house. She'd kept her dignity, however humiliated she felt.

As I reached the front gate again, Paul brushed past me as he strode off after her. He said nothing. I yelled after him, in an exponential fury not good for a dodgy heart, to leave her alone, she was worth ten thousand of him. He didn't respond, but then he always was crap at Maths. By then, Wendy and Hattie had come out. Wendy put her arm around me, and we trooped back into the garden. None of us, adult or child, knew whether to laugh or cry. We restarted Hide and Seek, with Wendy and Ruth joining in too. There weren't enough places to hide. There hadn't been for the previous ten minutes.

CHAPTER FIVE
October 2015

I can't find the time to watch Lancashire play cricket much nowadays, but we've been smiled on throughout the season, winning the T20 and being promoted back to the First Division. Lucky old Richard was at Edgbaston for Finals Day, with his son James. Life can still be pretty damn good

Wendy and I don't manage to get north again until the last week of October, half-term week. By now Jeremy Corbyn has become leader of the Labour Party and I've turned seventy. This is the start of my grandchildren's world, their equivalent of my 1963. It seems like every Millennial and Post-Millennial has joined the Labour Party, wanting policies that would have made Lenin blink twice. I now understand that the year of birth that's being used by sociologists to distinguish these two modern groups is 1996. Somehow, I don't think the reason for that to have been chosen is that Christ is thought to have been born in 4 BC, sorry 4 BCE. Sadly, I think they see this year as 0 SD, *Sine Dominum*, with everything from the intervening 2,019 years rejected as either harmful or inconsequential.

The Labour Party hasn't for a long time been the one I was a member of back in the early sixties. The abolition of the manual working class accompanied by the rise of the social worker and college lecturer has put paid to that. Even so, Jeremy Corbyn is the antithesis of responsible old Labour, and is encouraging the madcap ideas of impressionable youth. He's still crazy after all these years. I find it difficult to get my head around how a guy who's made his name from voting on every conceivable occasion against his own leadership can himself become Leader. It doesn't seem the right way to play the game. And he even has the effrontery to represent Islington, the epicentre of all that's wrong with Labour. Neither of these problems faze our family's teenagers, particularly not our Charlotte, who at 16 is really into politics in a big way. To be fair again, I can remember that in his early career Harold Wilson, along with Nye Bevan, resigned from the Government over prescription charges. That was only the once, and in retrospect could be judged a smart long-term career move more than the issue of principle he of course claimed. But at the time, well before I was old enough to know anything about politics, it must have appeared as self-indulgence to the others who were biting their tongue. Even Nye Bevan, the driving force behind the rebellion, saw through it. He had been the main instigator of the NHS to be free at the point of delivery and had every reason to be antagonistic to this breach of the principle.

"Where were you born, Harold?" asked the famously Welsh Aneurin of the professional Yorkshireman.

"Not born, Nye, forged…"

"Yes, I always thought there was something counterfeit about you."

That's the way politicians have to be, I guess, forged in the fiery furnace of political expediency. Unfortunately, I don't think there's anything counterfeit about Corbyn. I'd be very happy for him to become prime minister if he could make his way to the centre-left and become another Wilson. He doesn't have to become a Blairite red Tory. There's certainly nothing in his track record to suggest he will do either. Harold got a top first at Oxford, and Jeremy two E's at 'A' level, I believe. The Tories will really have to mess up to make him electable. Mind you, they'll no doubt do their level best to achieve that. I suspect that a hard-left cabal of older white men will end up in Stalinist control of the Labour Party, and the enthusiasm of youth will turn to disillusion, the fate of reaching middle-age, in a couple of decades.

We've heard from Ruth that Lucy has yet again been shocking the neighbourhood. Wisely, she'd kept her door firmly shut as Paul hammered on it. The next week, Bill Hardisty took an evening off from the pub, something unknown before. He and Lucy were seen together in a steakhouse in a village a few miles away. They shared a sticky toffee pudding sundae with two spoons. Bill must be trying to lose weight. The view of the school gate community is that he won't be able to provide all Lucy is looking for. On the other hand, I'm sure she could make him very happy. She seems to have thought the same and has preferred to plump for her own happiness. When Paul had tried to bump into her 'accidentally' as she walked Toffee the next week, he'd found that she was sharing her walk with Dave the bodybuilder, a 25-year-old with muscles bulging out of his leathers, accompanied by a female Rottweiler with no aspirations to be other than a dog who answers to the name Roxanne. Lucy has moved quickly. Whereas Toffee and Roxanne are still only at the bottom-sniffing stage in their relationship. Lucy and Dave, having met in a Preston night club the evening before, appear to have gone somewhat beyond that phase during the night. Several times, Paul sadly envisages. When Lucy saw him approaching, she'd said something to Dave. He'd laughed derisively in Paul's direction before giving an unambiguous finger sign. Lucy had giggled appreciatively. Paul wisely took the subtle hint. He didn't try to take a vanilla sandwich round as a peace offering. Bill Hardisty is back to eating a microwaved jam roly-poly on his kitchen table, and with just one spoon.

With school resumed, Lucy's reputation at the school gate as a scandalous woman has thus risen several notches. Dave has moved in at her house in the Breck. He seems to have no job, rides a Triumph Bonneville, speaks in monosyllables, and comes from lowly Kirkham. He only has one champion at the court of St Chad's opinion, my daughter Ruth, who after one brief conversation with him says that he seems a perfectly decent guy. I can't help feeling that she's never lived near enough to the tracks to know there's another side, but I'm pleased that she hasn't joined the rush to judge. Wendy and I are assuming that Lucy will soon be fulfilled in her wish for another child. She certainly seems to have found a more likely sperm donor.

There was a short respite from the rain this morning and we managed to take the four children to the park. Rachel, who's just started at her senior school, was sufficiently and necessarily glued to her phone. Ruth and I sat next to her on the slightly damp bench, old Hatts alongside, happily catching up on her shuteye. Year 4 Ben preferred the swings, as did 6-year-old Alice. Wendy was pushing Richie, who was in one of the round smaller swings for younger children. As uncoordinated as his Dad, he still hasn't got the hang of swinging his legs in unison. I felt the hair on my neck ruffled, quite sensually. I turned to Ruth, wondering what she was up to. She wasn't the culprit. Behind me, with an impish grin on her face, stood Lucy. She was guilty as sin and enjoying it. She's a new friend, whether I like it or not, and I think I do. It doesn't seem like I would have a choice even if I didn't.

"How's it going?" I asked her.

"Dave not with you?" said Ruth, also with a smirk on her face.

She's definitely living, vicariously through Lucy, the life on the edge she'd preferred all her life not to have.

"One at once," Lucy replied. "It's going well, thank you. He's gone off on his bike to North Wales with his mates."

"They'll be keeping a welcome for them in the hillside, no doubt," I said.

She asked me if I'd ever had a bike. Ruth has inherited her risk-averse genes from me more than from her mother, although neither of us have ever been likely to take up skydiving as a hobby. I had to admit to Lucy that the nearest I'd come was a push bike.

"With drop handlebars and a five-speed derailleur," I pleaded in mitigation. "And the second car I had was an MG Midget."

"No, not up to the mark, Bob. I need a guy with a big engine between his legs."

I can only assume that Dave fits that bill. I understand why the producer at Granada is interested in her turn of phrase, although I imagine that her body hasn't gone totally unnoticed with him either. She certainly has a way with words. Even Rachel briefly looked up from her phone, though seemingly unfazed at the antics of her former teacher. Lucy was breaking no politically correct taboos. But surely, she wasn't like that when she was teaching? I hoped the younger three swingers were sufficiently out of earshot. I would hate them to be hankering after a motorbike when they're older.

Ruth joined in the fun by telling Lucy that my new car was a hybrid, as at my age energy conservation was all that mattered. The real reason of course is that I don't want my carbon footprint to be another impediment to me passing through the pearly gates. In any case, Wendy had heard enough from the swings to shout over that she preferred me as I was, an old banger. She put her hand over her mouth the moment she said it, so hadn't meant the double entendre.

Lucy's cackle certainly assumed that she had done. It was as well that Paul appeared on the horizon at that moment or the sex education sessions at the school could have been declared redundant.

He walked up the path towards our bench, carrying a case, dressed casually while wearing shiny black shoes, incongruous unless you knew him. He must have been on his way to the station when he'd seen us. Wendy stopped pushing Richie and lifted him off the swing. Ben and Alice both leapt down, running to join us. By the time Paul reached the bench, an audience was fully assembled and looking forward to the show.

He looked haggard. "I can only tell you how sorry I am about that dreadful scene in your garden. I'm an idiot and I'll never change." He then spoke directly to the children. "I'm a rotten example for you boys and girls," he stuttered, before he broke down crying. Lucy put her arm round him, telling him he'd no need to beat himself up; we'd all no doubt made fools of ourselves in our time and would do so again. I'm not sure if Wendy ever has, but who knows what any of us can be like? Paul smiled wanly, saying that he'd loved those few weeks being half of an item.

He hoped that David would treat her well, then apologised again separately to Ruth and Wendy, before leaving as quickly as he had arrived, without any particular acknowledgement to me. I don't suppose anyone else noticed that omission. He's probably of the view that Lucy is worth ten thousand of me too.

"That was very brave of him," she opined.

"He was hurting deeply," agreed Ruth.

"Is that why he was crying?" asked Alice.

"His shoes were probably too tight," I suggested.

I was then accused of being unfeeling and unforgiving by Ruth, which was fair enough. I saw a faint smile flicker across Wendy's face though. She'd had enough of the plonker too.

"He's not a bad guy, Bob," Lucy said. "He can be charming when you get to know him."

Well, I'd known him for sixty years and he'd kept that well-hidden from me. I said no more. We started chatting about Lucy's writing. As told, her story seemed lightweight, involving incontinent pensioners, locked lavatories, and stereotyped characters failing to get on any better with each other than they had when younger, all with character quirks suspiciously close to self-parody. I guess that storyline does have the benefit of being similar to real life, as evidenced by Paul and me. She laughed a lot as she explained the ins and outs of the plot. Clearly, she was entertained by it all.

She was going to Manchester Media City that very afternoon to see her producer friend. She'd rung him that morning, she said, and he'd invited her over to discuss the project. I'd stopped listening to the story itself before she was halfway through. She must have noticed. From her coat pocket, she pulled out a couple of copies of the first two pages that she was carrying, ready for her meeting. She gave us one each. She'd already badly creased them both. She told us to keep them as she'd better take some fresh copies and put them in a folder before she went to Manchester. We both read while she looked on anxiously. What seems to me to be unusual is Lucy's ability to make the dialogue sound realistic but absurd at the same time. See what you think.

ACT I

SCENE 1

(The leaving of Lower Shuttlebottom)

A coach engine kicks into life above the general hubbub of chatter

52

DOREEN

Have you not got that seat belt on properly yet?

HILDA

I think there's something wrong with it. I can't get it in.

FRED

Never a problem for me! Take out a bit of slack first.

HILDA

He thinks we're making a coal fire with nutty slack.

DOREEN

Dad used to call it slutty knack, and Ma would give him an earful.

FRED

Must have been painful, getting an earful of coal.

HILDA

He was always having to have his ears syringed. Hooray, I've done it.

DOREEN

You've done it alright. That's where my belt should go.

FRED

How did you manage to have kids if you didn't know which hole was which?

HILDA

We tried them all and waited to see which one worked.

DOREEN

That's the way we picked the boys too!

(They cackle)

FRED

Both of you invited me to have a go, and both slapped my face when my hand reached the top of your nylons.

DOREEN

That was sixty odd years ago, Fred. We had to do that. You had to marry us to get past there.

FRED

What, both of you? That would have been bigamy.

HILDA

You could have married Doreen, and then married me if she'd died.

FRED

That's not allowed. Did you never read who you could or couldn't marry at the back of the prayer book? There was nowt else to read in the choir stalls. Wife's sister is prohibited.

DOREEN

Girls weren't allowed in the choir. I'm sure they did do in the Bible. Maybe that was the Old Testament, when they were knowing each other and then begetting.

HILDA

You were just too slow, Fred. Bill and Joe got in quicker.

FRED

I know they did. Ey up. We're off. Here we come, Bowness. On our Battle Bus.

"What do you think?" Lucy asked.

"Very good," said Wendy. "I'm sure the producer will like it."

"Superlative," I said, hoping that the insincerity wouldn't be obvious in my voice. "Sock it to them."

We wished her good luck as we all trooped back to the Breck to go our separate ways.

As a parting shot to us, she said, "I'll have the last laugh. Even if my play doesn't get on air, Jezza Corbyn will be the next prime minister, just you see. I'm fully signed-up to Momentum now, to spite Paul. Down with elitism. Close all public schools down. State schools are best. Hang all old Etonians, starting with David Cameron and Boris Johnson, even if it's courtesy of them that we're getting to escape Europe."

"God help us all," I replied. "But it is Labour's turn next time out, so who knows? I guess hanging them would save them from a lifetime of regret. Do you want to draw and quarter them too?"

"I think that may be a bit over the top," she giggled. "I don't really want to hang them. Just stick them in the stocks and chuck some rotten tomatoes at them."

"I knew you were too compassionate for the hard-left."

Going through my head as we said our goodbyes was an old rhyme of my Dad's. 'Tomatoes don't hurt said my Uncle Jim. But by Gum they do if they're in a tin.' The hustings were rough back in the twenties too.

I'd understood Lucy to be a moderate when she'd had her bash to get on Preston Council. I wonder if it's Dave that's radicalising her in bed. I don't blame her though. I've seen nothing to suggest that so much of Osborne's austerity is necessary or desirable. Undoubtedly, babies are being lost with the bath water. I'd be happy to pay a bit more in taxes, if not a lot, and we could probably comfortably fund a bigger deficit. But it would be hard to stomach the re-nationalisation of electricity after the blood, sweat and tears I spent privatising the bloody thing. Just toughen up the regulation and spend the dosh on something else, Jezza. We're an island, so how about a big tidal scheme? Maybe one across Morecambe Bay, linking Eric's birthplace with Stan Laurel's. That would hit all the right notes, if not necessarily in the right order, even if it did turn out to be another fine mess.

As Lucy clearly does, I try to enjoy what I write too, which then leaves me wondering if I'm indulging in futile self-praise, propping up and preening my sense of self-esteem, or if someone outside me is writing the words. Where does a joke come from? Are there really only seven jokes, as I've seen claimed? Or is there a companion volume to the *Book of Life* called *The Bumper Fun Book* permanently available to us all? Are the little foibles of Lucy's characters written for her by an alter ego?

And, crucially, does she stand a snowball in hell's chance of getting that play on to the radio?

CHAPTER SIX
December 2015

I've had a phone call from my great friend, Richard. The same age as me, he's from Bolton, as you'll have guessed from his football team. He now lives in the village of Monkey Mead in Hertfordshire with his beautiful, feisty wife Helen. One and a half of their four children are yet to fly their nest. The half is the second youngest, James, the lucky T20 Finals Day attendee, aged 20 and in his second year reading History at Manchester University. As we chatted on the phone, expanding further our solution to the meaning of life (Richard being a lay reader who conducts the services at his local Church), we found out that we're both going to be in the north-west this coming weekend. Richard is delivering a desk to, and collecting James from, Rusholme in South Manchester. Bolton Wanderers are playing Fulham on Saturday and the game is on their itinerary before the drive south.

Richard was originally planning to go into the Church as a young man, after reading Theology at Oxford. It was at theological college that he had too many doubts to continue on that path, making the leap into banking instead. He couldn't believe in eternal damnation, wanting all to be saved. In later life, he'd learnt how to hide his reservations with Church doctrine sufficiently to become a lay reader. It wouldn't be the doctrine that would be my problem: it would be the petty politics played by parishioners, particularly those on the Parochial Church Council. I've always avoided like the plague getting too involved. I just want to show up on a Sunday for a pleasant service, which definitionally has only a short sermon. The odd time I've been roped in for more, always when there's fund raising on the agenda and thus my cheque book is in demand, I've been astonished at the extent of the scheming and nastiness involved. A big company Board of Directors is a vicarage tea party compared with the committee organising an actual one at Church.

Richard is naturally much brighter than I am. I'm happy that I got where I did by a bit of, if not that hard, graft; he not only did it effortlessly but wanted everyone to know that's what he'd done. He can drive my super-conscientious Wendy to distraction with his genuinely last-minute brilliance. Of course, back in early 1963 he'd known about and watched Dylan in *Madhouse on Castle Street* rather than the Palladium show. As a banker, he's had to live his life among ex-public-school types who affect what comes to him naturally. He went to Oxford, too, but has never quite joined the set he's been with. The unforgiveable sin to people in that world is not to join, and that's what his conscience has always told him that he mustn't do. He even gave to charity what he thought to be an unearned bonus. That dichotomy means that he's a really interesting as well as a good guy, unfailingly friendly and a great advert for the northern intellectual that he succeeds in being.

We're driving up to Ruth's on Friday evening for a lengthy Christmas stay. All Ruth's children are home and Ethel next door is off to her son's place for Christmas. So, we've booked in at the Throstles' Nest Hotel, over the Wyre but the only Inn with any room. Hattie plans to spend most nights with us there but also will have her basket at Ruth's for if she prefers a sleepover.

Richard asked if I could find time to come to the game with them. I'll jump at the chance to watch any match, apart from Blackpool that is. The only time I'm allowed to watch them now is the odd game when they're in the Midlands, paying cash at the gate, so that it doesn't get into the wrong hands. Against Fulham, I'll happily stick up for the Wanderers. Wendy's not into football, but she likes Richard too much not to want to see him, even if he irritates her in equal measure. We all ended up going over to Bolton to meet them. Wendy went to the Vue cinema on the Middlebrook Retail Park next to the ground with Alice and Richie to watch a film called *The Good Dinosaur*, while I perched in the Lofthouse Upper Stand with Richard and James to watch a two-each draw. Wendy told me afterwards how Alice had cried at the sad bits of the film, which passed Richie by. As a lad, I was the same. It wasn't until adolescence that sadness started to evoke pity.

Afterwards we all met up and wandered round, looking for the least full restaurant while dodging the never-ending flow of cars. Eventually we found a table big enough in Nando's. It was as well that we'd ordered the refillable drinks option as Richard and I had both drowned our chicken in peri-peri sauce. The habits of our generation of going for the most macho sauce will, like good religion and sensible politics, seemingly die with us. James had more sense about which sauce to take, selecting two notches down. We were able to have what were called macho peas too, although I don't see how they can put hairs on your chest. Wendy picked the mildest sauce, which the kids also had.

Wendy and I had met James a couple of times as he was growing up. He's turned out a very pleasant young man, seemingly coupling his father's friendly disposition with his mother's good looks, while temperamentally somewhere between the earnestness of his father and the usually cool detachment of his mother. I could sense that he would be much sought after by the girls. And this was soon to be confirmed.

As I manoeuvred to the drinks machine with the children for a top-up, a familiar voice shouted my name as she came through the door. Of course, it could only be Lucy Fishwick. Anyone else would have come much closer before making their presence known. With her was daughter Maddie, who more than lived up to the photograph that Paul had shown me. She was a stunner. She'd dyed her hair ash-blonde since the photo, which accentuated the blackness of her eyebrows and eyelashes. They were on their way back to St Chad's from Sheffield. Lucy plonked herself down at the table which had just freed up next to ours.

"How did your meeting with the producer go?" Wendy asked.

"Total waste of time," answered Lucy. "He was disappointed that I hadn't done more to tidy the script up. I'd told him before we went that I hadn't got round to that yet. I've had other things I've had to do." She grinned at the memory of what and with whom those had been, before saying, "I could really do with some help on the editing."

She looked round for volunteers. Nobody met her gaze.

Maddie was sent to order their food. James' eyes followed as her tightly be-jeaned bottom sashayed its way to the counter, with frequency of wiggle identical to that of her mother's and with just as many secondary spikes on the wave form. It was like watching a tigress slinking through the grass before the fatal pounce. She was taller and slimmer than her mother, more conventionally good-looking with bigger eyes, a rounder chin and an almost symmetrical face. They shared the same slightly turned-up nose. I quickly did the Maths and worked out that Maddie must be a couple of years older than James. He'd already been the centre of attention with our Alice, who was doing her best to show how grown-up she was. He talked nicely to her, on equal terms.

61

On return, Maddie chose the seat facing James. Lucy's antennae picked up the immediate surge in male hormonal activity. Before they were ready for their first refill, she'd pumped Richard about his son for all the necessary information that her daughter might need to make an assessment. I suspect she was also sussing Richard out to see if he was a better bet than Dave to father her child, showing some disappointment when she found he was very married. Her work wasn't entirely in vain; as we prepared to leave there was a quick exchange of mobile numbers between Maddie and James, on the pretence that they were going to share some music. The noise level was high, and their faces touched in their strain to hear each other. Neither felt the need to apologise.

Outside in the car park, Richard, Wendy and I discussed when we could meet up again. Amy, aged thirteen, is their youngest, an unintended but delightful consequence of too spontaneous a coupling in later life. They are next planning to come north during James' reading week in late February, which coincides with Amy's school half-term. Richard suggested that they might stop for a night on the way up, at the posh hotel in Broadway, close to Nether Piddle. Wendy immediately volunteered to cook a dinner for them. Richard made a quick call to Helen, the executive sanctioning committee of their household, who happily approved the proposal.

That's still a couple of months away. We said our goodbyes to Richard and James before making our way to Throstles' Nest. We've not met the owner yet, an actor from Manchester who bought the place for a hobby he's become bored with, but the staff here are very friendly. There's no front desk at the hotel. Everything is run from the bar, which is just a normal pub with a restaurant in one section. We have breakfast in there every morning. The principal waitress multi-tasks as receptionist and occasional barmaid. Her name's

Fiona. She's from round here and went to school with Maddie. The main barman is Fiona's boyfriend, Jason, who's a Brummie. Each of them possesses a degree in American Studies from Birmingham University, where they met. Fiona says that the only use she has put her degree to so far is asking customers if they prefer their eggs 'over easy' or 'sunny side up'. They've been working like this for more than a year now, trying without success to find decent jobs in the area that could lead to a career, living at Fiona's parents' house, who for both economic and health reasons need them to stay around. We chatted to them while having a quiet drink. He's no brainbox and his 'Desmond' of a degree is not likely to make him an automatic choice in any short-listing process. She has a much better degree, and is pleasant, pretty and knowledgeable. You'd have thought the world would be her oyster, but, having lowered her sights to an entry level job in HR, she still hasn't come up with anything. She seems a sensible girl. Her parents had warned her to steer clear of 'that Maddie Fishwick' at school, advice that she said, with a sardonic grin, she'd usually managed to follow.

The next day, we went across to Ruth's for lunch and an afternoon with all the mob. In the evening was the carol service at St Chad's church. We were brave enough to take Alice and Richie with us. If they could survive *The Good Dinosaur*, we thought they could handle this. I bowed my head to say that little prayer intended to clear the head, as folk do. I always find that making up my mind what to pray for just produces more confusion. This was added to by Richie asking what I was doing. Fortunately, Alice answered for me. I was none too sure myself.

There was some noise in the pew behind as I prayed. As I sat back, head racing, Lucy's voice asked if we were fated to keep sitting close to each other. That wasn't the something I'd ended up praying for. I was more gobsmacked to find that sitting with her were not only Maddie and Dave but also Paul. Dave was in full leathers, Maddie a leather mini-skirt and knee-high black boots with black tights, Lucy a leather trench coat of many colours. Paul was in a suit. Such a gathering could only have been assembled in an Anglican Church or the pub. Paul wouldn't have wanted to be in Church, but the only thing Lucy would never get him to was a Momentum meeting. I guessed that he was the means to which she was reverting to tidy up her script. "Good God! Miracles never cease," I replied before turning back to the family.

"It was Maddie's idea," answered Lucy, as my head twisted back and forth. "I wanted to go to Mass."

"Ecumenism, Mum. You ought to give it a go. And you'll get better hymns here," said Maddie.

Alice looked spellbound at the star on the huge Christmas tree. Richie was more excited at the rows of pews. "It's like an aeroplane," he said as he jumped up and down. That's closer to what I'd just been asking for: that the kids will see Christmas the way I have these seventy years; God with us, the words written on our crib ornament, with us in the miracle of his birth. The faces of all my relatives who I'd spent those happy times past with, damn near all gone, went through my head. All had sat on these pews. Some of their coffins had passed through here on their way to the graveyard. Unseen, were they sitting alongside us? I don't have to wait for Easter to know that birth needs death. I miss them most at Christmas.

It's a pity that my other child, Ruth's slightly younger brother Robert, can't be with us. He's gone with his wife Sophie and family to his in-laws in Vancouver. We used to be so close, and still are when we meet, which isn't often enough. Accompanying them to Canada is my ex-wife Jane and husband Geoffrey. So, the quick of the present-day aren't to be together in full either. I'm even missing Jane, admittedly in the way that you can't feel a stone in your shoe once you've taken it out. Just sometimes I see her at Christmas. They're all mine, and I hope I'm theirs. Wendy, my saviour, is a wonderful partner and does her best to feel my past. Inevitably, that is learnt and not lived knowledge. We can't share the same memories, and we definitely don't listen to the same music! I do try to appreciate hers, and just occasionally something clicks, but there was a change of beat in between our eras. And, as life is but a short season, sadly we'll be together for only a very few games. I pray that peace on earth will prevail long enough for our two little ones to play their full fixture list. Someday, they will be the past too, remembered until soon forgotten.

A piping treble could be heard from the back singing 'Once in Royal David's City'. I know this is somewhat of an anachronism, like 'Abide with Me' at the cup final, rather than as the processional for our two kids' lives. But what a tragedy it would be if this tradition were to be lost in the wash, displaced as the community singing at Wembley has been. It already seems to be halfway down the plughole. I remember Arthur Caiger, the man in the white suit, conducting the Wembley crowd from a special podium. Not that we needed him at this service. Anglican congregations still know the old hymns. Once it was our turn to join in, Alice sang her little heart out as if she knew what I was thinking. Richie looked anxiously towards me and I gave him an encouraging smile, but my usual deep voice was wavering. Wendy gave me the smile I'd given Richie. Strength came in until the last two lines, 'Where like stars his children crowned all in white shall wait around'. I felt my voice crack again.

Behind was Lucy and crew, representing the Other in both physical and spiritual form, a Catholic, a Methodist, an atheist and maybe a hell's angel. As I said, only in an Anglican church... still, at least they add to the spice of life. Pity we didn't have a Muslim, a Hindu, a Buddhist and a Jew too, plus perhaps a Christadelphian and a Quaker to keep the peace or at least referee the fight.

After the service, Ruth asked us all back for a drink, on the foolhardy side of courageous given what had happened the last time Paul had been round. She'd put a big ham in the oven before the service, which went down a treat with barm cakes and mulled wine, supplemented with sausage rolls intended for later in the holiday. Paul was again doing his best to avoid me, latching on to Wendy. Ruth and Lucy discussed events at the school, with Maddie forced to listen. I was allocated Dave.

All I knew of him was that he's a body builder, has his motorbike and a Rottweiler, wears leather, and has derisively given Paul the finger. I'm happy about the last bit, more worried about the rest. But I've found out that the best way to tell the character of a dog is to look at the owner, and vice versa. Roxanne is a great girl on every measure.

I soon could see why. Dave is a salt of the earth type, the kind of individual who can only happily work for himself, which he does as an electrician. Contrary to what we'd thought, he has a job. Back at Kirkham, he owns a white van as well as a motorbike. He's not the reason for Lucy embracing the Momentum view of life. It was a reaction to Paul. I asked him where he'd trained. He'd been apprenticed with a small firm in Preston, and mainly works in Blackpool where there is always plenty of work to be had on the attractions.

The finger was out of character. He's never been a hell's angel, not that he's anything against them. He's very happy that Paul is back in Lucy's life as developmental editor. He says that he can understand

Paul, who's like most intellectuals. He has more trouble with me, who seems to be a bit of both. He asked a penetrating question: what I'd have done if I'd been ill on the day of the eleven plus.

"Could have been an electrician," I answered. "Though I'm none too good at making the wiring look tidy. Go back half a century and I'd have been a farm labourer." It's true, I'd have only been good for manual labour until having intelligence could earn you a living.

"I've heard the jobs you've had, and you've obviously got loads of money. Has it changed you?" he asked.

"You tell me," I answered. "Probably has done, and not for the better."

Maddie was bored with the parent talk. She came to join us.

"Mum tells me that you're a scientist who believes in God," she said. "You don't see many of those on the box."

"There's more than you think, particularly among physicists. The Big Bang Theory…"

"What, you mean Sheldon?" she interrupted. If anybody reading this hasn't seen this show, I can only apologise. "I bet you just fancy Penny. I certainly could. Pity she prefers men," Maddie added. Penny is a very attractive character in the show, one who is no better than she ought to be, but with the men. Of course, my interest in the show is for the snippets of science.

I have to admit that it never crossed my mind in my youth when lusting after a pretty girl that she might actually prefer another girl to me. Even at this late age, I was put off my stride. So, faced with this not-unusual-for-her-generation display of bisexual nonchalance, I forgot all about the guff I was building up to about a finite world implying a creator, and quite possibly an infinite world doing so too. Stuttering, I confessed to being an engineer and not a scientist, with no doubt Sheldon regarding me as he did Howard. But it wasn't humour or modern sexual preferences that Maddie wanted to discuss, any more than it was theology. It was that enemy of them both: morals, the devil's greatest accomplishment, a dose of which she was living through. Maddie wasn't wearing leather in sympathy with Dave or in opposition to Paul, at least not consciously. She admitted though that she hadn't yet come to terms with her Mum's relationship with either and certainly not both. As she spoke, she was teasing me and covering herself up simultaneously.

"Just don't think I'm a goofball like Penny though," she finished with. "Or as promiscuous as her. Or my Mum. I was, but not at the moment, anyway. My worry is that we're all meant to end up like our mother."

She was staring straight at Dave as she said this, in accusatory fashion. She then glanced towards Paul. I couldn't let that past.

"Both your Mum and Penny know how to live and there's nowt wrong with that," I said. "Life's to be enjoyed as much as you can. That way you can handle the sadnesses when they arrive."

Wendy heard the conversation. Worried that the children might be hearing too much, she suggested it was time for us to go to the hotel and put them to bed. Lucy was listening too. As we packed up our stuff, she squeezed me by the arm and whispered, "Thanks, Bob, you're a pal. It's something she's got to work through." They left with us. To show my solidarity with Dave, I asked what time they were walking Roxanne and Toffee in the morning. There are no decent dog walks to be had by the hotel, surrounded as it is by farmed fields. We've arranged to meet up. Paul asked if he could join. Lucy agreed. Dave looked bleakly at me. I said nothing.

The next morning, Hattie and I drove down into St Chad's from Throstles' Nest and rang Lucy's bell. Out came the other two dogs with Dave, Maddie and Lucy. It wouldn't have surprised me if Paul had stopped the night with them too. We did at least have to walk to his house to collect him. If it didn't seem that happy a band of pilgrims that trod onwards, the three dogs were having a whale of a time. Hattie is still sprightly for her age and ran rings around Roxanne who lolloped around happily.

"How's the radio play going?" I asked.

"Not great," answered Paul. "I can't tell when Lucy is being serious and when she's playing word games."

"That's what I'm always doing," said Lucy.

"Well, it would be helpful if the words were in the right order so I could know what it is that you're trying to achieve. It would be even better if the letters were the right order in the words as well."

Spelling isn't Lucy's strongest suit, nor diplomacy Paul's.

"How are you getting on with the course?" I asked Maddie. "Methodism suiting you?"

"I'm really not sure, Bob. It's logical and it's Christian. I'm not either. I don't think straight, and I can't turn the other cheek. I need more drama. Maybe I need something more charismatic."

"Come back to the Catholics then," said Lucy.

"That's not quite what charismatic has come to mean, Mum. And there aren't many opportunities for women in the priesthood. I can't see myself taking a nun's vows and keeping them."

"Nor can I, more's the pity," said Lucy laughing raucously. "Not unless they bring back chastity belts and I throw away your key. Even then you'd find a way."

I suppose it would be nice for Lucy if Maddie were to return to the old faith, but I prefer Christianity when it's messy and not homogeneous too.

"You could try middle-of-the-road Anglicanism," I suggested. "It works fine for me."

"That's just wishy washy," said Maddie. "That's definitely not me. I'd need more authority than that to stay on the rails."

"That's the last thing I want," I replied. "All denominations could do with forgetting about the creeds the early Church saddled us with, clever as they are. They've caused wars and worse. How are you lot spending Christmas?"

This last question, designed to change the subject, revealed a more practical application of religion's principles. Paul would have had nowhere to go on Christmas Day, while Dave has a sister in Kirkham. Dave really is a big-hearted guy and has already offered up to Paul his natural place sitting by Lucy for the day. Maddie didn't look any too happy with that act of charity. Lucy said that Dave would get a better meal at his sister's anyway. I gathered that her cooking, like her, can be erratic.

Maddie's mobile rang. She answered, and her next words were, "James who?" Only after the caller had said more did she say, "Oh yes, I remember," before moving out of earshot. She walked about twenty yards behind us for the next few five minutes. When she returned, she asked Dave what he knew about The Libertines. He gave a long and informed answer. She casually dropped that she was going to a concert at the Manchester Arena on 23 January to see their *Anthems for Doomed Youth* tour. "What passing-bells for these who die as cattle?" said Paul. Our old English master was keen on the war poets. My contribution was, "The pallor of girls' brows shall be their pall." The relationship between Maddie Fishwick and James Shackleton doesn't start auspiciously

Playwright Lucy is not so well read. "What are you two on about?" she enquired, looking up, head tilted, as eager to learn as puppy. Dave knew the poem and explained it to her. I thought then that she could be better off asking him to be her editor. The rest of the walk passed off without any quibbling. It's coming up to Christmas after all.

Before we left a couple of days after New Year, the editing had been finished and the manuscript sent off. Lucy seemingly has no more need for Paul, apart from that she has a heart of gold that wouldn't lightly let down a friend. Hattie and I saw Dave and Lucy walking their dogs most days before we left, usually with Paul in attendance. An unholy trinity indeed. Two's company, three isn't.

CHAPTER SEVEN
January 2016

Back in Nether Piddle, my son Robert and family visited us after their return from Canada. Robert is a partner in a big London law firm. He's made his pile. If Wendy and I want to join in with the economic trials and tribulations being endured by much of the population, not only do we have to do it vicariously, but also away from this side of my family. Despite being born in very modest circumstances as the war ended, and not being particularly well-off until the post-Thatcherite nineties, that's not the world I've inhabited, and I wouldn't be a good enough writer to venture that far from my comfort zone. It wouldn't surprise me if, as a result, there are no universals to be found in what I think, but it would be a pity. I'll keep on trying to fit that camel through.

Robert's still a grand lad, despite not even having poverty at the start of his life. His much younger wife Sophie is a cracking girl, of humble mixed-race origins, heavily involved in human rights law. She left commercial practice specifically for this area of work. I think this is her way of assuaging the guilt at having so much now when she had so little as a child, although the chambers she's in makes so much money that she's earning damn near as much as she was before on normal commercial work. The firm has also become one of the go-to places for environmental cases, often on the opposite side from where my past career would have taken me. They have with them their two children, also my grandchildren of course. Patrick is a year older than his Uncle Richie, and Susanna is three years younger than her brother. The four children in the house thus ranged between three and seven years in age. Entertaining them proved quite a challenge for a septuagenarian, and by mid-afternoon I'd delegated any residual responsibilities to wife and son while I had a chat with Sophie.

We've always hit it off despite our naturally different interests. We do both share the deep religious conviction that there's a God who we owe our life to, and that there's a judge and redeemer as our base for morality, which for me makes it odd that she thinks a humanist basis of rights should be viewed as primary.

"We don't live in a world where everybody shares our faith. What human rights provide is a template for all people to follow," she says. "As the Ten Commandments once did."

"They're both human constructions though. I don't think the Amalekites and all the rest of that crew around Palestine followed any Commandments. Forget that bollocks about Moses bringing them down from Mount Sinai. They're a priestly invention and Jesus came to replace them," I reply, not for the first time. "Only God could give us absolute rights. And he doesn't seem to have given us any. Our lives are totally contingent on whatever's chucked at us. The best response is to appreciate the absurdity of it all."

"That's nihilist. We need protecting from what can be controlled," she countered.

"That would carry more weight if the agenda hadn't been totally hijacked by special interest groups. Civil and Union rights were first won by black and northern voices, but they're now interpreted in condescending, middle-class tones. When one right clashes with another, it's the most fashionable that wins."

"No, it's the most liberal one that succeeds," she replied with a smile. "That's why you don't like them. You can't leave

73

your Victorian idea of duty-first behind, even when the duty leads you nowhere."

"Hey, there's not been one piece of liberal legislation that's been passed I haven't supported, not even abortion, despite my qualms. I just don't like things set out in lists. I'd rather find the principle, the equation that generates them. Lists are for life scientists and chefs. You lawyers should be brighter than that, and up for arguing from first principles."

"Lists are loved by most people. It's the way they catalogue, the way they store, it's the way they think. It's you maths guys with your equations who are the freaks of nature. Just because you lot can't multi-task doesn't mean the rest of us can't."

You'd have never thought that I'd run a multi-billion-pound business and she works in chambers with just a few others, who always seem to be falling out with each other from what she tells us.

"We integrate and not differentiate. Anyway, are you sure you're succeeding?" I said. "Rules put down in black and white are illiberal things. Look at social media. Everyone a hypocrite, casting stones when none need to be chucked."

"No, look at the bigotry out there right now, Bob. Hear what Trump is saying in his campaign. Build the wall, indeed. Not exactly 'love thy neighbour as thyself', is it? Look at the far right growing again in Europe. Read about the effects of austerity by our supposedly compassionate, centre-right Government here. It's time you changed to the *Guardian* from *The Times*. It's nearly as good a crossword." She paused briefly to smile at my professed reason for staying with Murdoch. "The battles still have to be fought on a daily basis. And it doesn't matter in what accent. Christ came to fulfil the law, not replace it."

She always gets the last word now. She wants to win the argument;

she's a lawyer. It sometimes seems to be more important than the truth to her side. So, I couldn't be bothered to say that most folk in the world aren't citizens of liberal democracies and live without any protection from their capricious masters, itself often made worse as a reaction to the moral posturing of the West.

"The accent matters to me. I'll only change back to the *Guardian* if they'll move back to Manchester," I replied.

Sophie sees my golden time, the early sixties, when for that short season the white working class got a real stake in this country's culture, as male-focused and at most a useful first step in the real feminist struggles that were to come. She's read her Betty Friedan about how fifties' and sixties' housewives used to pretend to live a domestic dream, needing Valium to take away the dissatisfaction they felt from missing out on a career. She claims, probably rightly I have to admit, that only the contraceptive pill changed that, although I don't believe that either my Mum or sister were on tranquilisers as a result of their supposed domestic captivity. The role of the engineer in making the world better brings a thin smile to her face. We caused global warming after all. When I point out how much, led by electrical engineers, the UK has cut its carbon emissions since the miners' strike, admittedly more by good luck than judgement, with conservation, wind turbines, nuclear power, and the switch from coal to gas, she says we could have done much more. She's totally antagonistic to fracking, dismissing the underlying statistics behind the safety arguments, or the security of supply for the nation. She takes it as a given that the lights will stay on. So, my former profession is either an irrelevance or part of the problem. It seems like the industrial revolution is finished. The future is entirely social. The lights will then stay on if a citizens' assembly says that they must.

When I say that you can't have the white working class forever on the back foot, apologising for things that happened when they didn't even have a vote to change things, she insists that they are still happening. I ask if she is worried that there might be a backlash coming in the upcoming referendum. It won't happen, she says, but if it does, so be it.

In that moment, I realised how much I face a lock-out, not only by her, but the educated of an entire generation, if not two. I'm humoured, but no more will my point of view matter to anyone, apart perhaps from Wendy. And she's a lot younger than me, so I certainly can't take her for granted. My natural friends from younger folk are only likely to be guys like Dave, blokes doing useful things from a white van.

Some things don't change though. I'm still Sophie's favourite in-law. Geoffrey hasn't managed to keep the peace between her and Jane in Canada. They'd had a big argument over gender identity issues, increasingly being handled by Sophie's firm. Older feminist Jane, inspired by Germaine Greer after reading *The Female Eunuch* in her twenties, doesn't think men can self-identify as women. Sophie disagrees, or at least says she does. I don't want to lose brownie points, so I haven't declared my agreement with Jane, confining myself to the practical. Seeing I don't know any who have so identified, I really shouldn't form a view. I'm not prepared to lose urinals, but if women want to have a unisex go at them, I'll promise not to look, or at least not to laugh, whichever way they face. Sophie says that to be the standard reply by all alpha males. I'm sure she'll be right about that too, not that I've ever discussed it with anyone. In any case, I'm only a beta double minus, and that's on a day when my sciatica's behaving itself.

Robert then came in to tell me that they'd made his firm's

Christmas bash a seventies evening. He only did it to wind me up, knowing that I'd rise to the bait and say how naff that decade was, at least until punk, The Pretenders and Elvis Costello came along. There's never been anything glam in my life, although to be fair, I did quite like Bryan Ferry when he out-toffed the toffs, giving a genuine depiction of grammar schoolboy aspiration. Mind you, I'm mainly talking about the earlier parts of the sixties as my time. There wasn't that much about the hippies or flower power worth bagging up and keeping. Folk don't recognise the difference between the sixties and seventies any longer, Robert then claimed, again no doubt rightly, let alone the different waves within them.

"I've just been hearing that from Sophie," I replied. "Am I not folk too?"

"No, you're Dad," he smirked. "It's our turn to patronise you now."

"I'd noticed. It's been your turn ever since that preening pillock Blair became prime minister," I replied as Wendy walked back in with the children. "The true voice of your generation. He took us to war because he couldn't tell fact from fiction. I never thought that Saddam had the weapons."

That was a below the belt last remark that didn't add to my arguments, if I had any. Political analysis was over as I was summoned to the kitchen to help lay out the place settings for tea. That's become my only sought-after skill set. I know which way to put the cutlery.

CHAPTER EIGHT
Late February 2016

I was putting the forks out the right way again, this time for dinner, in our Nether Piddle home on the evening of Helen, Richard and Amy's visit. The idea was for Alice and Richie to have an early tea and then put on their pyjamas before the guests arrived. They could join the grown-ups, a group to which Amy had been granted full membership, in the pre-dinner drinks and then go up to bed. While waiting, Alice helped me set the table in the dining room. See, I'm not so sexist that I'm not prepared to share the secrets of setting a table with a girl. I lost all my fine crystal when my marriage ended. I used to love savouring decent claret in the Thomas Webb glasses bought for us by my mother. At least I know that my ex's third husband, a good guy, will be appreciating them. The second one, not someone easy to like, at least by me, was good enough not to throw them away. Wendy's husband was in the antiques business, which means that her crockery, cutlery and glassware have become retro, being bought by her in reaction to him as the most modern available in John Lewis twenty years ago. She couldn't abide traditional stuff then, and she's still not too happy about it. The archaeologist in her is only happy with old stuff if it's from Roman times, or earlier. Hers hadn't been a happy marriage. But our changeovers have lost me the one bit of gravitas I'd ever had, decent glasses to drink decent wine from.

With great excitement, Alice opened the door. Hattie knew the visitors well enough to give them a raucous reception. Our cat Sheba scuttled upstairs. Helen remembered how much I detested the cheek-kissing routine, clapping me on the shoulder instead. Richard and Wendy indulged in the faux affection. To be fair, it's not false. We all like each other and in other lifetimes could no doubt have gone for each other's partners, apart from Helen could probably never fancy an ugly bugger like me. Richard is Richie's godfather, a role he has performed diligently to date and which he continued to do so for the next ten minutes before passing over to teenager Amy. She had no choice for this first part of the evening but to be one of the children. Alice and Richie hung on her every word. They showed her their bedrooms, and then their computer games. I've no idea what they were playing, and certainly had no intention of supervising. I can only supply the most general of guidance. It has to be up to them not to go off the rails. I'm pretty sure though that it wasn't *Grand Theft Auto*, whatever that might be.

Helen was looking as beautiful as ever, the lines on her face at one with her bone structure. She preferred the freedom of a pleasant glass of Pinot Grigio to childhood play, something she was pleased to have left behind after the four children of her own. She's a vet by trade, thus having no false sentimentality within her. While I chatted with Richard and her, Wendy popped in and out of the kitchen. She asked how James had hit it off with Maddie. Helen still hadn't met her but was already worried for him.

"I think he's a doomed youth already with her, Wendy," she said, although with a smile. "The concert was a success. She likes the same music as he does, or so she says. But he's like his dad, too keen to please. A couple of weeks ago, he was full of a trip they were taking to Chatsworth. His tail hasn't been wagging since. He's no Darcy, and she's certainly no Elizabeth Bennet. It didn't sound like that trip had pushed the right buttons."

"What's James like about the night clubs that used to be more her scene?" I asked.

"He doesn't like them much. Says you can't get served, the beer's too expensive and that they play lousy music."

She's been stalking James on iPhone's Find Friends, to Richards's disapproval, so she knew that James had actually spent the last two weekends in Sheffield. He'd know that she knew of course, but to switch her off would be something too rude for a Shackleton to contemplate. I deduced that Maddie hasn't yet plunged back into the Pope's bosom but is persisting in her course on post-enlightenment Wesleyan rationality. Apparently, that isn't totally clear, as James had confessed on the last mandatory weekly phone call home to being dragged to a Pentecostal event on the Sunday, after Chatsworth. Maddie is still testing all spiritual options. They do have an interest in religion in common. James is happy to share his father's liberal faith as a start point in discussion. Maddie wants a stricter interpretation, but she knows not of what. She's a non-spiritual seeker of truth. She could end up anything from Calvinist Marxist to Catholic Fascist, I said, but probably not a Quaker or a Buddhist. Nor an Anglican, as she's already made clear to me.

Richard's football team, the mighty Wanderers, have been sinking fast since we watched them a couple of months ago.

"It's not just the football. The whole town's wrecked," he says. "We've gone from thriving to desolate in twenty years, courtesy of Westminster and bloody Greater Manchester. The place used to have every activity under the sun going on, with jobs, great shopping and entertainment, a top football team, so you didn't have to leave. But I'm buggered if they're going to take my past down. I'm a proud villager from what's still the largest village in England."

Blackpool as a town apart has been fighting a losing battle for more than fifty years, deserted by many, including a Labour Party who find Brighton more their spiritual home. I think even that's still a bit far north for their modern membership. He and I fell silent with our memories, refugees stranded in the squalor of a middle-class home, drinking expensive wine before a delicious meal. Helen told us that it was about time we at least joined the twentieth century if not the present one, though we would both be over a hundred years later doing so than Queen Victoria. It was by no means the first time she'd said something similar. Richard pointed out that even she was born nearer to the end of Queen Victoria's reign than today. But she hadn't shared in that great Anglican revival from Victorian times that we've been brought up in. We're the runt of that litter.

When Wendy next came in, Helen asked again how well we knew Maddie. Clearly, she is concerned for her youngest son, who has turned soulful, with a newly acquired taste for the romantic poets, perhaps surprisingly introduced to him by Maddie. Helen had heard all about Lucy, Dave and Paul. We told her that we hadn't yet really got to know Maddie, but that Lucy behaved with great dignity and had a heart of gold.

"A tart with a heart isn't perhaps what I was hoping for, but I suppose it's better than most alternatives. James will be at least a bit more worldly when he emerges broken-hearted," she said.

Richard defended their son's choice of girlfriend.

"Maddie's not a tart, love. She's a serious young lady with an appreciation of poetry who's training for ministry." He continued, despite Helen's knowing smirk suggesting that she knew otherwise, "I don't suppose Lucy is one either. She's written a radio play, we're told."

I've had no information from Ruth at St Chad's as to how the next meeting with the producer went. Lucy hasn't been broadcasting, so we've assumed it's gone badly. Maddie has said something to James though, which he'd relayed to Helen in a phone call. There hasn't been a next meeting. The producer doesn't like the re-write, saying the magic has been lost. He's giving her one last go at a re-write before rejecting it.

"That will be Paul's doing," I reckoned. "He was only asked to tidy it up, but I bet he's made it read like a professorial translation of Cicero's speeches. With footnotes. He'll have sucked the life out if it."

"Zombies on a coach trip to Windermere. Sounds like he's made it more interesting to me," Helen sniggered.

She was brought up in Sussex. Heritage doesn't start at *Coronation Street* for her, although in fact she's the only one in this conversation who watches the programme. She views it with the same sort of interest as an anthropologist shows in a remote tribe. It helps her understand Richard better, she always claims. While refusing to disclose the breach in Maddie's social media security which she'd exploited, she was also the only one who knew that Maddie and James were sleeping together in Sheffield. That was until she told us. Helen isn't one to be subtle about such matters. She disclosed that Maddie is finding James reasonably to her satisfaction, which doesn't sound enough for a girl with a hearty and eclectic appetite.

Wendy gave the call that dinner was only ten minutes away and it was time for our little ones to go to bed. That was my task. I went upstairs to find they were off their computers and Amy was reading them a story. When she'd finished, they both went off without demur. Amy breathed a sigh of relief as she came down the stairs with me. She seems to understand all that's going on in life pretty well for her age. Even so, I hoped that she hadn't heard the conversation from downstairs. She probably had though. Young ears miss nothing.

At dinner, Richard was still in defiant mood about his, and my, disappearing past. The two runts of the Victorian litter didn't often get the chance to speak to like-minded souls. He was bursting to show me a YouTube video he'd recently come across of the Everly Brothers and Chet Atkins performing Mark Knopfler's 'Why Worry'. He ignored table etiquette to do so.

"Phil's gone. Never again will we hear those harmonies, Bob," he said. "But it was effing good."

It effing was, a magical performance. There should be sunshine after rain. Engineer and theologian, a few years ago we'd worked out our model of reality that suited both of us. All this was in my head when I was talking to Paul Eckersley in the graveyard and during the dog walks. The beauty of the King James Bible, the hymns, the teenage Church Youth Club, will remain until death or dementia in the recurrent assembly of neuronal connections in my brain that I call me. That vastly more connections occur that I am not aware of as I live an instinctual life doesn't negate this sense of personhood. We might by instinct make a mistake once, but we should have created a conscious circuit capable of preventing a second error. We do exist physically, and we do exist mentally. Physical and mental are almost separate categories, although I'm sure they must link somehow.

I remember reading something from a guy called Donald Davidson, a non-reductionist philosopher, who makes three propositions that sum up this problem. They are: 1. the mental can cause the physical; 2. everything caused follows a natural law; and 3. these laws do not connect the mental with the physical. He called this anomalous monism. But is this a logically possible formulation? Doesn't the third part contradict the first? Philosophers still argue over it. I suppose I've thought, ever since I read about the quantum in the sixth form, and the spooky quantum entanglement later from my nuclear colleagues, that physical laws may not be as deterministic as they seem. Maybe things can be willed. Everything caused doesn't have to follow a natural law as per Davidson's second proposition. The equations of Physics will never answer all the questions. And whatever else it can do, as Nagel has argued, looking at a bat's brain will never tell you what it would feel like to be one. So, folk should live life as if they may have just a bit of free will if they look hard enough. I believe that makes me a dual-aspect monist, a bit of a mouthful to wear on a label round my neck, but better than 'I believe in miracles'.

Richard reckons that we each have a moment in life, not at death, when we can take our spiritual body away from our physical body, ready for eternity. He claims to know the moment when it happened for him. I'm not sure if I believe him, but I'll continue to hope that the Almighty can do the trick, at the end of time if not before.

You've heard a bit about our grand model already. It starts with God as one at the end of time, which is also the beginning, setting things off with a Big Bang. He's already watched in preview how the story would turn out from our thoughts and actions, whichever if either takes precedence, maybe occasionally lending us a helping hand. He presses the 'Publish' button. The events then happen in the present tense. Sometimes we think we've willed an event, and that's because we did and do. Sometimes.

Richard has more doubt about our model today. The state of his town and football team at the moment are enough to have him in apocalyptic frame of mind. He can't understand why a loving God had blessed a story containing such a sad outcome for the great town of Bolton. I suggested that the story so far for the last 13.8 billion years has been worth the effort, but what with so many sides from the

South, on a demographic high, thriving in the Premier League well above their station in life, maybe a merciful God would soon have to press the abort button.

"Or else the devil took over right at the start?" Richard suggested. "God saw the draft up to this point and had to put his red pen through it. The devil sneaked back in later, picked it up out of the wastepaper bin, wrote 'Stet' on each page in green ink, and then masquerading as God took it to the publisher."

"Well, the devil has always been running the show, particularly the Catholic Church," added Helen with a wicked grin.

"What do you think, Amy?" asked Wendy.

"Dad and James are just the same, hopeless dreamers. I didn't realise your Bob was just as bad. It's an interesting way of viewing a world, but can you please get the apocalypse delayed long enough to give me a chance to live first? I don't want it now," she replied.

"What, with the possibility of Trump and Brexit?" Wendy replied. "I doubt it. I've a horrible feeling it starts here."

"And with climate change, not that Britain can do much about it, I'm pretty sure many will meet a very wet end," I said. "Or there will be a plague that just kills off humans."

"A partial apocalypse," said Helen. "Another species can replace us as top dog. Maybe it will be dogs, although I think they need us too much."

"Probably not cats," said Wendy. "Not sociable enough."

Sheba, sitting on Amy's lap, lifted her head and yawned.

"That might be an asset," Richard said.

I suggested that dolphins, living under the sea, will have survived sea water level rises yet wouldn't develop nuclear missiles, so they could have a role. Wendy didn't agree with that, pointing out the logistics behind Trident submarines. We went back on dry land, needing a herbivore who was big and bright and lived on high ground, but couldn't really think of one, even if the cow was rightly sacred and the elephant wouldn't forget what the plan was. Richard felt that trees had souls too and the land should be left to them, unless the waters reached the tree line. Wendy liked that idea, as it would leave nothing mobile to eat the fruit from the tree of knowledge. By this point, Helen was looking at us witheringly.

"It will be more of the same: rats and cockroaches," she said. "They'll leg it up the mountains."

"It will be artificial intelligence creatures, Mum," said Amy. "Cyborgs. I wrote that short story about it at school. They'll start thinking for themselves. They're already ten thousand times smarter than us, and they'll get smarter and smarter while we stand still. And they'll develop good feelings towards us like Buddhists have for cows. But not all of them will be good. They'll argue if there's a God just like we do, and, if there is, why he doesn't reveal himself in an app for him. Some of them will start to blame humans for that. A rogue robot will then release a genetic poison able to kill off the remaining humans into the atmosphere. It will probably happen in my lifetime."

That shut us all up. Wendy led everyone into the living room. I was a while joining while I made the coffee, loaded the dishwasher and soaked the pans. Having overdone religion, there was little choice but to discuss politics, something they'd already started when I re-joined. Our talk was sterile, as Corbyn is considered a loser outside the Labour Party and we're all Remainers on Brexit. We've assets to lose. We trusted that Cameron's luck would hold. The one who most doubts if it will is Helen. She's had to study the northern nation as an outsider and can feel the resentment that's built up even better than we can. She also knows that the non-urban south has very similar feelings.

"Outside London, it's mainly the better-off and the University educated, past and present, who are voting remain," she said. "I'm not sure that's going to be quite enough."

Amy was distressed at this thought. She couldn't envisage leaving Europe. She's got used to not paying roaming charges.

But nobody spoke of a future grand vision for Europe. I used to hope when we first joined that we'd end up with a Holy Roman Empire stretching eastwards from Vancouver to Vladivostok. Theologically unsound I know; the kingdom of God should know no boundaries. What we got instead was Jean-Claude Juncker. The absence of roaming charges does still make the European case sufficiently for me though.

So, it was a much less animated discussion. I guess I was pleased that the meaning of life stimulated us all more than political alliances. After a splendid evening, the Shackletons left at about eleven o'clock to go back to their hotel. It's nice to have such good pals and oddball times together.

Richie woke up with the slamming of the doors and was brought down to wave them off. Alice stayed asleep, upset the next morning to have missed the farewells. Hattie padged round the back garden for her needful while I finished the washing up. Wendy tucked Richie up again.

We were both ready for bed at the same time. We lay in each other's arms, talking.

"Maybe the world's not changed that much," I said. "Amy joined in well, didn't she?"

"She did, but she had to humour us to do it. There's been a massive shift. We mustn't forget that Alice and Richie are going to grow up in this new world. We'd like them to remember our world with affection. That's the most we can hope for. They'll go through a phase like Charlotte's, maybe after we're gone. They won't always be on our side."

"You'll still be around," I said.

"You can't know that."

We kissed briefly. "You will," I whispered after a few seconds, but I think she was already asleep.

I didn't sleep well. Dreams are never easy to remember, nor make great sense, but I'm pretty sure it was a Children's Home where I could see Alice and Richie. They didn't turn to spot me peeping through the window.

CHAPTER NINE
Easter 2016

Less than a month later, for a few days we're all up to St Chad's again. It's an early enough Easter, yet one with the daffodils already past their best. They seem to bloom earlier each year. We've been receiving regular progress reports on Lucy's affairs from Ruth, although I think we're learning even more from Helen, with her antennae focused on Maddie and James. Lucy has now been with Dave five months. According to Maddie, unlike Paul, he's firing on all cylinders but, as no pregnancy has yet resulted, Lucy thinks he could be shooting blanks. Maddie is going to make a very worldly youth minister, far too much so for her likely clientele in Methodism. She's probably too worldly for her boyfriend James too. Helen thinks, from his hangdog expression on a Skype call, that all is not well in that relationship.

I did briefly ponder if Lucy is showing her age in the egg production department, for me to be told firmly by Wendy that it's always far more complicated than that. It certainly was for her, but there had been an explanation, which is as well, or she would never have had our Alice and Richie.

Ruth informed us that Paul and Lucy are spending more hours together in the pub discussing the next re-write of the play than they spent actually writing anything. Apparently, Paul is drinking a bottle of Pinot Grigio most evenings, while Lucy tipples four or five whisky macs. Bill Hardisty looks on wistfully, wishing he was the beneficiary of Lucy's attention, but consoled by his profit margins being the best for years. Ruth is rightly worried what the play is doing to their livers. Dave is looking less and less happy as he joins them later in the evening after riding his bike with his Kirkham mates, usually up to the Lakes. He stays sober, only drinking a pint, while, in their cups, they're making total sense to themselves but not to anyone else. Dave is paying for that last round every evening too.

"I wonder if and how Lucy performs in bed that tanked up. Or if Dave still fancies her when she's reeking of alcohol," Ruth asked as she finished her reporting of the Fishwick News. I got the impression that she was asking with little personal knowledge of the likely answer.

We're staying Over Wyre at the Throstles' Nest again. I drive everyone over to Ruth's each morning and then take Hattie out in St Chad's for our morning constitutional. As we left this morning, the kids had an improvised game of football in the car park. Jason the barman deserted the breakfast plates and joined in until an exasperated Fiona summoned him back to his job.

Neither Paul nor I have bothered to restore full diplomatic relations since the incident in Ruth's garden. Somehow, I haven't been able to find it in me, which is totally at odds with my usual view that you should never let the sun go down on your anger. The others all find him a decent bloke, so it must be me. But as I walked past his house with Hattie this morning, he hailed me down, looking agitated. He asked if he could walk along with us. As we crossed the field, he described how Dave had angrily left the pub early the previous night when he was being ignored. Lucy and he heard the revving and roaring of Dave's agitation as he accelerated out of the car park. They'd staggered out to see what was up, only for Lucy to be promptly sick. Neither sight nor sound had been heard from him since.

"Lucy's just rung me up, wanting to know if Dave's alright. His phone is switched off this morning. Last night, I had to hold her up as she staggered all the way back down the Breck to the house," Paul told me. "I carried her the last hundred yards past the railway station. She'd got a bee in her bonnet that we could catch a train to Kirkham and find him there. When we reached her house, a very censorious Maddie opened the door."

"We could be just as judgemental when we were younger," I said, with a younger Paul particularly in view.

"Lucy fell straight through it, landing on the hall floor in a heap," he continued. "Maddie slammed the door in my face, but not before she'd called me a total tosser."

He was indignant at this reception, wondering what he'd done to offend Maddie. When I said that she was just wanting what was best for her mother, he didn't believe me.

"Dave must be OK," I reassured him. "We'd have heard something by now if he wasn't."

That wasn't strictly true as he might have been lying in a ditch with a motorbike on top of him on the back road to Kirkham. Paul was far more concerned about it being the end of their triangular relationship with Lucy than he was for Dave's welfare.

"Dave was never going to be happy with that for long," I told him. "Make this the end of it, if she's happy with him. You're just going to hurt yourself and them otherwise."

"I don't think she is happy. She thinks he's going off her," he replied.

"He might well be, if she's that rat-arsed in bed every night."

"You've such an uncouth turn of phrase. You always had. And what's the chicken and what's the egg there? Isn't she drinking because she's unhappy?"

"That's for you to find out. When you're both sober."

When we reached the top of the path, he turned back, saying he also felt a little unwell, and needed to go back home. I assumed he needed the alcohol to leave his body by one route or another. He scurried away. Hattie and I carried on up to the yacht club before turning to go back into St Chad's down the Breck.

I didn't have to wait long to discover Dave, and it wasn't in the ditch by the road leading to the River Wyre. He was waiting a few yards along from Ruth's house for when I returned. He greeted me with a handshake. He wanted someone to talk to. I asked him in for a brew. Wendy, Ruth and children were in the middle of a second breakfast in the kitchen, the greedy pigs. There were cheery hellos by them all for Dave, who they'd got to know well enough so as not to judge by appearances. I made two mugs of tea and the pair of us went into the conservatory.

Shafts of sun came through the windows causing us both to squint. The windows hadn't been cleaned, inside or out, since the rigours of the winter. I guess that's a job I'd better do. They won't look much better after I've finished. Dave spoke rapidly but quietly. He had a surprisingly understated persona.

"I've been a fool for thinking Lucy will find me, an electrician, as good a companion as Paul. There's only so much you can say about a modern printed circuit board. She's a lot older than me too. I don't think it can work."

"He's older than she is by more than she is over you. And the gap between how bright he pretends to be and actually is exceeds both of those," I replied.

Dave did a double-take, not sure if he'd heard what I'd just said.

"Are you saying he's a bullshitter?" he asked.

"We all are, but he's made an art form out of it," I replied.

"Maybe I'm envious. He got to Cambridge and I didn't."

"He's been encouraging about my efforts to read more stuff, recommending all types of novels. They've been good too. I'd seen you two didn't like each other much..."

"Never have done in sixty years," I laughed. "We're not likely to start now."

"He's not that bad a bloke, Bob. What he's not doing is helping Lucy to re-write her play. He's confusing her with ideas that can't work. And I don't think he minds. He's scared that once she's finished it, she'll not need him."

"If that's the case, wouldn't you be grateful? You'd have her all to yourself."

"It's not the case though, Bob. A few days ago, I popped by Lucy's on a whim as I was only working near Stanley Park. They were in bed together. He's got something she likes enough to do that."

I'd been trying to understand where Dave was wanting to take this conversation. I'm pretty sure he didn't know either. He was a quiet man unused to unburdening himself. I mentioned that I understood Paul was no longer capable and that they perhaps were simply relaxing.

"I heard them, Bob. Lucy's a fresh-air fiend. The window was open. He'd taken a dose of the blue pills. He made it."

I thought Dave had finally reached what had caused him to race off on the motorbike.

"It seems like you've got your answer, lad," I said. "You'd better let them get on with it, until the pills stop working."

"There's a bit more. The next day Maddie asked for a ride on my bike. I took her back to Kirkham. I hadn't noticed she was getting to fancy me a bit. I got my revenge on Lucy. We made love."

I saw red at that. Dave isn't that understated. I stood up, trembling with anger.

"Shit! Hey, that stinks. Her boyfriend is the son of my best friend. He's a smashing lad, and a sensitive soul. Did you bloody have to?" I snapped.

"I'm sorry, Bob. He's asked her to marry him, and she's not ready for that. She's told him to back off. She wants and needs something earthier than him anyway. Like it or not, that's me, for the time being. She'll soon get a better offer."

I was about to explode when the doorbell ring. Answered by Ruth, we heard Maddie's voice, asking for me urgently. A hung-over Lucy had walked past Paul's house on Toffee's morning walk and seen something slumped in the porch. It was Paul's body. He was dead, presumably from a massive heart attack. By then, I was down at the door with Dave close behind. Maddie looked different. She'd dyed her hair back to its original black. She scarcely gave Dave a second glance.

"Could Wendy and you come and console Mum, Bob?" she asked.

We didn't have much choice. As the three of us scurried own the road, Dave roared past on his bike, presumably Kirkham-bound. If he'd got any answers from coming to see me, they were God-given and not from me. More pressing matters had intervened. I suppose that Paul's body wasn't strong enough for the exercise and abuse he was feeding it, up to and including last night's bender, but I'd lay a galaxy to a planet that this untimely death wasn't in the first draft. It's the sort of plot twist which becomes tempting as the story unfolds.

Should I have gone back with him when he told me he felt ill? It never even crossed my mind. He certainly didn't ask me too. I don't believe his heart attack had started in earnest by then. I can't help but feel guilty though.

Lucy's eyes were looking very puffy. Waking up worried that one of your lovers was dead, only to find out a couple of hours later that he wasn't but the other one was, would test most folk's stability. Seeing the body had sobered her up. She'd called 999, unsure whether to ask for police or ambulance. The police beat the ambulance to the scene by five minutes. She'd just told the police that she was a friend of Paul's who'd happened to be walking past, and after taking her name and address, they'd allowed her to go back home. That might sound uncaring of her but was probably prudent. There was no need for any dirty linen to emerge.

She seemed to think Paul's death was her fault. She feared it was taking the Viagra that did it, or even the acts of lovemaking themselves, rather than the alcohol over-indulgence. It didn't seem that she and Paul had made love last night, and Viagra doesn't cause heart attacks. That's what I told her. She seemed prepared to believe me, which is perhaps more than I did. Manufacturers of drugs will say anything but their prayers. After about half an hour, Wendy and I felt it was safe to leave.

Maddie saw us to the door with a curl of a half-smile on her face. She was clearly interested as to why Dave had been in Ruth's house when she'd come round. I formed the impression that she knew we knew, but this was certainly not the time to raise it. In fact, there can never be a time. If she wants to forsake James for another, or indeed all others, that's her prerogative. As we walked home, I said to Wendy that Maddie's smile, under her black hair, was how I imagined Salome looked when presented with John the Baptist's head on a silver platter. We'd all heard the voice of one crying in the wilderness, poor old Paul, and this is what we'd done to him.

We went to St Chad's church as a family on Easter Sunday. Sat over on the far side were Lucy, Maddie and Dave. Why they'd come yet again to a wishy-washy Anglican service I've no idea. Maybe I've convinced Maddie of its value as a *Via Media*, although I doubt it. Congregation members were looking towards them and whispering. It was a great first Easter hymn, my favourite. The strife is o'er, the battle done for Paul, who isn't about to rise from the dead. That can't be in the script. He's not been the Messiah for anyone. He's made a worthy John the Baptist though, a bearer of tidings, but we know not of what. As in Herod's day, the age we're living in and the story I'm telling may yet demand a bigger sacrifice.

The coroner gave a heart attack as the cause of death. Paul's cremation took place ten days later, after we'd returned to Nether Piddle. I came back to St Chad's alone for the service held at Carleton crematorium. He'd asked for a non-religious funeral in his will. That's what he got. With no family or close friends, he had appointed professional executors in a recently written will, leaving his house and his substantial savings to Lucy, once the inheritance tax had been deducted. His ashes were to be placed in his parents' grave. A Civil Celebrant presided over the proceedings. Maddie, Dave, Bill Hardisty, Ruth, one younger colleague from Paul's teaching days and I were all sat in place when Lucy arrived through a side door, pushing a wheelchair. In it was her mother, brought by a special taxi from her nursing home in Penwortham. Paul must at some stage have been taken over to meet her by Lucy.

We could all have fitted on the front bench. Bill, Ruth and I sat behind to fill the place out a bit. The officiant had prepared a run-of-the-mill eulogy from the scraps of information provided by us all, but mainly by me. The younger teacher also had been given a slot. He described Paul as an inspirational teacher. I doubt that was the case for all his pupils, but it was good of him to make the long journey up to St Chad's. He was rewarded with a pork pie, cheese and pickle lunch on a table set aside by Bill at the pub. There I was formally introduced to Lucy's mother, Freda Fishwick.

"I know, my name sounds like a cartoon character," she said. "I was Freda Longton before I married. It could have been worse. I could have married Mr Freckles or Mr Frump." She certainly still had all her wits about her.

Bill had put a couple of bottles of Pinot Grigio out for us too, partly to impress Lucy and partly as otherwise he didn't know how he was going to get rid of the bottles he'd just bought in. It didn't seem a bad way to remember Paul, not my taste in wine but what he would have liked. It was what Freda liked too. She drank two glasses. It was at that point that Lucy cried, saying she really had loved the old bugger. She was planning to move into his house in the Autumn. Sitting by Freda, Bill listened intently; I think he had picked up that relations between Dave and Lucy were strained. Maddie was very good with her Gran, taking her to the Ladies, where no doubt she'd have had to show the more practical side of her character. Here I am writing about people who'll have many different aspects to them I have no idea about. But if I'm too careful in what I write, then you won't get to know them at all. Or me.

I found that I was fidgety rather than morose that evening, blaming the white wine. We should have drunk the blood by having red. I thought of the people who'd been at the funeral. We'd shared in a poignant, sombre and sad ceremony, despite its starkness. Yet I don't know which Lucy is the real one. Maddie hasn't found herself yet, and the blackness of her promiscuous adolescence does seem to be revisiting her. I can't weigh up Dave. Bill keeps his thoughts to himself. They're the future and they're all rank strangers to me. I don't know what's in their souls.

And I hadn't ever really known Paul either. He'd even walked away from me in order to die. I regret that we parted without becoming any sort of friends, and that's in two bashes separated by more than fifty years. I know he didn't make it easy, but I should have done better. Death does seem to end some stories before they've finished, both in the eye of the reader and the writer. Much more than that, I think death cuts off the story that every subject, every corpse, was telling themselves before they were done. We want to write our own final chapter and never to finish it. I hope you can see Paul as a hero out there in a wilderness not of his own making, however much I've written him up as a bit of a prat. I suspect though that our personalities would forever have clashed. If there is a next life, the differences are still be bound to there.

I wonder if Lucy is feeling pain, irony or meaningless emptiness. Her eyes suggest all three, with the irony perhaps predominant. A subdued twinkle is still there. There seems to be a sheet of steel recently grown behind Maddie's eyes which reflects away any attempt to look deeper. The angle of reflection equals the angle of incidence, no more, no less. Dave is the biggest enigma, a contradiction dressed in black leather. Is he still shagging both, one or neither?

Lucy both reminds me of my first wife and yet differs from her. They were or are equally highly sexed. Jane was, and still is, more intelligent, more focused, more educated, than Lucy, and less open, less happy. I think Lucy wakes up happy however bad the previous day has been.

I'm looking at Ruth sitting across from me. She'd woken up happy alongside her husband each morning until abandoned by him. He'd appeared to be enjoying their quiet life together, and indeed he did want that, but unfortunately with someone else. Ruth's resilience is internal, a grim acceptance of what has been, unready to risk another kick in the teeth. I'd wanted a quiet life with Jane but couldn't sit still long enough to let it happen, which was as well because it wouldn't have done. It isn't what she needed or wanted.

I've just rung Wendy, desperate to hear her voice. She's known the sadness of a marriage with Frank, a man with no zest for life, but who's still had the energy to betray her. She can't leave him behind altogether in the nursing home. She visits regularly. She doesn't see him as an unwanted ghost though. She knows what he's been and that's what he is. I need someone who isn't a dreamer to keep my flights of fancy.

I told her how much I loved her.

"It must have been a hard day," she said.

CHAPTER TEN
May to September 2016

I've had a phone call from my sister Joan. I haven't named her before because I thought I had quite enough characters running around the place too fast for you to read their badges, let alone remember what was on them. Joan was conceived not long after the war started, perhaps on the final night before our Dad joined up with the navy to fight against Mr Hitler. Right at the start of 1945, Chief Petty Officer Jack Swarbrick wangled some seasonal leave, and I was born after all the hostilities were over. There was thus five years between Joan and me as we grew up above the Ironmonger's Store in St Chad's Market Square, a rented property with not only an outside lavatory but also a galvanised steel tub for a bath. We didn't get full plumbing until I was twelve. The working class didn't just live in big city council estates. And if something went wrong with the plumbing on those, you rang the Council. Eventually, someone would turn up to fix it. We had to fend for ourselves when the lavatory froze up, which was most winters. None of that was much hardship though. I know that we were much more fortunate than our city counterparts, with green fields, an unvandalized park, a decent school and our thriving Church.

There was only the one year when Joan and I were at the same school. As was normal in those days, she was married by the time she was 20, with a husband a trainee in the engineering department at the Town Hall. Before then, she'd worked at Williams Deacon Bank. He was an ambitious enough young man at first, and they travelled around the country before settling in Devon once their children were at school. They had three of those, and today have many grandchildren and great grandchildren. Her husband, a heavy smoker, died in his fifties, and her life is now spent with her extended family. As children, the age difference meant that we weren't that close, but since our parents died, we've both been anxious to keep in touch. When I was younger, she was always the one whose judgement I trusted, who set the invisible boundary of taste that shouldn't be crossed. I guess Wendy does that for me now.

Joan hasn't quite the same affection for St Chad's or for Lancashire that I have; I know not why. Perhaps it's because the place didn't give her the opportunities it gave me. She is however being driven up there for a visit at the weekend by a Grandson and has asked if there's a hotel near us in Worcestershire where they can stop the night, halfway into their journey. Of course, we've offered to put them up at our house, with a hastily improvised arrangement of beds. She sounded frail, and I asked how she was. She said that she'd tell me in person.

So, it wasn't a great surprise to see that her face was drawn when she arrived. She'd had the diagnosis only a couple of weeks ago. It's breast cancer. She's to have a lumpectomy next week, followed by radiation therapy and then a daily dose of tamoxifen. The trip north is the trip down Memory Lane that she fears she won't be able to take again. They've arranged to stay with an old school friend of Joan's in St Chad's, although at our suggestion will visit Ruth and her family. Her eyes welled up when she saw our Alice and Richie.

"They seem three generations younger than me, although they're only one."

She didn't want to talk too much about her illness in front of them or her Grandson. It was when Wendy and I were making a pot of tea and slicing the cake that she followed us into the kitchen. Hattie came too.

"I was looking at that picture of us two in the old backyard when our Rover was just a pup," she said. "Me in a pinafore dress Mum made and you in your best Windsor Woollies that Grandma had bought on staff discount. Where's it all gone, Bob? Did I miss something by going away?"

"Maybe we both did. It all started changing as soon as you went though. Both the past and the people died, and what replaced it didn't have the same soul."

"I don't think I ever found that soul again after I left. I'd better hurry up and find it now. I'm not much longer for this earth."

"I've already checked the five-year survival rates on t'internet," I said. "They're pretty good."

"If you say so. You're the scientist. It doesn't feel like that though."

Her eyes were watering. We hugged each other, the first time I can ever remember doing it. Her tears rolled down my cheek. Up until now, she's always been older sister, me the younger brother. I've always taken for granted that she would be there, a permanent reminder of our parents and the happy childhood they gave us. She seems suddenly so vulnerable.

Wendy picked up my iPad and pressed a few buttons.

"There's that picture," she said, showing Joan. "He puts it up on Facebook every year on the anniversary of Rover's death. 'Big sister Joan, Rover and me, 1949' is its title."

The rest of her visit was more contained. She'd done the one bit of opening-up that she was prepared to do. Our farewells the next morning were of the 'good-luck' kind. She only spent a couple of hours at Ruth's while in St Chad's, meeting great nephews and nieces for the first time in many years. Back at home, her operation went as smoothly as could be expected, although I felt when speaking to her on the phone that she was holding something back.

We owed a visit to my son Robert's family during the next half-term. Wendy's parents came to our house for the week to look after Hattie and Sheba. We stayed in London for the first few days, reaching Richmond on the Wednesday, the first day of June. The house there, with its ultra-modern furniture, set my teeth on edge. Everything was pristine and would have to remain that way to continue to look good. Give me cottage-style any day of the week, where a few bashes only add to the charm of a place. You can't bang on about conservation and then change your furniture every few years. A Chesterfield is for life and not just for Christmas.

The children loved seeing the sites of London. We had a great few days. Who says children get bored easily? We saw Buckingham Palace and the Changing of the Guard, where Wendy sang 'Christopher Robin went down with Alice'; The Tower of London with me growling 'With her head tucked underneath her arm'; Big Ben, the Houses of Parliament, Westminster Abbey, and loads, loads more. If children get tired with London, they'll soon be tired of life, as Dr Johnson could have said. I pray ours never tire of either. I hope I don't too. On the whole trip, we had few tears and lots of laughter.

The time spent was also worth its weight in gold for reminding Wendy and I why we love each other. We might be different in age, we're very different in temperament, we bounce to a different beat, but we're always in harmony. The kids are the outward sign of a deeper grace we feel when we're in each other's arms at night, although, with both children sleeping in beds alongside, no further reminder of their incarnation could take place on this holiday. We've been together for eight years now. It's too easy to take each other for granted when engrossed in the chores of daily life. Despite all the noise of the city, all the attention the children needed, for the first time in my life I felt a peace that passeth all understanding while listening to Wendy's gentle breathing.

Sadly, that inner peace doesn't come from today's Christianity. Maybe it's something the Buddhists are better at. I can't stop the racing in my head for long enough to start meditating. As Richard says, it's not easy to feel peaceful if you're told every Sunday that all your friends and relations are doomed if they're not believers. Particularly, as in his case, if your father is to be counted among them. I can see why he thinks all will be saved, but still have enough fear that the Old Testament shows God the way he really is not to take anything for granted.

With so much to fit in, we didn't have time for the Natural History Museum. We promised the children that we'd see the dinosaurs on our next trip.

"I can see one now, Daddy," said Alice. "You."

I had to smile. It's important that children develop a sense of humour, not that mine's developed much further over the extra six decades I've had.

"The Daddysaurus is coming to get you," I growled, as I chased her round the bedroom to cackles of delight.

It's only three weeks to the referendum and the Cameron campaign isn't going well. It's all about what would go wrong if we left rather than the many things that have gone right since we joined. The leave side have Nigel Farage of UKIP seeing this as his chance to seal his life's work, along with Tory heavyweights Boris Johnson and Michael Gove. Corbyn is hiding, exactly as I expected, as we all know he sees the EU as a capitalist club, maybe not one of beyond-redemption Anglo-Saxon capitalists but not socialists of his hue either. Sophie is shocked by his disappearance though. As a human rights lawyer, younger person and a Canadian, she's assumed that the Leader of a Labour Party will be in favour. You have to know a person to judge a person, you have to know a country to judge a country, I said by way of a lack of explanation. Wendy then told Sophie you don't need to judge anyone. She's right as she always is. Sophie doesn't agree with her though. She can only see the Brexiteers as bigoted, not accepting her view to be part of an equally closed metropolitan mind fix. I like her enough to know that she's more than partly right, though I've just told her she's in danger of becoming a little Londoner and she ought to get out more. I know how welcoming Lancashire, and all the regions of England, even including Yorkshire, naturally are. Robert laughed but I don't think Sophie saw the joke.

"They've been condescended to for too long," I'd said. "It's their chance for revenge. Let's hope they don't take it."

We returned to Nether Piddle with the referendum outcome very much in doubt. Sadly, just before the vote, one deluded guy, influenced by right-wing rhetoric, savagely murdered Jo Cox, the Labour MP for Batley. Even that didn't sway the vote in the Remain direction. All uncertainty was banished with the exit poll on the evening of 23 June, followed by the results from Sunderland. My judgement had been that for the Nissan car workers to vote to leave would be tantamount to turkeys voting for Christmas, I guess that shows how badly a northern villager can be at understanding the industrial north, even if he is an engineer. Through-and-through southerner Helen called it better.

The nation has voted to leave in the ratio 52:48. This morning, Cameron has announced he's resigning. I think that, since the

105

referendum was his daft idea, the least he could do is to stay around long enough for us all to give him the good kicking he deserves. Noblesse isn't that obliging, not that his party would let him stay anyway. He'll have to spend the next fifty years effortlessly making light of it all, before Brexit is carved on his tombstone. Queen Mary at least had the decency to have Calais engraved on her heart. So, shouldn't this mean that MP's have to butt out and meekly act as delegates for the fifty-two percent on all matters Brexit? I somehow doubt they're capable of that, although it might well be easier if they did. That convention's not written down anywhere, and unwritten understandings can only be prayed in aid when the establishment find it useful. They should at least learn to talk softly on the issue and see if the public themselves decide to change their minds. Instead, we'll no doubt keep hearing about how the gullible ingenues were deceived by the proclaimed £350 million weekly saving available for the NHS displayed on the side of the Brexiteer bus. That's already started. I don't think the public are that naïve, although they wouldn't have known the difference if the number quoted had been a factor of ten higher or lower, or with a different sign in front of it.

They wanted to register their protest about the unforgiven banking crisis and expenses scandal. They've been laid low by austerity. Most of all, they wanted to recover a sense of national identity, particularly in England where the Britishness I naturally feel seems to be an anachronism now the Scots want out of the Union. I don't agree with my compatriots on any of this, but I can see how they think it. Sadly, all they've succeeded in doing is shooting themselves in the foot and also a bit higher. Yep, there was an anti-immigrant feel to it all, but it's only European immigration that will be halted. We English don't need to sort out who we are in Britain before realising that we are

European. I understand that it could take a bit longer to realise that we are also humans.

Ruth rang me today too. Lucy can hide the truth underneath a baggy jumper no longer. On some days, the weather can be too warm for that in June even in St Chad's. She's pregnant.

"Everybody at first assumed that it must be Dave's baby on the way. The puzzling thing though is he hasn't been seen around for a couple of months, which has set some tongues wagging that the baby might be somebody else's. Any chance it could be Paul's, do you think?" Ruth said, finishing with a nervous giggle.

I wasn't sure if I should tell Ruth what Dave had told me, so I did.

"There's some chance. Dave heard Paul and Lucy at it through an open window, which is why he buggered off. Whether Paul succeeded in transferring spermatozoa, I don't know. It's an even money bet whose it is."

Of course, I asked her not to tell anyone else. Up to that point, I'd been very good and only mentioned it to Wendy. Like Oscar Wilde, I can keep a secret but not all the people I tell them to can. Ruth only mentioned it as a small possibility to one of her friends at her Pilates class.

Despite the 'usual channels' having been abolished, or at least driven underground, the Tories have contrived by mid-July in their leadership contest that their time-honoured, back-stabbing methodology has left only one woman standing. To be fair, Michael Gove didn't resort to such underhand tactics. He's both cruelly and deservedly stabbed his erstwhile collaborator Boris Johnson in the chest. So, Theresa May is elected leader and thus Prime Minister. I hope that as a clergyman's daughter she'll at least be a safe pair of hands, but no doubt I'll be wrong about that too. She's started out by saying she wants to help those who are 'just about managing'. I guess that's more than what most folk were doing in the immediate post-war years of austerity. But then, there was a hope that things were going to get better. Generally, they did. Rightly or wrongly, people don't think that now. And I don't think Theresa has any plans for doing the first thing about it. She's offering no more than a prayer for economic growth to the deaf ears of the Chancellor of the Exchequer. In that role, she's fired Osborne, because she doesn't like him, and has appointed spreadsheet Philip Hammond in his place. There's to be no end to austerity, the one thing which might give a bit of hope, even joy, to the nation.

Before she'd kissed the Queen's hand, it had become the received view at the school gate that Paul was the father. By the time that term ended, the fact that Maddie hasn't returned home from Sheffield has also been registered. Inevitably, one parent at the gate has a relation in Kirkham who'd tried to book Dave for an electrical job, to be told that he's moved to Sheffield. Lucy bounces into school each day as if nothing has happened. She continues to walk Toffee round the streets with a cheery word for everyone. I can't help but be amazed at her resilience. She's as game as the old ladies in her play.

I rang Richard once I'd learnt from Ruth that Dave is in Sheffield, to find out what he knows and to see if James is badly affected. Up to then, I'd not wanted to expose James to the ugly truth. Richard already knew all about it from his suffering son. Apparently, Maddie is keeping both Dave and James on the end of a string, he says. Yet there is one key difference between mother and daughter. Maddie has for the time being turned celibate, with neither suitor any longer the recipient of her sexual favours. At least that's what she's told James. I don't know whether to believe her, but it is at least possible. After all, she is by birth a Catholic, and 'get thee to a nunnery' could be just the sort of advice she'd give herself when confused. James is home from Manchester, moping. It's fortunate that the worst of Maddie's betrayal hasn't emerged until after he's finished his second-year exams. Even Richard is now urging him to accept the inevitable and find someone new. James can't; despite everything he of course thinks that he's the mirror of Maddie's soul, and that all the other fish in the sea don't have any souls that he'd be interested in. Richard and I remember that both of us have also been besotted enough once upon a time to think that sort of thing, me unbelievably with my ex-wife both before marriage and years later after separation. We both know that words won't talk him out of it. The sheet of metal behind Maddie's eyes crying for no-one has become a mirror in which James can only see himself. It was a mismatch and never, as in the words of Lennon's favourite McCartney song, a love that should have lasted years.

"Good luck with James. Go easy on him. We both know it won't heal quickly for him."

"I am doing," he replied. "It's Helen who's having the more trouble. The lovelorn aren't a category she acknowledges."

That won't change with Helen, although as a vet I'm sure she must often see similar symptoms in bereaved dogs.

The schools have just broken up yet again, and we're back at Throstles' Nest and St Chad's. I've had another call from Richard. It seems Maddie was telling the truth about her celibacy, at least with men. Helen has been stalking Maddie's Twitter account. On that, she's announced to the world that she prefers girls, and is in a relationship with Amelia, a care worker in a Sheffield nursing home. Dave has been sent back to Kirkham. Showing no originality, I of course joked that such a move could well have become compulsory for a Methodist youth minister. Independent corroboration of Maddie's revised status has been received on my first walk here with Hattie. I've just bumped into Lucy, out with Toffee. Sounding shell-shocked, she's poured her heart out to me.

"I don't know whose baby I'm carrying, but I'm desperately praying it's Paul's. Dave is a shite, who's betrayed me and poisoned my Maddie against men with his behaviour. He ought to have his bollocks cut off."

I was pretty sure that this explanation for Maddie's passionate embrace of her own sex wouldn't be endorsed by the sisterhood, but I never know at any time which way is up on such issues. I wasn't being given the opportunity to respond at any stage anyway, so I didn't need to take sides. I don't know if this time we are seeing Maddie's true nature. Let's hope she's found herself. She may have more than one nature though. And whichever way she jumps, I suspect she will sometimes need to revert to the manic hedonism, schooled in her adolescence, inherited from her mother, but with an ability to cause pain that must be from her father. Lucy's next remarks, made with a nervous laugh, shed more light.

"Of course, she's only taking after her father, Fred Greenhalgh. He was certainly over-keen on the women. So much so that he married me when I became pregnant with Maddie, even though he was already married. In a Catholic church for both of us too. And he was only 21. I was 19. Fred ran up a mountain of debt secretly running two homes and tried to gamble his way out. The police were on to him for the bigamy, and debt collectors for the money. He fell off the back of a trawler before he was caught. My parents didn't like him from the start. He had style, and I didn't listen. They'd refused to come to our wedding."

"I met your Mum at the funeral, of course. I assume your Dad's gone."

"Long gone now, but Mum's still going strong, as you saw. She can't get about, but she's still all there. We did kiss and make up once Fred had gone. When I say fell, he either jumped or was pushed. An old boyfriend of the other wife was also on the boat. I don't think he was pushed though. He was on pills for depression the whole time I knew him. Fishwick is my maiden name, which I gave Maddie too when I found out."

"Bloody hell, Lucy, you've seen it all," I said.

"I saw more, Bob. I was pregnant a second time when it all happened. What with the stress of things, I had a miscarriage. It was a little boy too."

Lucy started to cry. I gave her the tatty hanky I had in my pocket. Toffee pawed her in sympathy

"Does Maddie know about all this?"

"She was very young but had been looking forward to a brother or sister. It's not something you can start to explain to a four-year old. I tried to keep the bigamy from her when she was little. But then, she needed her birth certificate when she first applied for a passport for a school trip. I had to tell her then that I was Lucy Greenhalgh married to Fred when she was born. She went off the rails from that point on. Then, last year, she met the daughter of the other poor woman at some happy-clappy event she'd gone to, another lost soul looking for salvation in the wrong place. Her mother had told her all the sordid details. I'd always intended to tell Maddie someday, but I never got round to it."

She peered at me to see if I was showing any signs of disapproval. There could well have been disbelief in my face, but certainly not reproach.

She continued, "She's always been a wild girl, but there's been a dark side to her since then. She was mad at me for not telling her. She blanked me for weeks"

"It must have been a big shock to her."

"Nothing like as big a shock as it was to me when I found out about Fred. Not that I ever loved him, Bob. It's only been Paul that I really loved," she said, grabbing hold of my arm. "He was special. He made me feel I was too, at least most of the time. When he lost it in your garden, you didn't know that I'd been impatient with him in bed the night before when he couldn't get it on. He kept refusing to try the pills, and it was like he was teasing me in bed. It was my fault. I'd been cruel."

"I guess he was special then," I agreed, I hope not through too obviously gritted teeth. I didn't really believe her, but it can be so difficult to know the truth of a situation. Unfortunately, I must have been grinding my teeth as well. Lucy pulled me up sharply, saying something penetrating out of the blue.

"Have you ever thought, Bob, that the reason you didn't like Paul is that you were scared he was right about religion? Particularly with the sterile stuff you go in for. He listened carefully to me about Catholicism. He liked literature. Another few months together and I've had him in with my mob."

She spat out these words with venom, even spite, and that was definitely aimed at me. The red devil was behind her eyes again. But, seeing she'd loved him, I reckon she's entitled to be angry with me. She's not the sort to hold a grudge for ever. I was quiet for several seconds and then changed the subject.

"Have Maddie and her half-sister formed any sort of bond?" I asked.

Lucy paused, considering whether to respond to that or to

continue to fight the good fight on Paul's behalf. Fortunately for me, she swallowed her bile and answered with only a slight tremor in her voice.

"They meet up a few times a year. Her name's Lisa. I've met her the once. She seems a decent enough girl. She's more got her mother's looks than her Dad's. She came round to our house just after Dave first moved in, before Paul died."

"She and Maddie could be a source of support for each other in understanding who they are," I suggested.

"Maddie never wants any support in that, Bob. Especially not mine. By the way, Dave turned up yesterday on my doorstep, begging for me to take him back. I used to do some kickboxing. I kicked him in the goolies and told him to fuck off. If he could father a child before, with any luck he won't be able to now." She smirked in triumph. "The kick-boxing place I went to had a punchbag too. I'd cool down using it. So, I started punching him. He tried to defend himself, but one got through. I had to drive him to Victoria Hospital. He needed ten stitches above the eye."

I'd definitely better not criticise Paul in front of her in future! The memory of this brought a smile to her face, the troubled face of a five foot four tall, over-forty, single, pregnant woman weighing nine stone. She'd waited the four hours while he had the stitches, and then taken him back to his house. His Bonneville was still on her front drive.

"He's coming back for it later today. Can you be here when he comes, Bob, in case there's more trouble? Mind you, it's probably only me that will cause it. Dave wouldn't hit a lady."

"You might, though, hit him again, or me," I jokingly protested. "Particularly if I'm rude about Paul."

"I'm a respecter of age. I wouldn't hit you."

"With malicious intent, you pushed Paul down the bank on that dog walk," I reminded her with a laugh. "He was the same age as me."

"He had it coming that time."

She then went on to tell me about her recent meeting with Maddie and her new partner. In the middle of a sleepless night, she'd driven over to Sheffield for a surprise early-morning visit. On the way over, she'd no idea what she was going to do or say when she got there. After she'd been ringing the bell and banging the door for ten minutes, Maddie blearily opened the door in pyjamas. Lucy pushed past her into the hall.

"Now where's this bloody dyke you've told everybody but me about?"

"If you can't be civil, get out of our house," Maddie replied.

"I'm in now, and I'm stopping until I've had my say. I'm not surprised. If you can shag your mother's lover, it's a miracle it wasn't the dog next. Get her down and let me tell her what you're really like."

"She knows, Mum, she knows. And she likes me anyway. She says I'm what she needs. She brings out the best in me."

"Is that any different from the worst?" At this point, Lucy had lost the little bit of cool she'd managed to keep. "Nobody can like you, you selfish slut. You buggered off without so much as a word and you're just pretending you've turned queer, so that once more Maddie can be forgiven and be centre of attention again. But once a Catholic, always a Catholic. You'll pay, someday you'll pay. I'll make sure of that."

With that, Lucy had started climbing the rickety staircase. She met the 'bloody dyke' Amelia edging nervously edging down the stairs, having been woken by the commotion. Wearing a short nightdress, she was small, dumpy girl with mousy hair and a pleasant face, and tired, hooded eyes. Lucy had been expecting a stocky woman wearing dungarees and perhaps with a moustache. Her good heart told her that she shouldn't take her anger out on this girl she didn't know. She calmed down in an instant. She hadn't expected her daughter to be so much the dominant partner, although Maddie's powerful body and her own prowess as a kickboxer could surely have suggested the possibility. She shook Amelia's hand. She said that nearly all women fancied other women if they were honest, and if she was twenty years younger maybe she would too. She then gave her a full-on snog on the lips. She went down to the kitchen and put the kettle on.

"Let's have a chat over a cup of tea," she said. "I've still more than a few scores to settle."

Lucy was no match for Maddie in her ability to harbour a grudge, or to get her own way by power of will. Once they had sat down together, there was only one outcome available. Maddie brought Lucy into her relationship with Amelia like a getaway driver being introduced to a band of thieves, which they all became as thick as. Within quarter of an hour, they were giggling together about the roughing up of poor Dave. Any necessary return to Catholicism was forgotten. Lucy accepted Maddie and Amelia as an item.

"She's not had the greatest childhood, I suppose," Lucy said in conclusion.

That was perhaps the only time I've heard an understatement from Lucy. Over lunch at Ruth's, I wonder what I've let myself in for this afternoon. Will it be peaceful, indeed so peaceful that by tonight Dave is back in bed with Lucy? Or will Lucy snap again? I'm not altogether surprised at her violent behaviour though. She's been atrociously treated. I'd seen she'd a temper when she knocked Paul over. Yet on all other occasions, she's stayed sweetness and light in trying circumstances. She does in the classroom too. What I can't work out is if the blips are random, triggered by an internal logic in her head that maybe I would sympathise with if I understood, or from that script written before time which she has no choice but to enact. Who can tell? I don't suppose she knows which one it is either.

As I prepared to leave for the arena, Wendy put her shoes on too.

"I'm coming," she said with a broad grin. "They might gang up on you."

I've always liked her nosiness. Ruth would have liked to have come as well but had to look after all the children. Hattie was left with them.

We saw Dave's crash helmet and gloves waiting in the porch for his arrival as we entered Lucy's house. Wendy didn't hang about, asking her how she was going to find out whose baby it was. I'd already rung Helen, on the basis that a vet is better qualified than a doctor and usually prepared to say more, which she was. Tests involving taking DNA from the womb, the way that Down's Syndrome is checked for, are invasive and she wouldn't recommend that unless Lucy as an older mother was already planning to do that. There was a non-invasive blood test that could be carried out, more expensively, which would be more accurate the longer the pregnancy had been going. It would be best though to wait for the birth, when plenty of baby DNA would be available. All tests would require the suspected male to provide a swab. Given that only one of the suspects is living, with the other having been burnt to cinders and pulverised, Dave is nominated, although that only gives an answer Dave or not-Dave. We explained all this to Lucy, knowing that the Catholic in her won't countenance testing for Down's.

She smiled as she replied that she knew we must think her, and her daughter, promiscuous.

"We are," she confessed. "We're not all collected and together, as you always seem to be, Wendy," she said, by way of explanation. "You never know, I might move on to Bill Hardisty next. I always fancied being a blousy barmaid. I've got the assets. I've been serially monogamous though, but the likely conception date is close to when I switched horses back to Paul."

"What about the testing?" I asked.

"I'm not doing any before the baby is born. Let's see if I can tell from looking."

"Looks can be confusing," said Wendy. "You'll really need to have a test."

Through the window, we could see Dave walking hesitantly down the Breck from the station. I joked that he was probably was wearing a cricket box and wishing he'd got his crash helmet on already. Lucy laughed happily.

"I'm going to be charm itself," Lucy said. "If he really loves me, let him come and prove it."

So, the only role Wendy and I played in that afternoon's meeting was that of gooseberries. The curtains were already being drawn in the bedroom window as we left. Bill had missed out again without even knowing that he was briefly in the frame.

A forgiven Dave gave notice on his Kirkham let to move in with Lucy in Paul's old place down St Chad's Lane. There was room in the driveway for both his bike and his van, though both were considered a bit vulgar by the neighbours. He promised to do the paternity test after the birth when asked by Lucy. She's taken Wendy's advice. Maddie has finished her course and found a youth ministry job in Blackpool, involving an active beach ministry in the summer months. I'm pleased about that. I was expecting her to jack it all in. She and Amelia have taken Lucy's old house on the Breck on a rent-free basis. Amelia has had no trouble getting a job at a local nursing home. Carers on minimum wage are in demand.

So, matters have been resolved. Maddie has found herself, or at least the aspect presently on display to her. Lucy has a baby on the way and a companion she's happy to settle for, if not actually crave, with quite probably a full bench of substitutes that can be called on if necessary. This solution has only required one old man dying and one young man having his heart broken. If God has written that, or at least if he has allowed it to happen, then it's not for me to judge. But you can see why it could well be the devil at the wheel right now, driving the world down a dead-end street. Or maybe you can't.

Our life over the eight years since Wendy and I got together has been what we'd hoped for and much more. For us, God is in his heaven, and all's right in the world. I think the only guilt we both have is that it was dementia that has permitted it, suffered, and suffered daily, by Wendy's husband. However badly he'd treated Wendy, he's been dealt a lousy hand. Wendy assuages her guilt with visits. For the same reason, words from *Bless the Bride*, a favourite of my Mum's, often come to me. These are our lovely days, but all happiness must pay. Have they been paid for already, or is there more owed yet?

CHAPTER ELEVEN
Autumn 2016

On cue, the answers started coming. Alice was playing with Hattie when she felt a growth by her ear. We were at the vets within an hour. Whatever it was would be inoperable without removing far too much, with several other growths of indeterminate nature springing up on her body too. The vet's advice is to let things progress a bit further and then bite the bullet, as all the alternatives are worse. I'd taken over as owner of little Hatts after her old mistress had died, on the day Wendy had told me she was pregnant with our Alice. She's been the herald from heaven, the bearer of the tidings of comfort and joy. Alice and Richie have known her all their lives as an interested, intelligent, sympathetic face who wants to be with us. She doesn't look like she's ready to go. I can't stop the tears falling out of my eyes as I write this. Sadly, this evening, a phone call with Helen confirmed our vet's advice. I'm scared that this time little Hatts is the harbinger of ill tidings. This has been immediately borne out by Sheba going off her food. Kidney problems are diagnosed, to be treated by daily subcutaneous injections. In the meantime, there's been the news of another harbinger of disaster from across the Atlantic. Donald Trump has been elected President. How on earth can that happen? It would be too unrealistic for any writer to contemplate putting into a novel.

Perhaps, the devil and God are taking turns. There's also been the wonderful news of Bob Dylan's Nobel Prize. We've been together through life. It somehow seems like a validation of the age I've lived through, but also the signal for me that, 'It's all over now, Baby Blue'.

Dave has helped Lucy re-write her play. His droll sense of humour has blended in quite nicely with her surrealism. She told Ruth that he's more gifted than Paul as a writer, possibly than she is. They sent it off to Manchester, only to find that the producer has left for the BBC in London. I'd call it the LBC in Britain if there wasn't one of those already. Lucy has contacted him in London to be told frostily that what they have isn't suitable for national radio. What, and on the telly, *EastEnders* is? This time Lucy showed no resilience. She's said she's giving up. I can see why. Just too much has been chucked at her while she's pregnant. Ruth says she's still looking well.

It's three weeks before Christmas. The injections stopped working for Sheba a few weeks ago. Wendy had to take her for that awful final drive to the vet with me looking after the heartbroken children. Yesterday, Hattie's back legs gave way on her walk. I carried her home and spent the night with her. She'd lost control of bladder and bowels. Today, I took the same drive with Wendy looking after the children. The vet told me that everything seemed to have packed up at once and it was time. I held her as the deadly deed was done. Old Hatts, like Sheba, had considerately made the decision for us. She looked so beautiful in death. She looked ready to wake up in another world, if only I knew where the invisible button to reactivate her soul was.

I have a recurring dream now, one where I eventually get to the celestial city, but then St Peter at the pearly gates says my name isn't on the list. Two dogs come bounding down the road behind him, Hattie and my boyhood dog Rover, begging Peter to let me in. I've not yet finished the dream to know whether he does or doesn't. I fear that means he doesn't.

The children are devastated at these two terrible defeats. There are tear stains on Alice's pillow every morning. Richie wakes up crying in the middle of the night, pretending he has cramp, but it isn't that. He asks time and again if dogs and cats really go to heaven. Wendy patiently tells them why it is a deep hope for all of us that death is not the end. I've never heard her say anything so overt before. But Alice's teacher at school has no time for what she sees as mumbo-jumbo from the past. Despite the fact that in rural Worcestershire her entire class is nominally Christian, she takes as little interest in the season as she possibly can. Fortunately, in the media from Bonfire Night to New Year, beneath the commercialism, all the signs and symbols that make our Christmas are there for all to see. But this year, no Christmas presents or parties can begin to make up for what our children have lost. The run-up to the most magical time of the year, the time when acting out a lowly birth in a stable gives us the magic of hope, is cancelled. I asked them if they'd like a new puppy or kitten. Alice cried at just the thought of it. They don't; they're not ready yet. They both take the view that Hatts and Sheba can't be replaced. Hattie Swarbrick was their dog, Sheba Smith their cat. Children are loyal.

Lucy's due date was December 11. In true Lucy style, she was a week late, then arriving at the maternity ward to give birth within the hour. It's what she wanted this time, a boy. But whose? Some cord blood has been taken for a sample. We're all agog waiting for the answer.

CHAPTER TWELVE

Christmas 2016

Our Christmas is taking place at home in Nether Piddle. Ruth is hosting Jane and Geoffrey this year, with us having Robert and Sophie and their two children. We seem to have fallen into an alternating arrangement almost by accident, which means that Jane and I rarely see each other. Perhaps as well. We have four bedrooms, so can manage a sleeping arrangement which involves Patrick sharing with Richie, and Susannah with Alice. The blow-up bed has sprung a slow leak since its last use, leaving Patrick rather closer to the floor by morning than he has been the previous evening. It's all part of the fun, but Richie has taken it seriously. Last night, he offered his bed to Patrick, saying that he could curl up in Hattie's old basket, which is still in the garage. He meant it. Wendy gently told him that he was too big to fit in. I looked at his disappointed face. An animistic view of the spirits must be congenital. I've heeled Hattie's and Sheba's ashes in around the big oak at the bottom of the garden. I often go down to talk to them. Wendy says I'm a big daft thing when I come back in. I've seen her down there too though. The kids go down together every day to say a prayer.

The local Church put on a good Crib Service for them on Christmas Eve. It wasn't a full-blown nativity so tea towels for shepherds weren't needed, but it did include the first bit of rock music I'd ever heard too, 'The Rocking Carol'. "We will rock you," we all sang. Queen's song can never compete with that. They were far too glam for my primitive tastes anyway, as you'll have already gathered.

This version had me wanting to lend a coat of fur to Hattie, wherever she is. As you know, Sophie's a religious lass, unlike that heathen son of mine, Robert, who follows his mother on such matters, so Patrick and Susannah were at home with it all. Afterwards, Wendy followed her Christmas Eve family tradition of ham, rolls (sadly, barm cakes aren't available down here) and mulled wine, with assorted drinks for the kids, followed by a gloriously gooey chocolate log. It went down well. Board games of different complexity were played, before the ritual hanging of both stockings and pillowcases.

It wasn't until the children went to sleep that the spectre of Trump loomed in the conversation. Of course, Sophie and Robert, from the metropolitan tendency, were appalled. Wendy and I from middle England agreed with them, more on grounds of taste than doctrine. I said that we shouldn't have been surprised though. Newton's third law has action and reaction equal and opposite. That law nearly got it right, but reaction had surprisingly prevailed, if only by the smallest quantum. Of course, family events like losing cherished pets quite rightly matter more than any political event, where outcomes are nearly always fudges as gooey as the Chocolate Log we'd had. A fudge though presumes leaders with a modicum of intelligence and conscience, however deeply buried beneath the layers of self-aggrandisement. That presumption no longer feels to be the central case. I think it was G.K. Chesterton who said that when people stopped believing in God, it's not that they would believe in nothing, but that they'd believe in anything. Maybe all this fake news will actually bring about people unable to believe in anything. For the time being, what's happening is that people will only believe whatever reinforces their prejudices. That little bit of free will that we might have to think straight is drowned out by the noise of the crowd who can't hear the still, small voice of calm in their souls.

As we moved on to issues in the UK, it was clear that the tendency still had a grand, reforming project in mind. I've preferred my politicians not to have grand schemes, ever since I had to watch Harold Wilson and George Brown trim from their National Plan and in so doing produce what in retrospect was a decent enough government. I guess that Sophie's soliciting role leads her to believe the opposite, at least professionally. She thinks that Corbyn is on the only track. While hating the idea of Brexit, she can't recognise how misguided is his notion that pure socialism can emerge from the wastelands of No-Deal. The moderate left has no answers to anything, she claims, be it economically, socially or culturally. I warned her not to follow leaders and to watch the parking meters. Best of friends that we are, it's as if I'm Dylan, no longer wanting either to lead or be in the movement, and she wants a life dedicated to a pure socialism akin to Joan Baez's Quakerist pacifism. She's committed to every bit of the left's agenda, even more so than in our last conversation a few months ago. Wendy gently asked if she was worried that it wouldn't work, making things much worse for everyone. Both Robert and Sophie can't see how things can get any worse. I resisted saying that a mansion in leafy Richmond, or indeed a large detached house in Nether Piddle with a glass of port in hand, are not the best places to judge this from. As things were getting a bit heated, instead I tried a bit of philosophy, not always a good idea when the vino is testing the ability to spot the veritas. They'd all heard me many times before argue that the sixties were the first and last time that the working class got a shout, and that a class analysis throws up a different view from the present debates preoccupied with identity. I think I surprised them when I said I no longer thought that was the most important aspect.

"Dylan knew that rationalism would overstay its welcome. He

wrote in imagery, maybe occasionally influenced by mind-enhancing substances," the drink had me say. "Rock became poetry and seized our souls. That's where Dylan wanted to go next, and not to every protest on every subject to inform the faithful that the answer was blowing in the wind. That's what displaced politics in my life. We didn't want then or need now too ordered a society. We don't want everyone thinking or believing the same. It's healthy to take an interest in politics, but not to make it the be-all and end-all. Most folk outside their bubble aren't thick; they just can't hack mouthing party lines, and they don't want to be a slave to a project which will only do harm with its false hope of a New Jerusalem."

Glastonbury has become a festival for the priggish and Labour the party of the prosaic, was the conclusion from near the bottom of the port bottle. Robert laughed at me. "Watching a bit of Glastonbury on the television doesn't qualify you as an expert," he said.

Wendy giggled too. Fair enough, maybe they have a point.

If I'm honest, I've known a long time that the grammar schools did more for the lower middle class than the workers. John and George were lower middle, as is Paul. Ringo isn't, and he didn't get to grammar school. Some working-class kids benefited though. And more to the point, lots of northerners have. The problem is that they're now retiring on their final salary pensions well to the south, stuffing money to their mainly unneedy offspring to avoid inheritance tax. Sometimes I don't like what I see in the mirror. Their privately educated grandchildren, if they haven't reverted to the mean, are now taking all the available good jobs, the natural end to a meritocracy defined by examination success two generations ago.

The happy morn had all the excitement of Christmas. God was back with us, the devil displaced. I didn't have too big a headache from the port. Briefly, Sheba and Hattie were forgotten by the kids too, as myriad expensive presents were exchanged. The contrast between this and the family Christmases of the fifties, when my Mum and Dad had scrimped and saved to give us as good a time as they could, was obvious to someone who had lived through those years but unsayable to those who hadn't. And nobody else here has, not even Wendy.

We had a family Skype call after lunch to Ruth's place. They'd had a similar morning to ours. One of their group, the only one I've been married to, commented on how presents have become so much more expensive, particularly the ones bought for children by their Granddad. I've outspent Jane again, and she isn't the one to let it go unnoticed. I admitted to being a hypocrite. Sophie said that we all were, cleverly agreeing with me without directly contradicting Jane. She's taken something from the last night's debate. She's a soul mate. I think she was pleased also that I seem to be moving somewhat leftwards again.

"St Chad's is on tenderhooks waiting for Lucy to announce who the father is," Ruth informed us.

"I really must meet this woman," said Jane. "She and her daughter are introducing you all to the world the way it really is."

"And you're the expert on that?" I foolishly asked.

"More than you are, saddo," she replied.

"Maybe not, Mum," said Ruth. "Lucy and Maddie confide in Dad like he's their life coach."

"No wonder they're making such a mess of their lives then," said Jane. "They'd be better off talking to a brick wall."

"Walls have ears," I replied.

The good thing is about Skype is that you can see if the people at the other end of the call are smiling. This was Jane being friendly.

A host of farewells had to be said, so ringing off took a long time.

With the delays over Christmas, paternity won't be known until the New Year. Lucy certainly does live in the public glare, doing nothing to shield herself from the spotlight. She must enjoy it. Maddie likes, indeed demands, to be the centre of attention, but jealously guards her privacy. There never seems to be a paradox in Lucy, not even between the physical and the mental. Is she a living argument against dualism? Or is her uncanny ability to spot details in others that she can't see in herself evidence for it?

At the end of the festivities, as we loaded the luggage and kids into the car, Sophie said with a grin, "I'm off back to slay the dragons. We shall overcome some day."

"You have done already. I'm too knackered to fight, so I've joined you. You've inherited the earth. Be careful what you do with it," I replied. "I'd like those bairns to have what I've had."

"You were white and alpha-male, Bob. And lucky."

I've no idea why I'm being accused of that again. I'm kind both to people and small animals.

"Don't forget you're married to a jammy, white male too, if not alpha," said Robert. "Long live working-class culture. Long live fresh air and fun. Long live Blackpool."

Sophie for once was taken aback. Robert didn't often get involved in political discussion. Thanks, son, I thought. I didn't know what Sophie was thinking. Eventually she replied, with a comment that didn't make much sense to me. It must have been a follow-up to something she'd said to him in bed last night. I'd stumbled on a sore spot between them.

"You hunter gatherers don't spend enough time in the township to value co-operation other than on one task at once."

"You're right," he said. "That way I can pick who and what to like. And my Dad's one I do."

"You know how much I like him," she replied. "He's real. He's so retro though. Sod old Labour!"

She was granted the last word. Wendy and the kids came out to wave them off.

Wendy had heard the final exchange with mild amusement.

"It was time Robert said something," she said. "You'll be losing out to Jane as favourite grandparent now."

"I won't. We buy better Christmas presents."

"More expensive doesn't mean better," she said. "Jane is very thoughtful. I'll be fair to her this once. She's never tried to sour your relations with your children."

I'd never thought of that before. Thank you, Wendy, for pointing that out to me. And thank you, Jane.

Before the kids go back to school, we've decided to make the visit to the Natural History Museum that we'd promised. With no dog or cat to be looked after, we were on the platform at Evesham station first thing on Tuesday morning, after the New Year, waiting for the London train. We'd booked a mid-priced hotel by Russell Square. When I say 'mid-priced', that's what it says on their website, but I reckon whoever wrote that was having tea at the Dorchester at the time, and not on expenses. The train arrived on the dot and was only five minutes late into Paddington. The children managed to keep their spirits high the whole way. Wendy told them how Oxford was once called Oxenford, the place where the cattle crossed the Thames. She's probably right, she usually is, though I suggested that most of the cows would have drowned until they built a bridge. This idea caused Richie to start making mooing noises, only for Alice to supplement the soundtrack with visuals, by simulating a cow drowning. Obviously, to achieve the full effect, she had to lie down in the aisle kicking her legs in the air and showing rather more than would have been considered lady-like when I was younger.

"Takes after her mother," I said.

Not to be outdone, Richie combined his mooing with his assessment of how a drowning cow splutters, not that hard an act after just having drunk a Smoothie, and consequently one pulled off too well.

"Takes after his father," said Wendy, tissues in hand.

That provided the entertainment until Reading, where my homily of how their football team used to be nicknamed the *Biscuitmen* until the Huntley and Palmer factory was closed went down like a stale digestive. I pointed out the spot, provoking yawns from everyone, led by Wendy. They're growing up in the post-industrial age and I'm obviously too old to counter that, saddo that I am. The history lesson acted only as a cue for a request for cookies, a word I can barely bring myself to write down, let alone say, even if I did then eat two.

The train entered Paddington, under its magnificent roof. The hiss of steam echoed in my head from a beautiful King Class engine, as shiny as an exhibit in a railway museum, maybe 6000 – King George V, pulling our carriages into the platform, rather than the droning diesel that I did my best to shut my ears from.

"What a piece of engineering!" I enthused, looking at the roof as we walked towards the Tube, this time not to yawns as the family did try to share the moment with me.

It was at this stage that we regretted Brunel abandoning his railway in the Wild West rather than continuing it into London. Still, half an hour and two trains later, burdened by luggage, as in what you have to lug, we emerged from the Underground at Russell Square. Richie was lost for words as he stared at the hustle and bustle; Alice acted as if it was what she was expecting.

The hotel was none too salubrious. We had to leave our cases with the concierge as our room wasn't ready. We decided to head straight for the British Museum as it was only round the corner. Kensington and the Natural History Museum could wait a day. Well, that's what Wendy decided, and life isn't a democratic process. Far better she made the decision than have the four of us all suggesting something different. The pull of the archaeology was too great for her to resist, I imagine. We had a big old Victorian sideboard back at home that I'd christened Tut's Tomb, in honour of her first love. My Grannie used to have a similar sideboard and that's what she'd called hers.

As we traipsed round, Alice was rapt, and Richie bored. He'd been promised dinosaurs. My singing 'Rosetta, are you better?' by the stone didn't help that much. But then we reached the mummies; some adult, some children, some with names, some with jobs like doorkeeper and barber. These caught Richie's imagination. I told him about the mummy's curse, that anyone who disturbs the mummy's burial place will not survive. All this of course was done in a bad imitation of Dave Allen doing Count Dracula, not a genre the children had encountered in their short lives.

Wendy said, "It will be your daft fault if he doesn't sleep tonight."

But then she couldn't resist embellishing the details. She told the tale of how a cobra ate Howard Carter's pet canary at the exact moment they entered the real Tut's Tomb; of how his colleague Lord Carnarvon died from a mosquito bite on his face; and how Tutankhamun had a healed lesion on his cheek when they examined his body. The kids still didn't seem that concerned as I told Wendy, "Now who's giving them sleepless nights?"

They were looking at a mummified cat and what might be

a dog. Thoughts inevitably turned to Sheba and Hattie. Then they were worried.

"I hope Sheba's alright up there without us," said Alice, with a catch in her voice.

"She's got Hattie to keep her company," Wendy answered quickly.

"The vet didn't make Hattie into a mummy, did he?" asked a worried Richie. "You said she'd gone straight to heaven, Dad."

"And so she did," I reply, feeling my eyes watering. "She was a good dog."

Well, you can hope, can't you?

The next day was Dinosaur Day. It was a relative success, but the kids had done enough traipsing. Cold as it was, we went on a river trip that afternoon. The London skyline can look glorious or an unplanned cacophony, depending on what angle you see it from. That sums up my attitude to the place too. It looked good on this holiday.

We were all sorry to go home the following morning. But school is about to re-start. One thing did puzzle us when we walked into our living room. Both the top drawer and cupboard door of Tut's Tomb sideboard were wide open. Neither Wendy nor I remembered leaving them like that.

"He's escaped," joked Alice.

That evening, just before Richie's bedtime, there was a groaning noise from the downstairs toilet. At first the children laughed about Moaning Myrtle from *Harry Potter*, before Alice suggested that it's either Tutankhamun or one of the mummies we looked at in the British Museum come to place its curse. Richie was really frightened. I went to investigate it, Richie following. The system was picking up a vibration from somewhere and acting like a trumpet.

I could only shut it up by holding the cistern. Richie found this interesting, no longer worried about the curse. I've got to say that I'm not so sure since I couldn't stop the damn thing permanently! I've not been an engineer all these years without learning something though, whatever Wendy says. I tied the ball cock up and the noise ceased. A real engineer, called a plumber, will be booked tomorrow to solve that.

"I've lifted the Curse," I pronounced.

"No, you didn't, Dad," said Richie. "It was something rattling."

It's been a good trip. I didn't want to see any clouds cast over it. I didn't try to explain how some would say it could be both, that a sign will have natural causes, that the physical and mental meet on edges. Live in the present, I told myself, you don't know how long it will last. Life's better than it's ever been. Wendy slept with her bottom pressed into my crutch throughout the night, leaving me dreaming in a state of pleasant arousal. The children didn't wake.

I was up first in the morning. I untied the ball cock. There was no groaning. But it hadn't stopped for good. It was back after breakfast. It was as well I hadn't cancelled the plumber. A new ball cock was fitted. The apocalypse is postponed.

CHAPTER THIRTEEN
January to June 2017

By the second week in January, Lucy had the results back. Paul hadn't died without issue. Ruth let us know that it was a non-Dave baby, registered with the name John-Paul, hyphenated. I think he's going to be brought up a Catholic!

"I knew all along that it was Paul's," Lucy told me in Booth's when we were up at St Chad's in February. "I don't have to feel guilty at living in his house. Pity I didn't know I was pregnant before he'd gone. I could have married him and got his pension."

She said this in her loudest voice. She does like an audience. I'm not sure if anyone listening could tell that she wasn't being serious. Mind you, I'm not certain if she knew that herself. She's been on maternity leave since the last Autumn half-term, with her return to the classroom not scheduled until next September. In the meantime, she and Dave are working together to turn her play into a novel. He's better at description than characterisation, she said. I've set my belief system on the assumption that the white, northern, working-class male is inherently intelligent, but in this instance, it was prudent to wait for further proof. I suspect that he's better at motorcycle maintenance, something incidentally you can rarely say about a nuclear engineer.

Bill Hardisty has joined a dating site, so far without much success. The joke among his clientele is that the photo he's posted of himself was taken at his wedding more than thirty years ago, and he looked old even then. On a first viewing, most women seem to be swiping left. One, Sharon by name, did make it as far as The Barn for a date, drinking gin and tonic in the Lounge with him. It seems that Dave and Lucy came down to the pub at around ten o'clock (Dave is doing a decent job of keeping Lucy from the whisky macs). They plonked down at the table where Sharon and Bill were sizing each other up. Seeing a putative rival, Lucy flirted shamelessly with Bill, and he showed more interest in her than he did in Sharon. There was no second date. Dave as usual said nothing.

Trump has been installed as President. If only more had swiped left on polling day! There's nothing more sinister than a clown, and he's proving a bigger one than people feared. On top of that, Kim Jong-un, who with that name we must assume is a wrong 'un, is goading him with nuclear weapons. There's no evidence that Trump has any fail-safe instincts. On one of our phone calls, Richard and I wondered if our chat about which species would replace us on this planet when we destroyed it is about to become a live experiment.

Richard reminded me that in our theory of creation God had blessed everything that was made concrete, everything that happened. "But could he really have blessed nuclear annihilation?" he asked.

"Universal bereavement, an inspiring achievement…" I started to sing in Tom Lehrer's paean of praise to the concept.

"And we will all go together when we go," we carolled together.

We were both back on the cusp of adulthood in the middle of the Cuban missile crisis, with the Russian ships approaching, unaccountably as happy as sandboys at the prospect of us all going to our respective Valhallas. We were somewhat concerned that we were taking the Donald too lightly though. JFK he isn't, and Putin doesn't seem like Nikita Khrushchev. He and Kennedy had known when and how to blink. We can only hope the Donald does, if only out of fear. Let's hope he's a coward.

I can't help wondering if the eternal Paul is as oblivious of being a parent as we could be if Kim dropped his bombshell. Neither of us could make up our mind if events occurring after our physical death will be transmitted to us in eternity, assuming there is such a place. We decided after due deliberation that they will be, as all links between the temporal and eternal terminate at the same point. I trust, dear reader, that you feel suitably reassured. If you are, you're doing better than Richard and me. In the rest of the conversation, he revealed the many doubts he was feeling in his lay-reading role, the self-same doubts as those that had assailed him when he was a young man.

"Salvation simply through belief in the fact of the one person's existence is something that even James, the brother of Jesus, seems to dislike. He thought that there's got to be some action," Richard said. "Any honest reading of the books of the New Testament, along with early Church history, shows Peter and John unhappy in places too. One reading of Revelation has it as John of Patmos raving against and abominating Paul's churches. Folk today also seem to find salvation by faith of no comfort, no good news. I'm comforting nobody."

"I bet you are, when you go off message."

"I'm never on message now," he said. "I try to tell it in secular terms. Like me, you see this world as the place where we make our souls. You'll use words like 'character' and 'bottom' to describe somebody who's getting the hang of it. I tell them that you need to believe that to be the case to start the process and then to live it out to become someone. There you are: St James and St Paul reconciled. And, because it's a person we're trying to build ourselves into, we look for a person who's done it. That's the Christ. He was authentic. The only sin he hated was hypocrisy."

"He was quick-witted but didn't wisecrack like we do. Perhaps he could see through the contradictions that we need a joke to make sense of. In just the same way as patterns re-emerge in nature, the Catholic, Reformed and Orthodox churches are in the image of Peter, Paul and John, aren't they?" I said. "There's no denomination in the image of James' original Jerusalem church. Perhaps as well, since they seemed to want to keep to the old dietary laws. Just think, we might never have tasted a pork pie. But when he tells me that I've heaped treasure together for the last days, I have to plead guilty. I should have given it away like you did that time. I've got two adult families to give it all to, though, one of which has been in need of it, and there will still be two kids to be fed after I've gone."

"What I gave away was no more than an act of vanity, Bob. I deserve no credit," he replied. "Hebrews was supposedly written for the Jerusalem church after James had gone and best synthesises the original disciples' competing views to me, particularly when describing how people who have never heard of Christ are still saved by a similar type of faith, one that leads to selfless actions. It's so well written that some think it's by a woman, an early follower of Paul, Priscilla, acting as peacemaker with the Jerusalem Church. Her counterpart today might be your Wendy. It certainly isn't my Helen," he laughed.

"Human monkeys had both to hunt and be hunted," I expounded, perhaps still trying to justify my greed. "We were bound to inherit selfish survival mechanisms. Trouble is, we learnt to kill each other too, literally and metaphorically. I'd like to be a better person, because I think I can be with help, whether that's from Wendy, or the Almighty. But, even if it is still our fault, my fault, it's his world that makes us this way, by design, or accident.

"The world doesn't seem to become a better place as a result of small kindnesses," Richard said. "But there aren't any other sort. Human and animal nature won't be tamed."

"We try. Once humans had language, people could collaborate together to get rid of the rogue alpha males, the dictators who did the real mass murdering. That's how we got elders and priests dominating us with laws. It's written in evolution that we end up with weasels in control," I said.

"Yeah. But we seem to be back with dictators again in half the world. Them or weasels, they'll both have it in for us for thinking for ourselves, whether we're alpha, beta or gamma."

"I'm aiming no higher than omega. You're right though, Hebrews does preach a gospel of the Holy Allegory from the Holy Cross pulpit," I told him. "Not that today's priests ever seem to hear it. Stories build from real events. You can't know exactly when actual events morph into allegory, but that's where the physical and mental meet. That's where the Rock of Ages is, cleft especially for us. To believe that the story is a revelation is what matters. There isn't an ha'porth of gap between those two holies."

Richard is despondent about the Church's future without a new message of hope. We both know it can't happen, unless we get the original Messiah back. But then again, if we see his return as an allegorical development of doctrine, it's not going to be on this Earth. Sometimes, it would be nice to be a fundamentalist, with Jesus riding a white stallion, and not a donkey, down the Garstang Road to raise the dead in the cemetery. Instead, we jointly concluded that God has written the decline of our religion into the script. After all that, we hadn't the time and energy for our usual football chat. We had our lives to return to…

…In which Theresa May continues to struggle with the challenges of Brexit. I've conducted a few negotiations in my time, some of them even successfully. These are not going to be in that category. You don't have to make your first bid the point where you hope to finish, so as not to upset anyone. You don't usually have more than half your own side wishing this wasn't happening anyway and insisting that you give any remaining bargaining chips you have away in your opening remarks. You don't have umpteen teams on the other side of the table, all hardened negotiators, to your one, from a civil service schooled more in diplomacy than cut-throat bargaining. You don't have to accept the other side deciding in which order things should be negotiated. You don't have a loyal opposition in your own company charged with taking as gospel truth everything said by the other side. You have to be able to pretend that you'll leave without a deal, almost certainly staging a walk-out at least once at some sticky point, even if you have absolutely no intention of ever doing so. Unfortunately, MPs aren't where they are today by prudently keeping their own counsel until the Prime Minister comes back with a deal. They are motormouths, not negotiators. It will be a miracle for us to get any sort of deal short of capitulation.

Then again, I was a Remainer, and not just because I could see all this coming. The world of free trade championed in days of yore by the *Manchester Guardian* hasn't been available since the last war. Disastrous Prime Minister as Edward Heath was, causing mega-inflation and splitting up Lancashire, he did take us into the damn thing for that good reason. Given that the whole shebang will quite possibly self-destruct anyway, we'd have been better staying in until the bitter end, heckling mildly from the side-lines, rather than behaving as perfidious Albion. It's looking ever more likely that we'll end up leaving even without the fig leaf of a fudged deal, particularly with Angela Merkel having lost her head-banging-together credentials following her Christian but, in worldly terms, too generous a response to the refugee crisis.

Yet I don't think we can stay in now. We'd look idiots. Worse, it would be yet another case of the metropolitan groupthink forcing their views on the rest, particularly on the working class I'd at last decided I'd left behind at eleven years old. They'd be ignored again. However painful it is, Brexit has to be writ in stone. Richard mouths the same view but doesn't mean it. He still hopes that something will arise so that we can all change our mind with dignity.

Wendy disagrees with me totally. She believes that leaving will be so disastrous that a second referendum must take place, when people are given the chance to come to their senses. Rare for us, we've even had a row about it all, with me saying that she's never been on the outside, and her saying that once you've come in from the cold, only an idiot would go back out again. It's perhaps typical of us that our disagreement is not about the primary issue, but a differential of it. Because we usually agree on things, we're now both avoiding the subject with each other. It's a pity everybody else isn't doing that too.

In including these Brexit snippets, I half-expected that they would mirror the main storyline in some sort of conjunction of the stars. Nothing could be further from the truth. The story is of a world and of people in energetic transition, like it or not. The whole Brexit debate is one of denial, one designed to stop the world from turning. The promulgators of fake news believe that the end justifies the means, unconcerned for the health of their own souls. There is a total disconnect between the personal and the political. I don't like the stance I feel that I must take as the person that I am.

Nevertheless, the snowdrops and then crocuses popped their heads up. St Chad's churchyard is famous for its crocuses. A blanket of colour to remind us of better things to come greeted us on our half-term trip to Ruth's. Nothing has changed in any of the relationships up here, making the visit a bit of an anti-climax. We attended the christening of John-Paul (to be called Jack in normal life), at the Catholic Church a bit further down the Breck from the village. The godfather was an ancient uncle of Lucy's, and the godmother a friend from Preston. Lucy apologised both to Ruth and me for not asking us to be godparents, but she wanted John-Paul to be nothing but Catholic. We didn't expect to be asked, so being told why not is a bit like walking past the Athenaeum and the doorman stopping you to tell you they won't let you in.

There was a bit of a crisis on the morning of the christening. Alice spilt orange juice down the dress she was due to wear. Fiona came to the rescue. She had it washed, dried and ironed within the hour, just in time for us to drive to the service. Wendy was effusive in her gratitude and I gave Fiona a £20 tip when we checked out, which was pocketed with alacrity and with mumbled thanks.

The Article 50 declaration, whereby we are in an irreversible process to leave the EU, was triggered on 29 March, having been voted through with a big majority in the House. In logic, that means we leave on 29 March, 2019, deal or no-deal, and there's nothing politicians can do about it. But many of the great and the good on both sides of the House are hostile to leaving, however they voted on Article 50. They're not about to lie down quietly.

The daffodils were already totally finished by the time of our Easter visit. Global warming is a complicated matter, despite the primary science being simple. I think though that their other name as Easter Lilies would suggest that something has changed. Fatefully, Theresa May spent the early part of the recess on a walking holiday in Wales. She's come back to call a General Election, the sort of daft decision that only someone who hiked with ski poles would make. She's hoping for a bigger majority so that she can steer Brexit through parliament.

I watched in disbelief as she then fought a woeful campaign single-handedly while Corbyn played the nice guy and Shadow Chancellor John McDonnell produced rabbits out of a bottomless hat. He claimed that all his proposals were costed, an assertion that would never be tested as he'd not have the money to pay for them.

At St Chad's, Dave is really making a go of his electrical business. He's now employing one of his mates, also an electrician. His van has acquired smart lettering on the side. He asked Ruth if she could recommend an accounting, payroll and taxation package for him. She's not only come up with one, but also, without any charge, entered all the initial data to get him going.

Dylan played the arenas in Nottingham and Liverpool on his latest tour. I liaised with Jane and Geoffrey so that Wendy and I would take oldest grandchild Tom to Nottingham, where he's studying Engineering, and they'd meet his sister, Charlotte, for the Liverpool show. Tom is now twenty and a happy-go-lucky boy. Charlotte is about to start her 'A' levels with a view to a Politics course. She's actually always been a very proper young miss, which was great when she was younger but can be wearing now that her range has expanded to include all matters dear to her generation. I didn't mind her flirtation with veganism, something that would massively help the environment. We're not that gentle a family though, and her Swarbrick carnivore genes proved too strong for her to persist with that. Perhaps as well, I can't imagine the fields of the Fylde without Friesian cows. Tom enjoyed the concert, or at least said he did. Charlotte didn't and did somewhat spoil it for Jane and Geoffrey. She'd read up on how, when Dylan left the sixties' movement behind, he'd mocked Joan Baez's attempts to keep him at it. She'd also read how Joni Mitchell described him as a fake. She'd decided during the evening to take that piece of blasphemy as her view, unknowingly siding with sister-in-law Sophie's political creed, mainly it seemed because Bob didn't talk to the audience nor, according to Charlotte, sing any protest songs. He doesn't often do the former, and he did sing 'Highway 61 Revisited', 'Desolation Row', 'Ballad of a Thin Man' and 'Blowin' in the Wind' from his early catalogue as part of his set, so it wasn't altogether surprising that Jane wouldn't agree with her. Nor incidentally does Joan Baez today. She's more recently said that Dylan didn't need be on the team because he'd written the songs. I wonder if I should encourage Charlotte to try the Quakers?

We'd arranged to go over to Evesham to meet some old friends, Margy and Mike Cornbill, for lunch on the day after the election. Margy is originally from St Chad's too. She'd been my girlfriend from before I'd met my ex-wife, a pretty girl with golden hair and a voice to match, which meant in those days that she was a folk singer. She'd been upset when Dylan left her scene behind too, but later relented when she realised that he'd moved to something more profound. She prefers the old songs though. Mike is her third husband, who was until recently a brilliant guitarist. They've just sold for a pittance their pick-your-own fruit and veg business, as he's developed Parkinson's disease. They're now living in a bungalow on the edge of the town. Not that I had many, but it seems like old age robs you of the talents that made you who you are. It's a struggle for him to get out of the house. We went to their place laden with puddings and wine, our contribution to the meal. As they were originally my friends, under the terms of a convention never documented but always adhered to, Wendy drove, and I was able to drink. There's a lot to be said for unwritten constitutions. They can be flexible as required, without anyone losing face. That can only hold true though if a public vote hasn't taken place first.

Margy greeted us warmly. Mike has deteriorated from the last time we'd seen him. Then he'd been awkward in his movements, but with a rollator and with Margy's help had been able to move about the house and garden, and to go with her to the supermarket as a treat. Mind you, if ever my idea of a treat is going to the supermarket, then I'll know it's over. Mike's since become wheelchair-bound, with getting him on the lavatory too big a fight against gravity for Margy. He has to wear pads, needing carers to get him in and out of bed. Parkinson's is a slow, progressive disease. Seeing him only every six months or so makes it appear to be developing quickly.

Exit polls have spoilt the fun of Election Nights. The shock news that Theresa was going to lose her majority was known within nanoseconds of the polls closing. By lunchtime, the die was cast. She was going to have to be a deal with the DUP, the Democratic Unionists of Northern Ireland, perhaps best described as the Ulster Calvinists. I can't think that this arrangement will be stable through the trials and tribulations of Brexit.

The Tories called for an unnecessary referendum when nobody but their own wretched backbenchers gave a damn about Brexit. They've now compounded their folly by holding an unnecessary election. They've become incompetent as well as unpleasant. A more complete comeuppance of a Labour victory might be preferable if only I was prepared to be governed by the metropolitan tendency, on top of the adverse tax consequences. The first of those rules out the second, so I'd copped out and voted Lib Dem again. Tim Farron is at least a Lancastrian and seems a decent guy, though his faith is more than a bit too literal for me. His party has been routed. Maybe we'll now see him on Blackpool Beach shaking his tambourine with Maddie! Wendy hadn't felt the need to cop out, so she'd voted for the Lib Dems too. We've become useful to forecasters; see which way we're leaning and bet the other way. Margy is more old Labour than Corbynite, but happy enough with the result, saying that we needed more money on health and social services. Mike has voted Tory, as he always does. He'd voted Brexit too. He'd be more country than folk if he was American.

"I won't be around long enough for it to matter," he said, his rich, Worcestershire burr lost in the weakness of his vocal cords. The last time we'd been he'd managed to sing along with Margy on their version of 'We shall overcome'. He's running out of steam.

Margy drank heavily from one of the bottles we'd taken. It was as well I'd picked up two. Mike isn't allowed alcohol with his medication, which is a shame as it might well lighten the load he's carrying. He and Wendy drank that wretched sparkling elderflower concoction I often have to resort to when I'm the driver. I wheeled him into the dining room. Margy had made a big steak pie and served us generous portions, with plenty left for seconds. Three sorts of vegetable and a big bowl of boiled potatoes accompanied it. Margy mashed up the food in Mike's plate and spent much of the mealtime feeding him. It didn't make for easy conversation. After lunch, we pushed Mike for a walk round the block to a local park. Again, not much was said, although after all the food and wine I was feeling sleepy too. Wendy and Margy never say that much when together, always seeming to be weighing each other up and never reaching a conclusion. Mike was still asleep when we reached the house, waking up as Margy brought the guitar out. With perfect timing, she sang a Dylan song only recorded by Joan Baez, 'Love is just a four-letter word', sometimes looking at Mike, sometimes at Wendy, sometimes at me. He grunted at the refrain, trying to join in. Their eyes smiled at each other.

We discussed the day in the car on the way back home.

"She still fancies you, Bob," Wendy said.

"No, she doesn't," I replied. "Her eyes smiled for Mike. I saw them."

"They glowed for you."

I'm certain she'd got it wrong, despite the ambiguity of the song and its title; indeed, the ambiguity of the day. Yet it isn't like Wendy to be jealous, not even about my ex-wife, who will always flirt outrageously with me at family events, when she isn't having a go at me.

At the computer, my sciatica's playing hell with me, my upper back feels like it's locked solid, and my fingers are aching with incipient arthritis. Seeing Mike has made it hurt more.

Book Two

CHAPTER FOURTEEN
June 20, 2017. Late Evening

There's been a change of author. Here I am, Wendy, the sensible one, also the one young enough to be able to sit at a desk and type without moaning about sciatica. Bob's asleep. I've often taken a peek over his shoulder at what he's writing. I'm still not sure if he knows why he's writing it, but it seems a good idea to me too. More than one story is emerging but the one that most interests me is whether Lucy and Maddie are to be tragic heroines. Or will they both succumb to domestic bliss?

I'm enjoying how he's written what's happened so far, and hope you are too. You must have reached this far for some reason. He writes exactly how I find him, so you're getting to know the real him. He is an alpha male, of course, whatever he says, sometimes a bull in a china shop, though one thoughtful enough to pay for the damage afterwards. He often hasn't seen the world from a woman's viewpoint. He was promoted quickly enough when he was young that he's never had to work for a woman, and it sometimes shows. I don't suppose that finding that out for himself is his only reason for writing. But I don't think he's bringing out the less upfront characters as strongly as he could, including me. So, let's see if I can remedy that imbalance. I'm a quiet thinker. That's why he's sometimes unsure about what I believe. I think I've said enough for him to have got the gist, but not all at once as a grand scheme. I don't think aloud. He often does, be it good sense or claptrap that he's spouting. You've heard them both.

What he's written so far would be ideal to hand over to Lucy for her to make a play out of, particularly as she seems to be the star turn whenever she's on the stage. We could do that; he hasn't taken many liberties with her character. He's been a shade nicer with her than I would have been. I wonder how she'd end the story if she could choose. It would be with a new man. But would it be for love or company? It wouldn't be for money, not the she needs it any longer. Paul has amply provided.

I'm glad that Bob still finds sex with me kind and loving, though that sounds like putting on an old pair of slippers. It's not necessarily the way I find it. He comes on much stronger than that. And he's not the one underneath. He does try to be gentle and can't help being a bit of a lump. After we've finished, it can be like pushing a beached whale back into the sea after the tide's gone out! He's really struggled with his back. But it's love, real love, that I feel, for him and from him. He still cares passionately about the future for us all. Once the children are in bed though, and after the second glass of wine, he's frequently morose about the past. I think he's happy with life now, while wishing he'd reached this point without anyone getting injured. He's short-changed nobody though, as far as I can see, and the person who's been most hurt is himself. He misses the previous generation so much too, with that graveyard in St Chad's casting its shadow over everything he feels.

On the whole, he has described fairly all the characters he's introduced you to so far. He could have made Lucy appear even more tarty than he has, because, believe me, that's what she is. Maddie is demure by comparison. He's caught Paul just as I would have described him, a non-humanist atheist. I wouldn't have got on with him much better than Bob did. He's not begun to get where Maddie's at, but I'll do no better at that either. The trend towards overt lesbianism in society is, I suppose, understandable, given the strong image of women and the confusion of men in society. I haven't felt that way inclined since pre-puberty crushes on 'Miss', transferred to a dishy male Maths teacher as my breasts started to grow. Thank goodness Bob doesn't go for Margy as strongly as she'd like. Ruth is carrying more sadness than he's conveyed, because she tries to hide it from him (but he realises this, which is why we visit her so often). He knows Helen and Richard very well and likes both of them to bits, a view I mainly share. I can though find both Richard's mix of diffidence and last-minute brilliance frustrating in the extreme. He would have achieved much more with his life if he'd only concentrated. I suppose he's the thinker, and Bob the doer. My Bob may be more the alpha type, but he's just as good with people, if not better. With feeling the need to work at problems and relationships the way I do, I can also find Helen's coolness with people particularly irritating. Bob still views James as a lad who could be wrecked by life's unfairness. With those genes, I'm sure he'll survive and more.

I know Bob's torch for Jane will never quite go out altogether, although he's very happy that Geoffrey is the one waking up to the new game of Russian roulette that each day brings. I've realised that from within a few minutes of meeting him. It's part of who he is.

Has Bob been fair to me? He'll be reading this in a few minutes. I do wish he'd mentioned me a bit more. Some of the others are such strong characters and he likes that. He's naturally a kind man, and shows this in all his relationships, even with Paul and his number one bête noire, Sir Charles Norman, the guy who got him fired from his Chief Executive job. Bob's actions are never mean, and his words always honest. He does prefer people to be stoical about their troubles, which mostly suits me fine. There have just been occasions when… no, there haven't, I mustn't be churlish. He's given me a wonderful life, from one of despair, just by being bluff, compassionate Bob, and never forgetting I'm here. My Bob, not Jane's, not Margy's, not Helen's, not Lucy's, not Maddie's, but mine, all mine in this earthly life. Beyond the grave, I'll have to fight it out with Jane again. Bob tells me that there is said to be no marriage in heaven, where we will be as the angels of God, but I think we'll owe it to ourselves to spend a few aeons in no-holds-barred rivalry, giving him hell, before we all settle down. I'm definitely leaving this in for Bob to read; it says it how we all want it to be.

I'm off for one of my regular visits to see Frank tomorrow morning, Saturday. He's in a nursing home a few miles away, one specialising in dementia. He's no idea who I am when I'm there. He also receives visits from the mother of his child, conceived some sixteen years ago while he was married to me. The lad visits just occasionally. I don't think my visits do much good, not even in assuaging the guilt I have little reason to feel.

And after that, I'm going on a dig with my friend Steve. I studied archaeology before moving into the big, bad world of finance, and I lecture on it from time to time. Bob's looking after the kids for the day. He may miss not having a job any longer, when I still have one of sorts but, if he does, he never says so. Steve was Frank's business partner and is still running the old business. He's now looking to jack it in and find a buyer as he wants to move north to Keswick, where his mother lives alone. He needs my power of attorney to approve any transaction on Frank's behalf. He's another kind man, but definitely not one to keep his problems to himself. Having said that, I have to admit that, with his personal life, Steve, who I think is by nature homosexual, also prefers keep things under wraps. He's almost the opposite of Lucy and Maddie, denying himself the pleasures of the flesh to the best of my knowledge. He and Bob get on just fine. They both like dark brown furniture, which now has them classified with the dinosaurs. I've always preferred more modern stuff, if I'm honest, provided it's understated. Today's furniture is too metallic and glassy. We've just got to hope there's a buyer who likes brown stuff too, as the shop is full it and it hasn't moved for months. Steve was thinking of setting up a new antiques business in Keswick. He's decided against, having found the sound of his head beating against a brick wall in Cheltenham none too edifying.

I've just read too that gradable adjectives and adverbs are fading from our vocabulary. I rather like them, and they'll be in mine a fair bit longer yet. But I'd better get the hang of this writing lark quickly. I'm meant to describe what's happened, not what's about to. I'll start on that tomorrow.

CHAPTER FIFTEEN

Summer 2017

I was only just back from the nursing home in time to hear the squeal from Steve's tyres as he skidded into our driveway. His driving mirrors his personality, up for a thrill until he chickens out. He'd already anticipated the monies from the sale of the business, acquiring a souped-up sports car, a new Fiat Spider, trying to regain a youth which in truth he never lost. Or maybe the one he's never had to lose. Bob and the kids waved us off, Bob telling Steve three times to be bloody careful in that car. I picked up Bob's vibes. For an instant, as we set off, I gripped my seat as if I was on a roller coaster. When we arrived, I realised that the dig overlooked the part-demolished nuclear power station at Oldbury. Poor Bob's career, I thought, as much an old fossil as what we'd gone there to look for, maybe even more so. They are planning a new power station there. I don't suppose for one minute it will ever be built. They never seem to be nowadays.

Not that we found any old fossils. Steve did drive very carefully, and we were home for tea. My parents, Audrey and Walter, are visiting tomorrow. They still live in my childhood family home in Cheltenham. They often come over as they can never see enough of Alice and Richie. I'm an only child, and they'd despaired of having grandchildren in all those long, barren years I had with Frank. They're old-fashioned enough not to be totally happy with the unorthodox relationship I'm forced to have with Bob. In truth though, they're not that much older than he is, and they have blessed our arrangement.

They've never been that religious. Nor was I, for that matter, before I met his nibs. They like Bob though, my Dad also being an engineer. They do see him as a sort of saviour.

None of this is carrying forward the story Bob was telling. He's told me not to start writing again until something's happened.

*

A little something does happen in this last week in July. The four of us come away on holiday and it's not to St Chad's, but to Disneyland, Paris. Now that Hattie and Sheba have gone, we're not so constrained. Richie, nearly six, can join in on many of the rides. He loves walking down Main Street between Bob and me. And if we'd left it much longer, Alice who is eight, going on eighteen, will be too old for the magic. She smiles benignly at us as if she's doing us a favour. We're able to pair up on the rides, usually on a gender basis. Our kids are almost the post-Disney generation, there being so much competition in entertainment for the young. In fact, I'm probably more at home with it. Bob finds it too Americanised, mirroring his own father's views when ITV was first launched. He complains about the ubiquitous smell of corn oil and tomato ketchup.

"Sacrilege, followed by heresy," I said.

"I once used to like cinnamon but not on overdose," he replied.

The people in the next room at the Hotel Cheyenne think he's my father and the kids' grandfather. He's not taken offence.

"You ought to be pleased that you're not down as grandmother and me great grandfather," he laughs.

I took offence when he said that though. I gave him a playful but well-deserved cuff round his ear. In reply, he kissed me. I think his dodgy ticker sometimes complains at the long days and

155

the huge distances we walk, yet he carries on regardless. We're in two gender-specific rooms too, so there's no further nocturnal strain placed on him.

I'd have expected him to be glad of the rest. As he's read this, he says not, and tells me that he'll make up for it when we're back home. He'll not admit that his best days are long behind him, and maybe I won't either. I'm realising that you still need illusions in later life to help live with the truth.

To counterbalance the contemporary culture of Disney, we also fitted in a quick trip to Venice before it sinks into the lagoon. Richie insisted we went on every single waterbus service. You do see culture from a different angle with children. Bob is more used to this from his first two offspring. Anyway, Venice is better from the outside.

*

It's now September and the summer holidays are over. There's much to report. After Disney and Venice, we then went up to St Chad's for a couple of weeks. Of course, the Fishwicks are still the talk of the village. Maddie has been working in an unusually inclusive Methodist youth team, wowing the youth of Blackpool with Carl, a married man some ten years older than her. He came up from London to help for the summer season, having lost his job as a fast-talking salesman. When we were in Blackpool with the kids, we couldn't resist going to see what sort of show they were putting on. As the tide went out, the evangelists set up their show, and yes, they did have tambourines. Maddie was in her tightest jeans, so a crowd formed quickly. Carl, dressed in a suit that looked two sizes too small for him, did most of the talking, bible raised and wielded in emphasis. I think he must have travelled in snake-oil during his salesman's career. I certainly wouldn't buy a used car from this man. As with his role model of Elmer Gantry, if we got closer, I'm sure we'd smell the sweat and eau-de-cologne. The meeting broke up with prayers for the future of humankind and invitations to the next Sunday's service, when no doubt they'd hear the same message again. And again, and again.

Maddie brought Carl over to talk to us. Creepily, he had his arm round her the whole time we spoke. He is a good-looking, powerfully built man and he knows it, but he speaks too dogmatically and too fast for my taste. He's over-confident. I know that Bob can appear that way too, but he has redeeming features. He's intelligent. He usually knows what he's talking about. He listens to the other viewpoint. He'll admit it when he's not sure or wrong. And he wears no cosmetic products, preferring to have a shower,

"Are you having much success," asked Bob.

"Loads," said Carl. "Look how many were listening."

"Who knows?" said Maddie, as Carl stopped talking. "They're mainly day trippers. There's not much repeat business."

Richie saw that the donkeys were arriving on the beach and wanted a ride. We smiled at their contradictory answers and moved away. As we did, we saw Carl pull Maddie towards him and kiss her on the lips while squeezing her bottom. Agape and Eros was on full display.

Yes, Maddie's been having the best of both her worlds during the summer, or at least she was until an anonymous phone call tipped off Carl's wife. Maddie assumed rightly that the call was made by Amelia. Carl was summoned straight back to London, with a smile on his handsome face that he wasn't entitled to. In retaliation, Maddie has kicked poor Amelia out of the house in the Breck. Amelia is at the moment having to share a bed with another nursing home colleague. Lucy and Dave are either too wrapped up in the book, or pre-occupied with Jack, to take much interest. Lucy is trying to get the book finished before the start of term, when she has to be back in the classroom. It's getting longer and longer, and further from the end, according to Dave.

*

Maddie wasn't actually in St Chad's as we left. We were perhaps the only people there who knew where she was. She'd driven down to London to pursue further the no-longer-secret part of her mission. On a whim, she'd first turned at the M25 to land on the Shackleton's doorstep. James was given thirty seconds warning of her visit with a mobile phone call from outside the house. The first inkling Richard and Helen had was the doorbell ringing as James came down the stairs to tell them they were about to have a visitor. I have to admit that I'm taking some liberties with what the exact conversation was as James opened the door, with Helen right behind him, Richard behind her, and Amy behind Richard. My only source of information has been Bob, who recounted to me what Richard told him. I hope that the subsequent conversations weren't quite as sharp and explicit as I have to report them to you.

Maddie, bronzed and toned (God knows how she'd done that from a summer in Blackpool, even though they had managed to sing some hymns on the beach), was wearing a summer flare frock which left little to the imagination. She'd obviously raised Richard's spirits. He said she looked a million dollars. The outfit was probably acquired at Primark. That wretched girl doesn't need money to look stunning. Her hair was still black.

Before anybody had spoken, the old Shackleton family

dog, Trotter, rushed out, wagging his tail with a welcome normally reserved for his most intimate friends. Helen wasn't as easily turned.

She spoke first. "Well, that's the dog seduced. Who are you going after next? James or me?"

Perhaps this was better than Maddie was expecting. At least Helen didn't slam the door in her face. I rather wish she had, particularly after what Maddie said next.

"Are you both offering then?" said Maddie. "Have you a bed big enough for the three of us?"

Her face fixed in a defiantly insolent grin. Helen's anger stayed cold, liquid helium in her veins.

"You wrecked my son's life without as much as a second thought. You betrayed your own mother, and your girlfriend. You are not welcome here to do the same again. Bugger off, I'm telling you, bugger off."

James walked out to be next to Maddie.

"Let's just drive somewhere quiet for a chat," he suggested.

They drove off without anything else being said. Back in the house, Richard told Helen that, whatever her feelings on the matter, it was down to James.

"What, and leave him moon-eyed for the next twenty years like you were with Emma Greenwood? We've got to save him from that."

Emma Greenwood had, he always readily admitted, been somewhat of a trial in the first half of his life. He didn't pursue that James has a God-given right to exercise free will. Helen would only have said that he wasn't showing any.

James returned an hour later on his own. Maddie wisely dropping him off at the corner. With a sheepish grin on his face, he told them that she had to meet someone in London. She'd only intended to say hello on the way. He looked a little dishevelled.

"And you've just bonked her in the back of her car in that pull-in by the woods," said Helen. It was molten metal she was pumping round her circulatory system this time. "Don't think I can't tell. That's all she wanted from you. She'll be meeting that guy she met as part of that damned mission. Don't forget, she'll be shagging him tonight. The only thing you can say for her is you do know where she's been. Does she adopt the missionary position for men? She'll have got used to being on top of her girlfriend, I imagine, wearing a dildo. When she's not using her fingers or her tongue."

"That's disgusting, Mum," he muttered as he retreated upstairs.

"True though," she shouted after him.

"You shouldn't have said any of that, love," Richard said as he put his arm around Helen. "I don't even know what they get up to, not that it matters. Fancy a cup of tea?"

"I'll say what I think. He's being taken for an idiot. Yes, make me a tea."

Whatever the words actually spoken, Helen is determined to make the love between Maddie and James no more than a four-letter one. The debate as to whether it is more than that rumbles on in the Shackleton household.

Meanwhile, James has returned to Manchester for his fourth year. He's got a first and is doing a master's course. Both Richard and Helen know that he hasn't looked elsewhere because he wants to stay near where Maddie is, in a forlorn hope.

*

While Bob and I were up at St Chad's at half-term, Steve came down one afternoon from Keswick to see us. He'd had an offer for the

160

business which we'd agreed to accept. He'd managed to sell it as a going concern, and we'd completed the week before. An ongoing concern, more like, I thought, but the price we'd obtained hadn't put much of a value on future earnings. In fact, we'd no doubt have made more money selling to a property developer. At least we aren't going to be the ones who feel guilty when that inevitably happens. Steve is letting out his house in Cheltenham, while living with his mother to look after her.

We went for a walk around the village with him. There never being any show without Punch, we were bound to meet Lucy and Dave, and we did, pushing Jack in a pram. They were full of the way the play was developing as a novel. I have to confess that, listening to them, I was even less convinced than Bob was, and he thought it stood no chance. Steve though was clearly taken with them both. Lucy never misses an opportunity. She roped him in for an editorial session on Friday, once he'd had chance to read a draft. Phone numbers and email addresses were also exchanged. I'm sure Dave must have been thinking, "Not another bloody Paul." If so, he didn't betray it.

*

We arranged to go out for dinner at the local Italian with Steve on Friday, once he was through with Lucy. He arrived late with her in tow. Looking after Jack had been delegated to Dave. I wouldn't have been happy to do that. In nature, doesn't a stepfather kill the offspring and then have his own? The table was a tight squeeze too, as it was in a corner meant for a maximum of three, which is what we'd booked for. Bob was good enough to avert his eyes from looking down Lucy's cleavage whenever I looked his way.

Steve was adamant that trying to turn the play into a novel had been a great mistake. Lucy's gift was in dialogue. What it needed, he claimed, was a sub-plot that had nothing to do with the coach trip. He spoke with all the authority gained from writing a skit for a scout camp entertainment show forty years ago. On the back of that, he suggested that a gang from Manchester could have been raiding the Windermere post office while the group of pensioners were buying souvenirs to take home to their grandchildren.

"Sounds good to me," said Bob. "The robbers get pelted with Kendal Mint Cake as they make off with the loot, one falls over a rollator in the confusion and is stabbed to death by its owner with a Swiss Army penknife from off the shelf."

"I'm certainly not asking you to help," said Lucy. "Try and explain all that in dialogue in either a novel or a radio play. You'd make a terrible writer."

"He does," I said.

I wish I hadn't said that. Bob looked hurt although, when I apologised later, he said that it was his sciatica playing up. Steve was disappointed that he couldn't stay longer, with the drive home to Keswick beckoning. We picked up the children from Ruth's and went back to the hotel.

We left Throstles' Nest the next morning. Our kids treat Fiona and Jason there as if they were part of the family, with Alice always telling Fiona what we've been up to. They waved us off. We returned to Nether Piddle after a final lunch with Ruth and family. There'd been nine of us at the table, with all four of her children including the older ones present. She still has her hands full, with nobody to share the load. She's the Swarbrick most like me, or at least how I'd like to see myself. Thank you for welcoming me with such open arms, Ruth.

Bob received a text on the journey, which he didn't get to read until we were home. Mike Cornbill had died.

CHAPTER SIXTEEN
Autumn 2017

Bob waited until both children were in bed before ringing Margy. I think he was showing me how our family came first. I could tell that he was itching to pick up the phone. Full marks to him for resisting. He even read a story to Richie before coming down to play a game with Alice. I joined in with that. Of course, by the time the children were in bed, Margy's phone inevitably gave out the engaged tone, which it continued to do for the next half-hour. Bob decided to have a shower before he tried again. Sure enough, our phone rang as he was mid-shower. So, I took the call. Mike had suffered a bad heart attack that morning, and never looked like he was going to pull through. Margy was able to talk without breaking down, with the occasional pause to recover herself. We had the usual conversation that maybe it was for the best, he'd been spared that slow decline, he was a proud man who would have hated the indignities, but we both knew that, given the choice, he'd have plumped for a bit longer. He'd died in hospital, so there would be no problem with a death certificate. The funeral arrangements hadn't yet been made.

Margy sounded a bit disappointed when I'd told her that Bob was in the shower earlier in the conversation. He never takes long, and he was soon down again, in his dressing gown. She decided to punish him for not being there in the first place, telling me to pass on the news. She would ring later on in the week with the details. Bob, who'd been walking over to collect the phone, arm out-stretched, succeeded in not looking disappointed. To be fair, he probably wasn't. Spending ten minutes making repetitive sympathetic noises isn't one of his life skills.

He did ring her back the next morning though, while I was out shopping. She'd checked out with him if he thought it was a good idea that she sang something at the funeral. He'd advised her not to, saying, "Grief hits you when you don't expect it and you don't want to break down two bars in."

She'd insisted and eventually they'd decided on singing 'Rock of Ages', to the tune Petra, the one that Victorians would have sung in churches in Britain, and not the more upbeat American version.

"Good choice, but better not, if you can talk her out of it," I'd said. "Was Mike much of a believer? Has the rock been cleft for him?"

"I think he was. If he wasn't, Margy believes enough for the pair of them," Bob replied. "She'll wangle him a ticket."

"I'm not sure it's meant to work like that," I'd said.

"Does now."

"Do the same for me then, will you?" I asked.

*

There wasn't a lightning strike at the church in Evesham where the funeral took place, which Bob regards as sufficient evidence that his theology is sound. I don't think he's based it on Richard's wish for everyone to be saved. Bob has a view of the Almighty more derived from the Old Testament, and a more jaundiced view of humankind, than that. He'd like to find a theology to wangle Hattie and Sheba into heaven, as well as me. I told him that, as he's seen in his dog dream, it's more likely that they'll have to smuggle us in.

"Nothing in my hand I bring, simply to thy cross I cling," Margy

165

sang to a congregation for whom this was no more than a concert, other than for Mike's few relatives.

The cross is Bob's desperate hope, one I'm beginning to share now. Before I met him, I didn't think much about religion, although nominally an Anglican. It seemed a bit far-fetched to think that the truth had been uniquely entrusted to just one species of animal on this very planet. But I've still not had to face the death of a parent. I realise that Bob, Richard, and Margy are later-life orphans for whom the graveyard has remains still living in their heads. I now wonder if Bob's holy allegory in many different forms is open to all thinking creation as the best salvation from the absurdity of despair. It's not open to Frank any more though.

Bob tells me how he imagines that, once the coffin lid shuts down, contained within are all the events of our lives which are then re-lived as our brain decomposes, until all the bad ones have been excised and the good ones transferred to our resurrection bodies. During that time, it's like we're both living and dead in there, like Schrödinger's cat, unable to do anything about it. I do like his analogy that Brexit could mean just that for the country too, only it will be the bad characteristics that cross over.

"Or maybe, t'worms will come and eat you up," I suggested, scepticism again rearing its head.

"Ay, then duck'll eat t'worms, and thou'll eat t'duck. I'll be able to rest happy until the next time you have a crap."

"In metaphorland, I only powder my nose," I said.

"And in that green and pleasant land, the coffin will represent the memory of my life in God's mind, from outside the system, where I can't get to while I'm living."

A hymn so poignant as 'Rock of Ages' definitely merits eternity though. And Margy did sing it beautifully, playing the guitar too, with no Mike to do it for her. The quavering in her voice was more down to old age though than either emotion or in tribute to Joan Baez. I hoped she really had sung it for Mike and not Bob.

In the congregation were Margy's son and daughter. Her daughter is a vicar but hadn't felt it right to take the service for a stepfather, in case his blood relatives thought she was being pushy. Neither of Margy's children is much younger than me. Perhaps I'm being silly, worrying about her trying to steal him. She does have form though, with three husbands.

Bob was more worried about his metaphorical coffin. "There should be no time dimension in the box, it all being in eternity, but there has to be. We know that some good events are caused by prior bad ones. The fault must come before the redress, so there is some sort of time going on. You can't mess with any part of the story. I'll have to give up on the physics and start studying the metaphysics."

"You won't," I replied. "You only do science and religion. And it was only a thought game, wasn't it?"

"Was it?" he replied. "I only really do religion. And not very well."

I did have the grace to look interested. Well, it actually would be quite interesting if I could get my head around it. Sometimes. I imagine that Jane in their early days thought so too, though she'd have tried to prove him wrong, whichever way he argued. But does any of it matter to Margy? Isn't she an artist and not a thinker? She sees meaning in a melody. I wonder if that's why Bob finished with her for Jane all those years ago? I'm worrying about nothing. He does like his music though.

CHAPTER SEVENTEEN
December 2017

We stayed at the Throstles' Nest again when we went up for Christmas. As soon as we arrived in St Chad's on the 21st, Lucy and Dave decided to reciprocate for all our hospitality, inviting Bob, Ruth and me, with the smaller children, over to Little St Chad's Lane for tea. Jack is only 12 months old, and about as reasonable in his demands as you'd expect in a son of Paul's. Lucy has had trouble weaning Jack off breast-feeding and on to a bottle. Her return to work had to be delayed until half-term, exactly twelve months after having left. By then, she'd managed to find a childminder that she's happy with. Jack isn't walking at all yet. He is, of course, ahead on talking, knowing the names of his toys.

"He'll be writing his first treatise on Leavis before he's at pre-school," said Bob.

"As long as he doesn't criticise my novel like his Dad did my play, that's fine by me," said Lucy.

Another nappy change was required. Lucy and Jack disappeared to the changing mat upstairs.

"How are you coping with fatherhood?" I asked Dave.

His face creased into a worried frown. I realised that I'd asked the wrong question.

"It's hard, when you know you're not the father. At this stage, it's all give and no take. And, though Lucy's done it all before, she was a lot younger then and didn't have a full-time job. She's struggling but won't admit it. She's looking dreadful."

Lucy could be heard coming back down the stairs, carrying Jack. I hope she didn't hear that ungallant remark, true as it is. She said nothing if she had. She tried to put him in the big plastic Wendy house to play. It didn't work. She had to carry on feeding.

"And how's the world of electrical engineering?" Bob asked. Unusually, and differently from the former colleagues of his that I've met, he's never been that bothered about the academic distinction between engineer and technician. "None of the Victorian engineers had a degree," he'd say.

"Business is good," admitted Dave. "A bit too bloody good. It's as well Ruth helped me out on the admin or I'd be floundering. The Taxman and the VAT man have caught up with me at last. Living in just one place has made me a sitting duck. I've now got to pay most of the profits over to fund other people's snotty kids to go to University, where they'll be taught how to despise their previous pals and where they've come from. They'll then get jobs on twice as much money as us in something that never used to need doing, and still doesn't, if we're honest."

"Don't get too chippy, love," said Lucy. "You've got work, and life's pretty good." She turned to us to explain: "We're just tired after the sleepless nights with Jack."

She then focused on me.

"It's true though, Wendy. We vote for Brexit and we're told we're xenophobes. Dave and I like watching those comedy quiz shows together, but they're all middle-class southern boys making out they know better. That's except for the mandatory woman, who's usually even more patronising but not as funny as the men. Half her jokes will be about tampons. I know me voting leave was just meant as a gesture and it's probably a bad mistake, but I'm still glad I did it. I wanted to tell Londoners that they're only a small bit of England."

She then looked guilty. "Sorry, perhaps I shouldn't have said that. They are people, after all."

"I suppose they are," grinned Bob. "It's just that some of them do a good job hiding it. And none of them's anything like as funny as Peter Kay or Lee Mack."

"You should say it if it's what you think," Dave snapped at Lucy. "The Labour Party's been taken over by college lecturers and the like, all smarmy sods. The public sector's all middle-class now, pretending they're not. The one thing I've liked about austerity has been to hear their moans when one of their little privileges has been removed. The real working class are in, what's it called, the gig economy, or they're white van men like me. The smarmies then try to pretend we're National Front, BNP, UKIP or whatever. I voted for their precious Labour Party last time. And of course, I voted bloody Brexit. And I'll quite likely vote for the same Labour tossers again once we've left, since all the others stick their noses up in the air too."

I've only just read that the best indicator of whether someone is a Remainer or a Brexiteer is whether they're university-educated or not. Bob and I both voted to remain, as you know. He'd been strangely quiet through Dave's diatribe. I knew he must be preparing his considered response.

"Brexit won't do you any good though," he finally said. "After Brexit, if it happens, the BBC will still think the world starts and ends in London, even if they're all moved to Salford Quays. All the public sector jobs will be protected. Bankers will find different ways of making even more money to nobody else's advantage. The car workers at Sunderland and many other places will lose their jobs. The Labour Party will likely win the next election on their disaffected votes. You'll pay a bit more in tax. I'll pay a lot more, but I don't mind that." He then grinned. "Well, maybe I do mind, but I can take it. The panel show comedians will look even further down on the pair of us, until they realise that they're paying more tax too. But the railways in the north won't be improved, nor will a swing in trade to the Irish Sea ports take place. The South and the East are too strong. It's not only London. All the cities around the country are too powerful, nabbing all their region's growth for themselves. The Mancs and Scousers are doing fine. They've all got both this Government and the next Labour one stitched up. Maybe as a matter of honour, we now have to leave the EU, but it's a colossal mistake for all of us."

"I'm still glad I voted that way, Bob. You only voted Remain because you're loaded."

"I guess you mean I'm well off, which I don't deny, but doesn't the word usually mean something else nowadays?" Bob replied, trying to lighten the mood.

"It can do," said Lucy with a grin. "Not that I'd know, I'm a good Catholic girl, as I'm sure you know, so I hadn't noticed."

"Bob's got something to lose," Dave grouchily continued. "That's what I meant. In fact, he's got a hell of a lot. We've never had much. The longer we stay in the EU, the more it feels like we're losing ground, and not just in what we own. I used to know who I was. I'm buggered if I do now."

"Maddie's not forgiven me yet for voting for Brexit. She says we've wrecked her generation's future," said Lucy, as if to me but looking at Alice. "It's cultural with me too, so I guess both Dave and me can be accused of being racist, sexist and all the rest. I like here, it's where I belong. Maybe I'm not urban enough for the Labour Party, but it's good fun being a left-wing Catholic. It confuses people no end. What I can't handle is Theresa May. She's just stubborn and wishy-washy at the same time."

"She seems a nice person," chipped in Alice.

"I doubt that, love," replied Lucy. "She went into politics."

Alice had been listening intently. I can remember doing the same during the Falklands War, when my parents disagreed vehemently. Bob can recall his Dad's furious denunciation of the Suez invasion, with his mother patriotically in favour. It's not as if Bob and I are disagreeing violently about Brexit itself. He's just said exactly why it would be stupid to leave, and yet he still thinks we have to, as a matter of honour. Nobody cares about honour any more, if there's any left.

"You're all cutting off your noses to spite your face," I said. "When it's so damned obvious that we'll all be worse off, then admit you misread things, and change your mind. For pity's sake, let's stay in."

"That's what I'd like to happen, Mum," Alice said.

Alice joining in of course changed the tone of the conversation, if not for long. All it succeeded in doing was change the subject matter, and who was disagreeing with whom. Dave is in favour of fracking for gas in the Fylde, particularly with the prospects of plenty of electrical work for his company that it might bring with it. Cuadrilla, the company pursuing the idea, are trying to get their planning consents relaxed. Lucy is viscerally antagonistic to the idea, at odds with her vision of black and white cows in green fields as the view she likes to see on her walks. Alice said that she liked the cows too. With Bob quiet again, and oft-times having heard him on this subject, saying how we ought to trust our engineers more, I took it on myself to present the case for it; that wind power isn't much use on cold, still days when the winter peak for electricity takes place, so we'll still have to burn the gas then, and that we'd be better having our own than buying from the wretched Putin. Bob was now ready with his next, big thought.

"It's the sweep of history. Us power engineers were heroes not that long ago for keeping the lights on. Now, the public view is that we've spent the last two hundred years wrecking the planet, and that there's no need to any longer. Let's see if they're right."

I've never heard anything like that from him before.

"No, let's at least squander the Government's money on something which employs engineers, if we have to spend it at all," Dave replied.

"It would do far more good on the Health Service and social services than on fracking," said Lucy.

"The two don't need to be exclusive," I said. "Most economists now agree that austerity needs relaxing."

"Fracking's just not going to happen," said Bob. "I'm not going to bang my head against a brick wall. No government's going to have the balls to relax the earthquake limits they're not allowed to exceed, which has put the kibosh on any testing. I don't suppose the civil servants advising Ministers realise the Richter scale is logarithmic, or even what that means."

"Nor do I," said Lucy.

Bored by this time, Alice ran off to supervise Richie, which was as well, as mild-mannered Dave slightly lost his cool.

"You don't understand it, but you still want to ban it? Nothing can ever get done. Yet you'll shove money into the NHS willy-nilly. That is a bottomless pit, keeping folk alive when they'd rather go, always presuming hospitals don't kill more than they cure," he ranted. "Did you see all the wastage going on in A and E when you put me in there?"

"You mustn't say that," said Lucy. "You'll need them again one day."

173

"I probably will, knowing your temper," Dave snapped back.

Both Bob and I both chose to laugh at this at the same time, to lighten the atmosphere. We didn't want a row like the one in Ruth's garden with Paul. Lucy chose to grin too.

"You'll always get some inefficiency when something's managed as a cost centre," said Bob, who's worked in both public and private sectors. "But God forbid the NHS becomes a profit centre. On the international comparisons, it comes in pretty cheap and it's reasonably efficient. I doubt if we can improve it much. There's no need to spend public money on fracking either. That just needs sensible planning permissions and a steady nerve. They're not available anymore."

"No, Bob, we should spend a lot more on education," said Lucy. "There's plenty of untapped talent in the children I teach."

"You're right about that," said Dave, calming down. "But then they'll only go down to London and sell out as plastic socialists."

At that, they smiled at each other. They'd found a point of agreement, and one which we all could go along with. Dave's never expected or got much help himself and would prefer it if others didn't. He's not succeeded in developing any reason as to why leaving the EU would help change things. Perhaps he actually does want things to turn so sour financially that further austerity is inevitable. If others are thinking like that, the Tories will win again. I doubt if most women do, though. Or that many men for that matter. And Alice doesn't! I'll take her opinion to represent the whole of youth. Engineers are a different breed from the rest of us.

The rest of the afternoon was pleasant enough, with an interesting chocolate cake baked by Dave. Lucy doesn't do much of the cooking. The red wine was excellent too. Dave had chosen it.

*

The next morning, two days before Christmas, saw much action in Little St Chad's Lane. Dave rode off on his motorbike early to return three quarters of an hour later from Kirkham on the train. The few belongings he had in the house were soon packed into his van. He'd decided to leave and had arranged to stay temporarily with his sister. He rang his new confidante, Ruth, to tell her where he was going. I suspect this is for the best for both him and Lucy, but it still seems a shame. Political differences are not the reasons he gave. It would have been better if they had been.

"I've stopped fancying her," he told Ruth. "Nothing against older women, but it's time for someone younger. I feel like I'm wasting my life."

Ruth joked to me that she was mortified. "I was about to abandon the kids, forsake my feather bed, and move in with the raggle-taggle gypsy-o myself."

Lucy has taken it all in her stride. Ruth went round to see how she was. She claimed that Dave had beaten her to the punch. Her eyes were looking very puffy, and Ruth didn't believe her, but I'm sure in the end it will be for the best. She then asked Ruth about how to cook the turkey, for which Dave had been lined up. It was a big turkey that she'd ordered, and she only has Maddie to share it with.

Steve will now become a necessity to Lucy though. She can't live without company. He's already been summoned from Keswick on Boxing Day, ostensibly to help turn the novel back into a play. There should be plenty of cold turkey left, provided it hasn't been burnt to a frazzle.

"All that prose is too dull for me," Lucy asserted.

I won't ask her to read this then.

CHAPTER EIGHTEEN
Christmas 2017

We're facing payback in real time. Jane and Geoffrey are coming to Ruth's for a second Christmas in a row. The central heating system has gone kaput in their apartment. Not only that, they've managed to book themselves in the Throstles' Nest for three days. I'm not going to find the time to carry on with this while we're altogether, so reports from the front will begin once we're back home. We'll be close enough for hand-to-hand fighting in the short corridor between us at the hotel.

On Christmas morning, as we set off after breakfast for Ruth's house, Fiona's mask slipped. I hadn't even realised before that she was wearing one. Father Christmas had been told where our children were overnight, and so their gifts from him and us had already been delivered, including new iPad Minis for each of them. While Bob was loading all the presents for the rest of the family into the car, the two children were speculating to me in the bar about what other presents they were going to get, particularly from Grandma Jane and Geoffrey, who had already left for Ruth's. Jason had been late arriving at the hotel, leaving Fiona to do the work of two. I saw her looking askance at our children as they happily prattled on.

"Your kids think the world owes them a living," Fiona said to me. "They've no idea what it's really like."

"Excuse me...?" I spluttered, shocked.

She wasn't finished.

"With your lah-di-dah accent, I don't suppose you have either.

Someday, when Lord High and Mighty Swarbrick isn't around to protect you, maybe you'll find out."

As you can imagine, I was livid. It was Christmas though, and not a day to allow bad feeling, if possible. I thought I would try to emulate Helen, and be ice-cold and factual, although I would have preferred to be more Jane-like and torn her limb from limb metaphorically, or better still, like Lucy, and performed the task physically.

"You might have studied America, but maybe you'd do better if you understood your own country. For your information, my accent is from Gloucestershire, more in the Midlands than the south-west, where I went like you to a state school. I had my own successful career for many years after that before I hitched up with Bob."

My remarks were calibrated so that Fiona could see a way to back-track. The fiery nature of her next comment to me demonstrated her temperature still on the rise. She was feeding her own demons.

"Don't you get snotty with me, you middle-class cow, with your 'thank-you-so-much' and 'that's-so-kind of-you' patronising attitude."

Or perhaps the devil really was in her. Alice joined in.

"You're being horrible, Fiona, after being so kind to us up to now. My Mum's nice to everyone because she's nice. Anyway, my Dad's from round here, and you sound much posher than he does."

"Hark at you, Miss Airs-and-Graces. Entitlement's oozing out of every word you say. Your Dad's not from here. He left what was then here half a century ago. It's a different place now. We'd all be a damn-sight happier if he didn't come back, and the rest of his stuck-up family went and buggered off to wherever you're really from."

Richie ran out to get his Dad. It was as well. Enough heat had entered me that I was incandescent.

"How dare you say that?" I shouted. "No wonder you can't get a proper job with that chip on your shoulder."

I shouldn't have said that. I'd flipped from Helen to Jane, which doesn't sit happily with me.

"So, this isn't a proper job then? Did you think that when I brought you your breakfast this morning? I should have spat on your scrambled eggs. Perhaps I did do," Fiona said with a triumphant smirk at Bob who had just hurried in with Ritchie. She walked out into the kitchen as he arrived.

"What the hell is going on?" he said to me.

"Nothing," I said. "Forget about it."

Unfortunately, I wasn't the only family member to have been involved. An equally angry Alice relayed to him the gist of the conversation, including all the insults against him, me and her. He marched into the kitchen, with me following him and the kids behind me. I was waiting for his volley of abuse.

I was surprised. He obviously had been thinking about what Fiona had said long before she'd said it. Perhaps his northern instincts had spotted that she'd been wearing a mask, not that he'd ever said so. As we walked in, she busied herself putting some pots and pans away.

"Fiona, never try to understand anyone from where you're standing. Put yourself in their shoes. You've just badly upset people who up to now have liked you," he said in his deepest voice.

"I'd love to be in your shoes now, Mister Rich Guy. I'd have liked to be in them fifty years ago, when you left Uni. But we can't be, and you bloody know we can't."

"I don't bloody know that," he growled. "I started out in life with much less than you've had so far in yours. Just think how rundown the nation was as the war finished. It all looked hopeless.

We had our worst bit right at the start of our lives, not that we knew differently. But our parents had hope. It was drilled into us and it was eventually fulfilled. Not that quickly either. After the false promise of the sixties, I spent the next two decades trying to keep the nation's lights on against attacks from both sides. We were still a rundown country. Now we're just an unfair one. I can understand how that bugs you."

"Well, do something about it then," she snapped, still avoiding eye contact.

"I'm an old man who can only do my best for my family, apart from the odd drop in the charity bucket. I've fought my battles and, like everybody does, I've lost more than I've won. You've got to do the something."

"Fat chance of that!" she said, then realised that she had just jeopardised her only source of income. "Are you going to snitch on me to the owner here, if you can ever find him, and get me fired?" she asked reluctantly. "That would make my Christmas complete."

"Of course not. There's still enough old Labour in me to believe that protecting a job and the person in it is what matters. Shake hands with us all, and let's be friends again."

As usual, Bob was being presumptuous that Alice and I would be equally happy to bury the hatchet. But it was Christmas. We did all shake hands, with ill grace in my case. Has something corrosive been let out into the air, or were we wrong in thinking that things would always get better?

"I'm sorry," Fiona said to Alice, unconvincingly. "You were a brave girl coming to the defence of your mother."

"I was coming to your defence really," said Alice. "I was trying to calm Mum down."

Fiona made no personal apology to me, nor Bob. If we're

honest, it was us, and not the children, who had got her goat. In fact, it was probably more me than him. I tried to make light of Alice's comment.

"Well, I'm calm now," I laughed. "You'll succeed soon, Fiona, with that spirit."

"Not as long as I stay round here. And I can't leave."

"I wish we could help. There will be something," said Bob. "Life always prevents you from being in a rut for too long."

I'm not sure there will be. And nor was Fiona.

"Can I sue if you're wrong?" Fiona joked. "Get my hands on your money that way?"

She doesn't like us. Bob finished packing the car. Off we went for a traditional Christmas at Ruth's, a tradition formed after just a few years.

*

I nearly had to start this by eating humble pie. Until the last day, until the last minute, Jane was sweetness and light, and didn't flirt with Bob at all, apart from one playful fight over the tea towel when doing the washing up together. Not a single hand-grenade had been rolled down the corridor. Geoffrey was the droll commentator of the living room, with his glass of port scarcely touched but permanently in his hand.

Ruth's self-compiled Christmas album included Joan Baez singing 'Silent Night' as well as the usual Nat King Cole and Frank Sinatra. The spirit of Margy was invoked. Inevitably, even on her best behaviour, Jane felt the need to remind Bob of how Margy had sent him a Valentine while she was in the last stages of pregnancy before giving birth to Ruth.

"She could be a bit persistent," he answered.

"She could indeed," I said.

Jane giggled mischievously. "What, still, even with you two? Just think of the sweet music you could have made together, Bob."

"I can't sing," he replied.

Tom and Charlotte were both at home. Charlotte was the only one not to go to Church. She explained at length how it would not be right to support such a repository of antediluvian views on gender and homophobia. She's not yet quite out of her serious phase as revealed at the Dylan concert. She had tried to show solidarity by making friends with Maddie and Amelia while those two were still together. Amelia was friendly, but Maddie had been less so. I believe she might have made a pass at Charlotte and took offence when it wasn't reciprocated. She'd then made some cutting remark. Charlotte had stopped hanging round them before Amelia was given the order of the boot. I know from the way Charlotte blushes when the name of one young man from the village is mentioned that her tastes are for the boys. He did have a girlfriend. Apparently, he's just become available. Charlotte is a pretty girl and looks very pleasant today in a long beige skirt and tight brown jumper showing her pert breasts to good advantage against us older women. She has a spring in her step too. Let's hope she's soon on to something.

Unfortunately, Bob took her bait and remarked that it couldn't be the case the Church had antediluvian views as the flood came before the Council of Nicaea. That irrefutable piece of history was wasted on Charlotte. Doesn't he know that function and not historicity is what matters? Geoff played the wise old owl to perfection, only to be told by Charlotte that the sole purpose of politics was to change things.

"Not too much, I hope," he'd muttered, at what he'd thought was under his breath.

Unfortunately, his rich, ringing tones were not so readily dampened. Charlotte heard.

"I can't believe you said that," she snapped at him, accompanied by a patronisingly astonished smile that wouldn't leave her face. She can't have scored with her young man yet.

"Someday you'll say it too," Jane answered, in defence of her husband.

I think Charlotte was most disappointed that arch-feminist Jane, her Grandmother, would give her views no backing, just as she hadn't at the concert. As per her argument with Sophie, written up by Bob, Jane wanted nothing taken away from her pride in being a success as a woman. Charlotte thus reserved her most condemnatory comment for her, saying that she'd lost her will to fight. Jane managed to bite her tongue, something she's not normally known for, rolling her eyes. In my direction, would you believe?

Over lunch, Bob of course came to Jane's defence with his usual class analysis, that the real victims today are the working class of either gender. I like it that he's still so loyal to his ex-wife. He was told by Charlotte that inclusivity is a class matter, which palpably as expressed from her middle-class, educated mouth, it isn't. Ruth had heard enough. She told Charlotte to stop being so aggressive. Charlotte stormed off in a huff before the puddings had been brought out.

"We've been no-platformed by her," laughed Jane.

"It's like our whole generation is being buried before we're dead," said Bob. "At least we don't have to take it personally."

Ruth and Tom both went after her. We could hear Ruth tell her she was setting a bad example to the younger ones, followed by Tom accusing her of spoiling Christmas for everyone. It used to be her putting his naivety straight until recently. He managed to bring her back to the table by making her laugh, threatening to eat all the trifle, her favourite. I don't think he's quite as bright as his Granddad, but he's just as full of common sense and gruff bonhomie. Peace was restored.

*

Later that afternoon, Ruth confided in me that, in all the years she'd had the children, this was the first time she'd felt at a loss. She wondered if Charlotte was developing something of her grandmother Jane's erratic disposition, of whom even third husband, psychologist, port-drinking Geoff believed had manic depressive tendencies. He'd told Bob this many years ago. Funnily enough, on one of the many things that Bob and Jane agreed on from opposite ends of the spectrum, both couldn't see the point of attaching a label to the problem, if indeed it is one.

"Jane in the end has controlled it, whatever it is," I said to Ruth. "Charlotte's rejecting all that's gone before, probably because she was the one that accepted the conventions without question as a child. Yet we mustn't forget our past. It would mean disowning our own parents and grandparents."

"She seems to be having no problem with that," Ruth said ruefully.

I discussed this with Bob later. He doesn't think that the sixties' revolution was about getting rid of the past but recognising it for what it was in all its glory. That's not the case this age. There's Oedipal father-slaughter taking place, with mother-slaughter as a second stage, a national identity crisis to go alongside the personal ones. When I suggested that could be an inevitable consequence of a less homogeneous population, he shook his head. He's always said that we have a duty to be welcoming.

"Bloody funny place to be having it then, here in St Chad's," he said. "We've not had any immigration since us Saxons arrived, apart from the few Micks who stayed around after they'd built the railways. The Church was in the Domesday Book, for God's sake, not that Charlotte is impressed."

"It's all been structure and not history in academia for a long time now, Bob. That's what wound poor old Paul up all his life," I told him. "That's why we can't tell Charlotte that today's fads will be forgotten tomorrow."

"Great pity he died without knowing of his son. He'd have seen some hope in that. You know, Charlotte carried on down to my sister's place in Totnes after she went to Glastonbury. Joan said that when she showed her our Grannie's old milking stool, she got a lecture on the exploitation of women. Grannie was so proud of that stool too. Granddad was a farmer's boy. They all mucked in together."

"Everything's seen too much from today's perspective, but with the science misunderstood. There's no religion, no ethics, no philosophy. Everything's politics. That's the real problem," I said, to save Bob from saying it.

"It's the rational outcome of the Enlightenment. Apart from the science, everything has turned out not to be rational, with no-one bothering to tell the humanities folk that they're still in control. Not that most scientists get it. Brian Cox was on the box again, eyes focused on infinity, telling everyone that the idea of a creator solves nothing, because then you're left with the question of who created God. He'll never see to infinity though, even with those eyes. It's definitionally outside the system."

I know I've got that down correctly. I've been able to check what he wrote himself earlier.

*

Back in the real world, as I said, Jane behaved well, until it was time for them to go home, leaving from Ruth's in the late afternoon. She'd been spared Bob's philosophical insights on this trip, which I thought she'd be pleased about. She and Geoffrey had checked out of the hotel after breakfast; Fiona had been sweetness and light with them. Their Liverpool address was perhaps to their advantage, or it was maybe that Fiona noticed they had bought fewer presents. Bob and I were part of this later farewell party. With Geoffrey already in the car and all the goodbyes done, Jane pulled me to one side.

"What have you done with him. He's not the Bob I know and love. He's lost all his spark, all his energy. Where are the corny jokes? Where are the sweeping generalisations? He's turning into another Geoffrey."

"No, he isn't…"

"My Bob's man of action, not wisdom. This doesn't suit him. He must be drowning in your sweet syrup."

"How dare you…"

I was too late. I'm glad I was, as I was becoming tired of acting as if I was indignant. She'd abruptly turned and jumped into the car. Everyone else was waving their cheery farewells. The first Bob is going to know of this is when he reads about it here. In the meantime, I'll inwardly seethe. How could she think or say that? I am indignant. There's a devil in her.

"When she dies, we'll get the vicar to drive a stake through her heart," joked Bob when he'd read this. At least she's wrong about the corny jokes.

185

"If you can find it," I replied.

But what with Fiona and Jane, I'm having my doubts about the much-vaunted friendliness of the North. People don't turn on me like this in Gloucestershire or Worcestershire. It didn't often happen in the City of London. Resentment is running high in these parts. They're not behaving to type.

CHAPTER NINETEEN
Early 2018

It's still Wendy at the typeface. Under pressure from his party, the Leader of the Opposition has finally come out in favour of joining a customs union (not necessarily with the definite article or capitals) with the EU, the words sticking in his craw. Assuming we leave, we all know that's the only logical way to prevent a hard border with Ireland and the subsequent risk of the troubles restarting, which otherwise looks more than possible. Corbyn's been reluctantly dragged to this point, clearly himself wanting to leave altogether. And hapless Theresa is still trying to negotiate the impossible knowing that a substantial minority of her MPs, including quite a few in the Cabinet, and most of her party members, are pathologically opposed to anything other than a clean break. All she can hope for is for the EU to facilitate a colossal fudge. They won't; they've got us just where they want us. Bob is torn between honouring the Irish Peace Treaty and the intention of the vote, whatever that was. He's so silly sometimes with his sense of honour; he wants us to stop in the EU with every fibre of his body, but he can't allow it.

The news from Ruth continues to come thick and fast in weekly telephone calls. Maddie's still living on her own on the Breck. As a postgrad James has his car with him in Manchester. He's been seen twice leaving her house in St Chad's first thing in the morning for the drive back to Manchester in time for classes.

Bob wasn't sure if he should pass this piece of intelligence to

Richard. We discussed it and decided that we must. Richard wasn't sure if he should pass the news on to Helen. He discussed it with us, and he concluded that he had to. Helen wasn't sure if she should raise the matter with James. Thank God that she and Richard discussed it and resolved that they didn't need to. Richard says that James really seems to have knuckled down on his master's course, as he wants to get a distinction, and then move back south next year for a PhD, either at Oxford or in London. Maybe he's learning the game, and he's using Maddie, but if so, it's not a game he'll win. That girl has got too much low-down cunning. There will be more tears, of that I'm certain.

Steve is also ringing me up regularly. I decided to ask him if he and Lucy have become an item.

"Not in the physical sense," he said. "I've never felt attracted to anyone like that, Wendy. I thought you knew."

"I thought I knew too, petal." That's been my occasional name for him since he moved north, the sort of epithet that could be used in *Coronation Street*. "But it sounds like you two are getting on like a house on fire."

"We are, but that's not going to spread down my trousers," he laughed. "Look at the trouble everyone else gets into. I can enjoy people for what they are, if they've anything left to reveal once the sex has been taken out. I know you don't much like Lucy, but there's plenty left with her."

That was me put in my place. Still, I'd learnt a bit more and Steve never held a grudge.

"I think she's taking time-out from that anyway," he added. "She lets Bill Hardisty from the pub take her out occasionally, but she's not letting him get any further from what I can tell."

"That's a shame. It would tie up a couple of loose ends. Have you got to know Maddie at all?" I then tried to ask casually.

"Relations between mother and daughter are a bit strained. If I'm zero on the sex drive front, and Lucy's 50, then Maddie's 100. Her religion is sex-worship. Lucy hates the way she's using that James. She thinks he's a better offer than her other three options of Dave, Amelia or Carl."

"Is Carl still with his wife back in London?" I asked.

"Sometimes. Lucy says he pretends he's religious but really he's a God-hater. I think he's the one Maddie wants. And we've come to learn that whatever Maddie wants, Maddie gets."

I fear that's the case. It's dilemma time again. Do I tell Bob? Does he tell Richard? Does he tell Helen? Does she tell James? Definitely not. I'm telling no-one. Let James have his day. Oh bugger, Bob will read this. I'll swear him to secrecy.

*

Margy's started the folk singing again, with Mike not that long buried. She invited us to a folk evening at a pub local to us where she was singing. Of course, it wasn't the sort of evening when I was prepared to give up a precious babysitting pass, so Bob went alone. He came back late, and with Margy in his car. He explained at the door that two breakdowns had happened, one to Maggie's voice while she was singing, the second to her car as she'd been leaving. That must have meant that he'd hung around to make sure she'd left safely. But then this is Bob, and he would have done that for anyone. He'll have carried her guitar to the car.

"We've called out the RAC and they'll ring us 10 minutes before they get there," he said. "Could be more than the hour. It just wasn't firing at all. Most likely the battery or terminal connection, or maybe the solenoid or starter motor. I couldn't see anything obviously wrong but then it was pitch black and I always was a crap engineer. That's why they made me a manager."

Margy lapped up the self-deprecatory comments. I wanted to tell her that my Bob was bright enough to have been rehearsing them ready for this audience, and for me particularly. Her voice had given way while she was singing 'Barbara Allen'.

"Didn't the briar get to grow round the rose?" I said, maybe a little too tartly. She gave me a sideways look. She'd taken it as a hint I didn't really mean to give. Or perhaps I did.

"It was very good of Bob to give up his evening for me. I won't ask him again, I promise. In fact, I think I'd better give up on the singing at the Clubs altogether."

There was a tear in her eye, left unexplained as to if it was caused by the prospect of not seeing Bob again or not singing in public again. Of course, Sir Galahad was straight on to either case.

"You were singing beautifully until you got the croak," he said. "You should have had a sip of water between songs. We'll get Audrey and Walter over to look after the kids and come together next time, won't we love?"

The question at the end was addressed to me. I answered, "Of course," with as little conviction as I could muster, hoping that her next concert would coincide with my parents' bridge evening.

Bob made a cup of tea while Margy and I discussed the strange ways of the world. She's still on message to the left's agenda, hoping for great things from Corbyn. Bob was gentle with her when he returned with the tea. He did say though that Corbyn worried him and that he wasn't up to becoming a second Harold Wilson. They then had argument that surprised me with its intensity, Margy claiming that Harold had sold out, Bob believing he'd done a good job. They were both back fifty years, finishing off something that had started then. It was as well Margy's handbag rang and that they were wanted back at her car. Bob didn't return for another two hours. It was the starter motor. Her car had been towed to the nearest repair centre. Bob had then driven her back home to Evesham.

"I told you she still fancies you," I greeted him with as he walked through the door. "Did she drag you in for a nightcap? Or ask you to tuck her up in bed? With you in it?"

To be fair, he looked genuinely astonished. I can usually tell when he's holding something back, so I was pretty certain that nothing had happened yet.

"I escorted her to her front door, as a proper gentleman would," he growled. "She said that she'd better not ask me in, because it seemed like you'd be jealous, and she didn't want to cause problems between us. I don't know what the hell's got into the pair of you. There's a set of mind games going on independent of what the reality is. Which is I haven't the slightest interest in Margy as other than a friend. We finished fifty years ago for a reason, and it wasn't her bloody stupid politics."

I didn't answer him. We'd never really had a cross word with each other before and I didn't want one now either. I went to bed, resisting the modest advances he made when he clambered in alongside. He was drooping like stick of celery left out in the vase for too long anyway. The tension I'd created had got to him.

*

I've made a fool of myself, I know. My mind has got ahead of the action. But somehow, that's how it feels. The action might not be imagined, only delayed. He always tells me that the mental and physical have to coincide; it's knowing which one is the agent that's problematic, he says. I dreamt of Bob making love to Margy in the back of the car. The celery was fresh enough in that dream. I felt like I've seen the future before it's happened. But it was in Steve's new sports car, with a functioning starter motor. I must have been hallucinating. That can't be the future. Neither of them would fit in the back of Steve's car individually, let alone both together. I started kissing Bob's face frantically to wake him up. He did do, bemused.

"I'm sorry for being stupid," I said. "Are you up for something now?"

At his age, this did necessitate first going to the lavatory for a pee, followed by some lengthy foreplay to get his circulation up and then him coming suddenly as I was just starting to enjoy it. But we'd made our peace, still without having said too cross a word.

Margy rang the next day. Having given Bob the car news, she asked for me.

"Can you go somewhere Bob can't hear what you're saying?" she asked.

I went into the kitchen. She told me that she'd been a fool. She could tell that I'd guessed that a flame had been rekindled in her heart. Even though Bob had already got his car keys out and was edging back down the path, she'd asked him in for a nightcap. He'd reluctantly agreed. Inside the door, she'd put her arms round his neck and tried to kiss him. He'd pushed her away, saying that was a bad idea. He'd told her he was truly happy with me, the happiest he'd ever been, and nothing was going to spoil that. She'd burst into tears, to be told that on this occasion he couldn't help. He'd turned and left.

Ok, he'd lied about what happened on the doorstep. But he'd

been thinking only of me. He'll find out that I know what happened by reading this.

Margy told me that, once her car is repaired, she's going to put her Evesham house on the market and then go to stay with her daughter in the Northumberland vicarage.

"I must have been wanting to play one last silly game before the final end. I'd be better preparing to face my maker living the reality of my life. And they have a great folk club there. Maybe my voice will come back with all the fresh air. When we ring off, would you tell Bob? We really said goodbye fifty years ago and there's no need to do it again now. I'll still send you a Christmas card."

The phone was dead as I tried to reply. She'd at least gone with dignity and style. Bob picked some classy women in his time, and sometimes she was one of them.

Margy is going back to the future, the past not open to her. Paul has returned to the only location he could call home, to his parents in a graveyard, never to know the son who could have changed the shape of his eternal soul. Bob and Jane have carved out new lives with me and Geoffrey respectively. I do wonder if they ever hanker for the deepest past still available to them, each other. I hope not, but I guess they both will on occasion. That's the human condition.

The television news is on as I write this. All I can hear is of leaders elsewhere in the world obsessed with power: for starters, the buffoon Trump who, crazy as he is, may be less dangerous than the pumped-up Putin and the ludicrous Kim Jong-un. Putin is a judo and not a chess player, and they're all more opportunistic than strategic. The one exception is the apparently fully-clothed but increasingly autocratic Chinese emperor Xi Jinping, who certainly looks as if he has a plan, if not one honouring western liberal traditions. The future of the world is in the hands of these and some even worse regional contenders. I suppose it would be yet more perilous if a deep-thinking megalomaniac was at the helm. The only religion that gets airtime is Islam and that's more out of fear than respect. Our compassionate Labour Party is led by two guys with eyes as cold as the Siberian gulags, even if the senior one can look like Dave's smarmy college lecturer on a good day. They've made me realise that I'm too county-set to care for the organised resistance of socialism, unless sorely provoked, and perhaps not even then. Quiet dignity in defeat seems the best way to salvation here and in eternity.

But that view of life holds no sway. Power matters, with many parts of the world preferring strong government. Christian values are not universal even in the West. Nietzsche's philosophy remains attractive to some, and dictatorship to many. The God of the Old Testament is written up like that too. I suppose Christianity and liberal democracy do need the rough stuff to have happened first. Is it really necessary for that to continue during and afterwards too? Is there to be no progress in history? Is the devil to be forever in charge? Other than Brexit, the only British news is either of safe spaces for students judgemental of our past, or of 'inappropriate' behaviour by male MPs. I'm sure you can't be in favour of anything inappropriate by definition, which makes every sentence ever uttered using the word no more than a tautology. I would certainly like to know what's really happened before casting the first stone at the member's member. The trouble is that the facts are never proved. You're left judging which one is telling the truth by the look on their faces. That's probably how juries work too. The truth isn't often available.

What we need is an antidote against all who believe in themselves. I'm certainly a full believer in other than me. I look at Bob and think that he must feel part of some of the most uncool groups in the country right now: straight white males, engineers and Christians.

Despite coming from the working class and of liberal disposition, he's still tarred with the sins of stereotype. It seems unfair to me that he's having to spend his later years hearing so many disown the meaning and purpose of his life, and that of his ancestors, as if he really were a member of the elite. In his lay readership role, I know Richard feels that strain too and he is as hip as his generation gets. He reckons that Europe's had a half millennium on top and it will be at least that long again before we know who or what we are. And that's in the unlikely event that humanity hasn't destroyed the planet first. Bob still says that he's been blessed. He looks neither bloodied nor bowed.

The planet will recover with or without humans. Whatever's happening must have been accepted by the Almighty. So, what's suddenly come over me? Something's bugging me. I do now have the hope of faith and yet keep inventing a Godlessly bleak future. It feels like payback time is starting for these years of happiness we've had.

CHAPTER TWENTY
Easter 2018

It's still Wendy writing. Bob's sciatica is a bit better, but he says he's enjoying what and how I'm writing. I can't think he meant that last page. It's true though that a man couldn't say what I've just written without being assailed from all sides. I don't suppose a woman can either. I'm not giving out my Facebook or Twitter handle.

*

We came up at Easter for a full visit. We felt we had no choice but to use Throstles' Nest again, as Alice wanted us to. We didn't need to have worried. Both Fiona and Jason have left. They've been replaced by other graduates searching thanklessly for better. It's Jason who has found a job in HR, in Warton. Fiona has taken to selling advertising for a Preston-based free newspaper. It should have been the other way round of course, but recruitment is bound to be hit-and-miss when there are so many candidates. Perhaps it's not so much that the ladder has been taken away since our day, but that all but the bottom two rungs have been sawn off.

Charlotte is finally walking out with the young man of her fancy, who's called Seb. She's very happy with life, though of course she won't allow herself to admit the proximate cause. Provided her results are good enough, she'll be starting a Politics course at UCL in September. Seb will be not far away in Reading if he's successful.

A much more cheerful Ruth asked Lucy and Steve over for a coffee on our second day, so that we could hear all the news about how the play was coming along. They'd finished it, they said. Not only that, but James had put them in touch with Kieron, a BBC trainee based in Manchester who'd been in his football team at the University. They were on a fast track to a new radio producer, or so they hoped. We know enough about James to think he'll have introduced them to the real McCoy, however starry-eyed he is about Maddie. Mention of her brought a frown to Lucy's face.

"She's keeping James on a string while carrying on with Carl. She's trying to get Carl to leave his wife and move here permanently. You proddy dogs have a strange view about marriage."

Then she grinned before continuing, "I didn't, which is why I've never married. I just thought I did once. Fornication is a lower level sin than divorce."

She really does have a friendly, open face that smiles so sweetly when she's being at her most provocative. I looked at Steve and wondered if he'd taken on board that she'd be after some real action once her play had been heard. She hasn't conceded joint authorship rights to him, despite the post office robbery being a crucial part of the storyline. Bob's contribution of a robber tripping over a rollator has made the final cut, but with no throwing of Kendal Mint Cake, which would have been truly sacrilegious, nor any stabbing with a Swiss Army Knife. He definitely isn't getting a credit!

*

Charlotte and Seb went to the pictures in Blackpool last night. They bumped into Dave, there with a new girlfriend, who were leaving as they arrived. The girl did look slightly familiar. Charlotte soon

197

found out why. Her name was Lisa. Dave explained to Lisa who Charlotte was.

"I've heard a bit about you from my half-sister," said Lisa.

The penny dropped with Charlotte.

"Who, Maddie? I can see the resemblance. You're a bit taller than her."

"And nothing like as beautiful, I know," admitted Lisa.

"More beautiful to me, and with a much nicer disposition, thank God," Dave added with feeling.

Charlotte was about to say that with three from the same family in a row Dave should win the jackpot but stopped herself in time. It was possible that Lisa didn't know about Dave sleeping with either Lucy or Maddie. Not likely, however, given the nature of gossip in the Fylde.

"Our family obviously has something that Dave goes for," said Lisa.

So, as Charlotte had correctly surmised, the game for all the family hasn't remained a secret. Ruth is still Dave's confidante, and has dished out more of the dirt to us. But it's not that dirty. He's moved into Lisa's flat in Cleveleys, while they save up enough for a deposit on a house. He's asked Ruth where he should deposit his savings. He's taken to full respectability. He's also told Ruth that Lisa is the best of the three in bed as well as being both young and straight. Bonneville or not, in twenty years' time, I expect he'll be in the Rotary Club.

*

Steve and Lucy visited us last night too. Her big news is that James is coming to see Maddie from Hertfordshire on Good Friday.

198

"Carl obviously can't get away from his wife, so the substitute is called off the bench. She's shagging them both at the same time. I always left a gap in between my conquests," she claimed.

"Measurable in nanoseconds, if I remember right, between Dave and Paul," chortled Bob.

"No, there was a day," said Lucy, trying to be indignant, but laughing too. "I stopped with Dave when I started with Paul again. I just didn't tell him that I had."

She put her arm round Steve and squeezed him hard. I could see him squirm with discomfort.

"I'm not letting go of this one," she said. "The best friendships are platonic. That sex stuff just befuddles the brain. James wouldn't pick my Maddie if his head wasn't ruled by his cock. She's picked him for his brains though. Carl's the one with the cock for her. That's who she'll end up with."

"What about Amelia," I asked. "An aberration or a big part of her."

"You tell me," replied Lucy.

Steve wriggled free from what had become a headlock. "Whatever Maddie wants, Maddie gets," he repeated for the new audience. "It will be Carl for evenings, but afternoons with Amelia. James will receive his marching orders."

As Steve so often is, he is soon proved to be right about the marching orders. James spent Good Friday and Easter Saturday in Maddie's company and bed. Carl rose from the depths of Hades on Easter Sunday, abandoning his wife. He arrived unannounced just after breakfast, having driven up overnight. While he was unloading a suitcase and a whole load of stuff thrown into the back of the car, Maddie, unable to contain her delight, made it clear that James had to pack, telling him it was always going to end this way. She was laughing as she told him.

"It's always something cruel that laughter drowns," a line from Roy Orbison's wonderful rendering of Elvis Costello's song 'The Comedians', was what I thought of as Bob told me what happened. That's a song which links Bob's musical tastes to my time, so I thought he might know it. He did. Maddie was so preoccupied that James left without even saying goodbye. "It's the bitter way that I was told," sang the Big O. Has that girl no time for some charity?

It was a few hours later that Lucy found out what Maddie had done. Appalled, she immediately rang Ruth to ask if she had Richard's phone number, so she could check out that he was back home safely. Ruth passed the phone to Bob who volunteered to call Richard, promising to be back in touch with Lucy when he had some news.

Richard answered in Monkey Mead with a cheery, "Happy Easter. He is risen indeed."

"Maybe not time for the Alleluias yet, pal. Maddie's given James the elbow again this morning and Lucy thinks he's driving back home pretty distraught. Has he arrived? If not, can you ring his mobile to check out how far he's got to?"

Helen's 'Find Friends' app located James' phone as somewhere near the cemetery on the edge of St Chad's. It wasn't being answered. A very few minutes later, Bob's tyre wheels skidded through the gates. Fortunately, it being Easter, there wasn't a hearse arriving at the same time or he might have tried to overtake it. There were though a few folk paying their Easter respects. As he pulled up behind the chapel, he could see James stooping over Paul's grave.

James didn't look like he was about to thrust a knife into his own chest or collapse from hemlock potion, so Bob was able to walk briskly towards him rather than run. He even wondered if he should pretend that he'd come to see his parent's grave but decided that the entry velocity into the cemetery of his car, that of a bat into hell, would then require an explanation he didn't have. The tears on James' face had dried. He looked up at Bob and smiled blotchily.

"I've seen a couple of graves in here with Swarbrick on as I've walked round," he said.

"That will be my parents and grandparents. Why seek ye the living among the dead, lad? Come on back to Ruth's place for a cup of tea and a piece of cake, and then get home to your parents. They're worried sick about you. Where's your car?"

James took one last look at Paul's grave. "He was another victim of the Fishwick curse," he said. "They seem friendly, but they cast a witches' spell on you."

Bob told him he must have read too much *Harry Potter* when he was younger. I'm writing this conversation as remembered by Bob. I bet it's close to word perfect.

"Maddie's not the one for you," he'd continued. "I married someone who wasn't quite convinced I was the one, but she was a damned sight better fit for me than Maddie is for you. I got her pregnant, we married, and she'd been right. We weren't suited. Your Dad pined for that Emma Greenwood for twenty years. She's Lady Norman now…"

"They still exchange Christmas cards," said James, with a little break in his voice. "Always with two kisses."

"Of course they do, and that's what you should do with Maddie. You can go as high as three kisses if you like. You don't have to forget her, just recognise her as another flawed member of humanity like the rest of us, and one whose needs will always carry her away from you. The first cut is the deepest, but it's a cut all the same, not a kiss. There'll be other times for you. Your

201

Dad found a proper match in your Mum, and I did with Wendy. Neither of them is perfect either, but both suit us down to the ground. Do your Mum and Dad proud and get that distinction. Let time look after the rest."

"I can't forget her, Bob. I want her. She's so dynamic, everything about her. The way she talks, the way she walks…"

"You see, she's nothing special. That's what Elvis sang and that was about the girl of his best friend. It's your Dad's favourite Elvis song, he told me once. I'd tell you mine was 'Heartbreak Hotel' but I don't think that's where you should be staying tonight. As I said, let's get you home to Hertfordshire safe and sound."

James smiled for the first time in the conversation at the Elvis song choices. He grinned a second time to say, "Mum will be insufferable telling me that she told me so. She doesn't like Maddie at all."

"You don't need me to tell you that your mother is a woman of strong opinions. They're nearly always right though, damn her. Yes, sure, she won't be able to stop herself saying it. What was her maiden name again? That's it – Helen Durell. She won't greet you with a hug. Helen Shackleton will though, even if it takes the form of a sarky remark. And so will Richard Shackleton, though that will definitely be in the form of a weak joke. We specialise in them. You'll know who you are there, James Shackleton. And not someone under a spell."

James thought for a moment and then started walking. The two of them slowly wandered back to Bob's car. From there, Bob rang Richard and explained that everything was fine before passing over to James. He spoke to both his parents, and thus suffered Richard's weak joke and Helen's sarky remark in Bob's presence. Helen asked for one last word with Bob.

"Well done, big man," she'd said. "You're still a contender."

He didn't tell me that. She did, when she rang to thank us all once James was back home in Hertfordshire much later in the evening.

James had left his car in the main car park back in St Chad's. They were able to rescue it from there, having exceeded the maximum stay period but with no parking attendant noticing. They drove back to Ruth's separately, Bob staying close behind. James had a sandwich, cake and cup of tea, while Bob rang Lucy to tell her that all was well. As James left, our Alice said that he would remain sad for a long, long time.

We drove back to Nether Piddle a few days later, leaving Lucy, Maddie and their affairs to find their own solutions and confusions. I'm not sure how much I care any longer.

CHAPTER TWENTY-ONE
Summer Half-Term 2018

We've come up for the summer half-term too. Our kids seem to prefer it to going away on holiday. Miracle of miracles, the BBC has accepted Lucy's play. It's to be called *Battle Bus to Bowness*. As we walked through the park in the afternoon with Alice and Richie, we saw Lucy and Steve with Jack and Toffee. Lucy told us that she didn't like the title but hadn't been able to come up with a better one. Steve, whose idea it was, said that he'd resorted to alliteration when he couldn't think of a joke.

"That's what we've done with the script too," he'd added. "You'll think you've terrible static on you set with all those esses in a row."

A small team has been assembled to prepare the piece for broadcast in the Autumn schedule on Radio 4. It's in the hands of the professionals.

"I'll probably listen to it and won't recognise it at all," said Lucy.

She seems to be on good terms still with Steve. There's no physical contact at all between them. She too now seems to prefer it that way. She has no plans to write another play, although that isn't what she'd said to Kieron's boss. She thinks that once is more than enough.

"It's new experiences I like, not repeating old ones," she told us in a rare piece of self-awareness.

"You'll be sodding me off soon then," laughed Steve.

"You'll still be a friend when I find the next one to make a fool of myself with. You're good at picking up the pieces," she said, looking him straight in the eye.

"Not sure about that. Picking up the shit after the Lord Mayor's Show isn't the career option I aspired to."

He then rapidly apologised for not being careful what he said in front of the children. Silence ensued until Bob suggested that's what most jobs entailed in his experience.

"How are Maddie and Carl getting on," I asked, mainly to change the subject.

"Not sure," said Lucy. "I don't see much of them, although they're only ten minutes' walk away. They've both left the mission. I always expected that once she joined the Methodists, she'd end up as an atheist. Carl was a salesman before he found his phoney God, and he's gone back to that, this time selling advertising. That will suit him better. He's really a God-hater, which is almost as bad as a protestant."

She did say that last bit with a grin.

"He knows I don't like him," she continued. "I'm sure the feeling's mutual. He's a hunk of a bloke, but he knows it. In fact, he thinks he knows it all. I can't see Maddie standing for that for too long."

Inevitably we then bumped into the pair, also taking a walk. It all started affably enough after the "Hello, Stranger" greetings. Maddie told us she had been intending to do the Post Graduate Certificate in Education next year with a view to teaching philosophy and RE in a secondary school. We all waited for the follow-up in a pause that she allowed to run for an indecent length of time.

"I'm not sure if I can manage that now. I'm pregnant," she said eventually.

"I knew you were," said Lucy, rushing to hug her. I'm not

sure she really did, from the previous conversation. "Even though you were hiding from me, I could see the signs," she continued. "When's it due?"

"That's why I was hiding from you," admitted Maddie. "It's due in December, but we're thinking of an abortion. I don't know which one the father is, and Carl's not that keen anyway. He wants us to have time to ourselves first."

These revelations took place in a secluded area. That was as well. We had three young children with us though. And, as we've seen, Lucy is forever a Catholic.

"You'd murder a child for a bit of time together. Don't you dare be so wicked. And don't you give me all that crap that it's your body. It isn't. Holy Mary, what have I brought into the world?" she shouted furiously.

She let go of Maddie and walked towards Carl. Knowing her reputation for kicking out, I feared the worst. In a sense, that's what I got. She turned away from him with a disdainful sniff. She asked me directly what I as a woman thought of abortion. If there's a moral issue I've never fully reached a conclusion on, it's that, having been childless until late, and for the last thirty years I've kept my own counsel on the subject to avoid upsetting either side of the debate. Coward that I am, I muttered something about how it depends if you think potential is an entity, words borrowed from Bob and his electrical engineering brain, and that Maddie would need to make up her own mind on that.

"We all think that potential does matter once a child is born. It's a massive responsibility to bear either way," I concluded.

"Wendy's right, you've got to make your own mind up about that. It's not something for priests or lawyers to decide," Bob added.

"Only you know how that baby feels in your womb."

He only looked up to Maddie as he finished. Time stood still. He'd hit the right note. Maddie's face slowly changed. She walked to her mother and hugged her.

"I'll keep the baby," she said. "The chance might not come again."

She moved back to Carl, as if to hug him too. He turned away from her.

"You said that you'd have an abortion," he said. "How do I know the baby's mine? It might be that idiot James's you pretend not to care about. Don't listen to this lot. It's your choice."

"You're right there, it is my choice. I'm choosing to have the baby. If that's the way you feel, go back to your wife, Carl. See if you can get your religion back. I don't want to be the reason you lost it." Maddie hissed. "You belong there. I won't ask anything from you if the kid's yours."

At first, Carl looked shell-shocked. I think he was on the point of asking to stay with her, even if she kept the baby. But Maddie hadn't finished.

"And I'm going to ask Amelia back. That's who I want. She'll come."

This hurt Carl's pride too much. "Too right, I'm going. I'm escaping this fucking madhouse. You've just used me to give you two dykes a kid, with James as back-up in case I misfired. You hate men."

Lucy said nothing to defend her daughter of this accusation. Bob and I didn't either. The reinstatement of traditional Catholic teaching was short-lived with Maddie. Lip curled, she thanked Carl for his services, before adding that he'd been cheaper than a sperm bank, but less good company. Lucy showed more grace and shook

207

him by the hand as he made his exit, wishing him well. He asked for half an hour to collect his things from the house before Maddie returned.

I suppose this episode is a good introduction for Alice and Richie of the ambiguities in the study of ethics. We reassured them as best we could as we all lingered in the park chatting inconsequentially. I'm sorry if Carl is an underwritten, one-dimensional character, but that's all we've seen of him. I can only hope that in the future circumstances will allow him to find the gentler side to his nature he must have had when he entered the ministry. And before he met Maddie!

Bob was asked by Lucy to walk back with Maddie after the half-hour was up, to make sure that Carl had exited the scene peacefully. Lucy and Steve went in the opposite direction, back to her house, with Jack and Toffee. The rest of us made our way back to Ruth's.

When he got back to Ruth's, Bob said that he'd asked Maddie en route if she'd told James yet. She hadn't and had no plans to.

"He ought to know if there's a chance it's his. He's the one who cares about you. You tell him," Bob had said.

"I'll think about it. He wouldn't care about me if he stopped to think what I'm really like," claimed Maddie. "He treats my body as if it's a temple but it's nothing more than a façade around a mass of sexual compulsions that I can't, won't and shouldn't resist. They're what my life is."

Bob has written about how Lucy seems to be displaced in time, perhaps temperamentally more suited to the sixties. Her daughter seems to be absolutely in sync with the age she lives in.

"Statistically, it will be Carl's anyway," Maddie had added. "We shagged far more often. He had and was the bigger prick."

"Does size matter? Amelia doesn't even have one of those," the ever-logical Bob had said.

"There are other compensations," she'd replied. "If I have to put up with one, it may as well be a big one."

As they'd walked down the Breck, they'd watched the proud possessor of the profane object in question zoom away from the madhouse. He must have seen them but there was no wave of farewell. Maddie had then asked Bob if he could pop in to help her move some furniture before Amelia's return.

"You know she's coming back?" he asked.

If Maddie ever lacked confidence, she was good at disguising the fact.

"I'll ring her now. She will."

And ring her she did, with Bob listening. She obviously found it easier to speak to her ex-girlfriend than ex-boyfriend. Bob only heard one side of the conversation, but they appeared to make up straightaway. Maddie accepted Amelia's apologies for tipping Carl's wife off. She didn't express any regret for having kicked Amelia out. It was all very business-like, with no kisses or tears. Amelia is moving back in next week.

When the call was over, Maddie asked Bob to stay a bit longer.

"Do you really believe the religious stuff you spout, Bob? I shouted out for Jesus at beach rallies all last summer, proclaiming a relationship with the risen Lord to the few weirdos who stopped to listen, probably because they liked my bum or my tits, maybe both. And I was lying. I've never had one."

"And not with the Holy Dove, the Spirit?"

"Not that I know off."

"You will have done. The Dove's always there. She works with all creation. You remember our little dog Hattie who died late last year. I dug in her ashes, along with those of our cat Sheba who went at around the same time, at the bottom of our garden. I looked out of the window a couple of weeks ago. Two muntjacs had found a way through the back hedge and were standing at the exact spot. They saw me looking at them, stared back and then slowly walked away through the hedge. When I'm dead, I'm going to follow them through that hedge."

"Bob, in my head, you're the technical guy. It's not what I want to hear. I've heard too many miracle stories from Mum and the Catholics to believe in them. Just tell me, why do you believe? The science students I know at college think religion's a psychological defect. You seem to think it's rational."

"I can't quite think that, but a bit of animistic thinking never did much harm. Because it's primitive doesn't mean it's imagined. Science can't ever explain creation. Nor can it explain how our sensations feel. It can't give life meaning and purpose, so many scientists assume there isn't one."

"And you think there is?"

"With all these thoughts swirling round my head, I've got to. I bet your head is full of semi-processed ideas too. If you can't hear the Spirit, if you can't find the risen Christ, start with the dead one. You don't have to believe that the miraculous events happened, as described in the Bible or by the Church. But the place of those tales in history has enabled a bigger story to be written, bigger even than immensity of the natural world."

"Whatever, we all end up dead in the last chapter," she said with a sardonic grin. "Did you know that Mum had a miscarriage when she found out about the bigamy?"

"She told me," he said.

"It's probably the real reason I didn't have an abortion. I wake up

210

at night thinking about the poor little soul. Was having the potential to be a person that you talked about enough to make him one? If so, where did he go to, Bob? Did he just die or is he lonely in some sort of limbo, without even having known a teddy bear as a friend?"

"Bloody hell, that's sad. Lucy said that you were looking forward to having a sibling. It obviously hit you harder than you knew. I think he was, maybe is, a person. I hope the good Lord has given him a resurrection body of the older man he could have become. You'll meet him someday up there and be the best friends you would have been if he'd lived."

"That's too good to be true. It's illogical."

"The curse of life, time, isn't fundamental," Bob replied. "That breath you just took is no nearer to now than the beginning of time is. Apart from you can remember breathing it. It's consciousness that's the only key. And we're conscious in the womb. We all have deep memories of it."

"I hope you're right, but that's not the key I'm turning right now," Maddie replied. "I've overdosed the physical since puberty, and yet I still wake up wanting more. It stops me from thinking about it all. Amelia's coming back. We'll be in bed within half an hour of her getting here."

"That's very considerate of you. She'll be tired after the long journey from Sheffield and will need a sleep," Bob bravely joked.

"She'll be a lot more tired before she'll get any sleep, Bob. I'm a highly tactile person and a vamp…"

"I'd love to know what you get up to, but that's enough vamping," grinned Bob. "Is there, are you, the dominant one?"

"Mainly me. She can be sometimes too, and I go along with it. Weakness is out of fashion. Ask Putin, he'll tell you why. If I met the right one, maybe I could prefer a man for the shagging bit. James was too gentle though, and Carl too rough. Men today are so bloody confused as to who and what they are. And you don't have vaginas to play with."

I don't think Bob has ever been able to understand his women, at least until he met me. Surprisingly, despite or perhaps because of, encountering overt lesbianism for the first time, he's better at it now.

"We always have been confused," he admitted. "It's you girls who are castrating today's blokes though, one by one, by expecting too much. And there's me thinking you and Amelia held hands on the couch watching chick flicks."

"No, you didn't, Bob. You're taking the piss now. Any more and I'll cut you and your bollocks down to size too."

He stopped smiling and winced, before turning serious.

"Not much need at my age, love. Try writing something, Maddie. See if you can find yourself that way. It sounds like you've inherited the gift from your mother."

"Nobody reads books any longer. I'll maybe try that when I'm old and grey, if it's back in fashion," she replied with a shrug.

"That happens quicker than you think," Bob said ruefully.

"In fact, in no time at all, if I've just understood what you were spouting."

"You're near enough," said Bob. "I'd better be going. You and Amelia, enjoy yourselves while you can. Look after that child you're carrying. The Holy Dove has wished that upon you. Do that education course too. You'll be a good teacher. Teach them both the sacred and the profane, but please never that bloody secular crap most RE lessons consist of. Don't try to make it relevant."

Maddie's phone rang. It was Lucy, asking if she could pop round with Jack to discuss the afternoon's proceedings and revelations.

"Bob's just leaving, so that's fine, Mum."

Maddie rang off and then turned to Bob.

"Mum's on her way round. You'd better get back to your Wendy before the senior Fishwick vampire decides to suck your blood. She's on the look-out for Paul's replacement."

At the door, Maddie pulled him to her and pecked him on the cheek. This was one cheek-pecking routine I bet he didn't shirk from. He said though that he was scared she was going to suck the blood from his neck.

*

As Bob got back to Ruth's, Steve was just arriving. He'd been told to amuse himself for a couple of hours while Lucy went to celebrate the baby with Maddie. Apparently, we represented the best entertainment he could find in the area. Another man might have gone to the pub. Bob related the unusual conversation with Maddie almost verbatim to Steve, Ruth and me, clearly thrilled at this rare insight into a world he didn't know. In mentioning the goodbye kiss, he said that she'd smelt young and feminine, and not too much like a vampire, wherever she'd been and whatever she'd been up to. She'd impressed him with her honesty. I can't say I've noticed much of that in her dealings with James. Steve disclosed that Maddie had described Bob as like an old grandfather clock in one of their conversations.

"One wound up a week ago, and ticking hesitantly before finally running down, I imagine," Bob said.

"I think she sees me as a Victorian sideboard, too gloomy and taking up too much space," reckoned Steve.

I'd still prefer a modern kitchen, but I feel happy nowadays that I'm here with the solid, brown furniture, sitting comfortably. Modern clocks very often have so much unnecessary function and decoration on their faces that it's difficult to tell what the time is. And the storyline has moved on so quickly that we're right back where we were. We've got to watch the movie again with some old and some new actors. Maddie and Amelia are getting it back together. Lucy has accepted Maddie's sexuality. They're all going to have a baby to look after. And who's baby is it? Like Lucy, I'm pleased the admission price isn't an abortion though. The repeat of history should move from tragedy to farce, and that's what I hope it's doing. It can't seem much like farce to James though.

Despite his new-found admiration of Maddie, Bob doesn't trust her to tell James about the baby. He's already on the phone to Richard. James rang Maddie before she'd bothered to inform him. She almost begged him to stay away, saying she was pretty certain it was Carl's. She'd ask for a swab after the birth and let him know whose baby she'd had. In the meantime, she intended to make the most of the time with Amelia before the birth. I'm sure they'll have great fun.

CHAPTER TWENTY-TWO
Summer of Discontent 2018

The State of the Nation is nothing like as settled as this period of stability in the Fishwick households. The Brexit dance involves one step forward and then two steps backwards, with Theresa May's weakness seemingly her only strength. The irony is that if this makes her position stronger then she becomes weaker again. We've made tactical as well as strategic mistakes in our negotiations. We triggered Article 50 too quickly, before we worked out what we wanted. As a result, we've conceded to the European Union that the negotiations will have to be in two stages, with only the first part, the Withdrawal Agreement, being concluded before we leave. As part of that, we've already agreed to pay a £39 billion divorce payment. It's an unusual negotiation where you agree to a payment without knowing what you'll be left with, even if you did owe the money. But that's the least of our worries. There's then to be a Transition Period when all future commercial arrangements are to be agreed. All that's to be done on that before we leave is the penning of a non-binding Political Declaration, newspeak for kicking the can down the road. The EU are insisting on the rights of European citizens in the UK being guaranteed in these future arrangements, which I'm sure won't be a problem. They are also demanding that there has to be a 'Backstop' in the Withdrawal Agreement, which means that we will have to guarantee that we'll stay in the Customs Union until a trading arrangement with the whole EU is reached, and that this agreement must require no hard customs border with Ireland. The Irish are understandably insisting on this. The EU's preferred solution if a suitable agreement hasn't been reached is putting the border in the Irish Sea with Northern Ireland effectively still in the EU. The DUP in Northern Ireland, equally understandably given their reason for being, cannot accept that they will be treated separately from the rest of the UK. There seems to be no technological fix currently available which can replace traditional customs posts, another randomly plucked suggestion by Leavers to avoid the issue. I'm sure that every possible fudge of words will be explored but this problem, as framed, has become one of logic. The intention, if not the formal text, of the Good Friday Agreement effectively requires customs arrangements to be the same on both sides of the border. So, we're stuck with that as far as the eye can see. I don't remember hearing anyone say this during the referendum campaign. Unfortunately, Erwin Schrödinger is no longer available to have us both in and out of the Customs Union simultaneously. His equations work better on more spiritual matters.

Mrs May seems to be arguing that the EU originally wanted more obstacles in the 'Backstop' and to have got it down to one is a good outcome. That's akin to arguing that there is only one stretch of sea between Alcatraz and the US mainland. Ostensibly, we could reach trade deals with other countries during the transition period, but which couldn't come into effect until afterwards. And, as long as we remain in the Customs Union, they probably wouldn't be valid anyway. I'm sure the EU will not readily give way on this in the next stage of negotiation. So, we could well be leaving while having to follow all the rules, without being able to vote on them. All we seem to be getting in the Withdrawal Agreement is control of fishing in our territorial waters, and perhaps the ability to replace European immigration with similar numbers from elsewhere in the world, provided we don't want to stay in the single market. Either way, this is not going to be an easy sell. I can't see any reason why the DUP should support it. Nor why any Labour waverer would defy their Whip to do so, unless the clamour from their constituents becomes too loud to ignore. The whole notion is unbuyable even if it's not unsellable. Surely, somebody saw this coming. Yes, somebody probably did, but they were employed by the EU in their 'stitch-up the UK' department. I know that, when Bob was writing, he said some rude things about MPs behaviour, all justified, but even if they'd behaved well, we'd still be in this fine mess. This conjunction of negative effects has been designed by a malign intelligence.

Of which there is plenty of other evidence. Russia has apparently been poisoning its exiles in Britain once more, in Salisbury this time, the scare 'em in Sarum way of discouraging dissent. Its ally Assad is doing the same to his rebels in Syria, using chlorine gas and perhaps worse. On this, Theresa has been able to look calm and rational in a limited response, with Jeremy struggling to be the same. With his political past, he tends to favour the old soviets even in their capitalist reincarnation. Bob still reckons we ought to be friends with Russia too, saying that if we'd got them into the EU when Yeltsin was in power, we would have voted to stay in. I think he's wishing for the impossible there, although the drinking sessions involving a resurrected Yeltsin and Juncker would add to the gaiety of life. Putin is a gangster, and there's nothing else to be said until the Russians realise that for themselves. The far-right nationalism elsewhere in Eastern Europe shows that serpent also still to be around and with an unbruised head. Jeremy is also struggling with left-wing anti-Semitism emerging from the shadows to haunt him. Those old conspiracy-theorist Marxists aren't going to let go of any of their prejudices. More moderate voices are being shouted down. Some of the young who joined the Corbyn bandwagon are already seeing how this old guard dislike any differing opinion. I can't see him winning the next election at the moment. But I can't see anybody else doing so either.

Trump is pre-occupied. The EU owe us nothing. The UK has become Billy No-Mates, something we have to get used to. We're even, shamefully, offending our own citizens, the early immigrants of West Indian descent, who we've been trying to deport in some enormous Home Office cock-up, sadly sometimes succeeding. I remember one lovely carer at my husband Frank's nursing home being deported because she didn't have the right papers. I wonder if she'd fallen foul of some modern-day version of this. These cock-ups quite possibly have their roots in Theresa May acting in a grotesquely uncharitable way when she was thought to be halfway to competent as Home Secretary. Bob reckons the West Indian guys are the closest thing to soulmates he has in modern Britain. I've told him he's got to welcome everyone; he can't pick and choose, but I do think we're all bound to have favourites. Almost to prove the point, the African American Presiding Episcopalian Bishop gave a corker of an address at Prince Harry's wedding to mixed race Meghan Markle. We both loved it, particularly the uncomprehending looks on the faces of the stuffed shirts, except possibly for her Maj, who looked like she was enjoying it too. There's not about to be a spiritual revival if only three of us are ready to join in. Yep, I think I'd be onside for that.

"When she's gone, there'll just thee and me," Bob said.

"In the end, there'll be none of us," I replied. "We'll be dead."

I regretted saying that. While I'm coming back from an offside position on matters of belief, I mustn't interfere with play when there's a scoring chance. Yes, as you can tell, we've both been watching too much football from the World Cup. It's made a pleasant diversion from the travails of Brexit. England have done quite well, although Bob grouches that they've beaten nobody they shouldn't have. He's never let sentiment sway his judgement, as far as I can tell, apart from with Jane. Or maybe it's that the dismissed Sam Allardyce is more his character type than Gareth Southgate is.

"Wearing a waistcoat and doing the bottom button up, indeed. He's not eaten enough pies," said my beloved, as we lost in the semi-finals.

"Is that how we won in 1966?" I asked him.

"Of course. And sausages. The Germans were on Bratwurst and out lads were eating ones with 30% fat. We were bound to have more energy in extra time."

I don't think Bob takes his heart condition as seriously as he could.

CHAPTER TWENTY-THREE

Autumn 2018

We went back home to Nether Piddle after a hot summer visit to Lancashire. There have been wildfires on Winter Hill, scorching heaven and earth but unfortunately not the television transmitter. The News keeps getting through, and it keeps on surprising. There's even been a blaze on the sandy nature reserve at Lytham St Annes, only a few miles from Ruth's. What once would have been thought apocryphal has become apocalyptic. We left hoping that a worse Lancashire monsoon season than normal would soon be with us to dampen the madness down.

To make Bob feel worse, the county cricket team have been relegated again. That's depressed him greatly, and Richard too. It's proof positive that the Lord's face isn't shining upon them. Apart, that is, for the good news. James, having worked much harder than his father ever did, has got his distinction. He's won a place at Oxford for his doctorate, which he's accepted. He told his parents that he hoped Maddie's baby isn't his. I'm sure he didn't mean it.

*

The Tories are split in two over Theresa May's middle way in attempting to find a form of words to mitigate the impact of the 'Backstop'. It's pretty obvious that one can't be found. Whatever, Johnson resigned as Foreign Secretary over it and then upped the ante by being naughty about burkas, playing the cultural nationalist card. He seems his own worst enemy, incapable of acquiring gravitas. Is he planning a coup? I'm not sure. Planning isn't his core competency; blundering is. As that seems to be the basis of the new world order, if he ever does get in, he'll be in his element. He's made so much noise that he's going to have no choice but to challenge for the leadership at some stage. He may also have a rival in a backbencher named Jacob Rees-Mogg for the most outrageously ludicrous caricature of the modern Tory. He looks and sounds like a throwback to the twenties. The 1820s, that is, if not the 1720s. This Jacobite is a leading light in something called the European Research Group, eighty-odd backbench Tory MPs who are seeking the hardest possible Brexit of leaving with no deal at all. For all Jacob's old-world courtesy, his acolytes are unfortunately not in the business of gradable adjectives and adverbs.

There doesn't seem to be a majority in the Commons for anything; not for leaving without a deal; nor for leaving while remaining in the single market; nor for a separate trade deal; nor for Mrs May's valiant attempts at fudge; nor for a second referendum. Theresa has given a successful Tory conference speech however, by shimmying to the rostrum to 'Dancing Queen' without falling over. I suppose I have more in common with her than I care to admit, but not enough to feel much sympathy. It was the job she wanted, after all.

It would just be nice to get a few of the old certainties back. One of those was that Russia was good at spying, and at assassination when deemed necessary. No longer, apparently. The poisoning job at Salisbury was so badly botched that an innocent woman has been killed by picking up a perfume bottle containing the actual nerve agent used weeks later. The harum-scarum culprits have been photographed in situ in Sarum, and their identities with the Russian secret service confirmed. Then, another load of their spies has been spotted and photographed in the Netherlands, trying to compromise the chemical weapons agency's investigation. Putin blusters, but he must be seething at the incompetence of it all. The worry is that he will be even more dangerous if he's wounded. And it's quite possible that Trump, blundering around playing trade wars, will badly upset the Chinese and the Russians soon, although, to be fair, he has been less bellicose than I expected. Even so, Artificial Intelligence, take over from us, for God's sake. Provided you're on the side of the good guys.

*

We travelled up to see Ruth and her brood at the Autumn half-term. Murderous behaviour is catching on with senior statesmen. Just before we went, the Saudis butchered a dissident journalist in their Turkish embassy. And when I say butchered, that's precisely what I mean. The details are too grotesque to read, let alone joke about, but human beings actually did it. Power corrupts, and it's getting nearer to absolute in too many places.

This time our visit coincided with all of Ruth's children being home, Tom and Charlotte taking a reading week off from their courses at Nottingham and London. Both Charlotte and boyfriend Seb passed their exams well enough to get their chosen universities. Tom's in his last year now. Not having planned for them all being there in advance, and our children having decided that they didn't want to go to Throstles' Nest with Fiona and Jason having left, Bob and I took Ethel's spare room next door again with Alice and Richie shoe-horned in at Ruth's. The introduction to university life along with the new boyfriend seems to have improved Charlotte, who is as considerate and well-mannered as the girl we knew as a child. Bob says that she still avoids discussing any social issues with him. I tell him that she's no different with her mother or me. She'll no doubt mellow further with age.

To compensate, he has plenty of debates with Tom on more worthy subjects such as the Duke cricket ball or video referees at football, on which they always seem to make common cause. Richie never misses a word and asks about anything he doesn't understand. Alice takes a healthy interest in all these crucial issues, as well as happily discussing the meaning of life as seen from a ten-year old's eyes, which frankly isn't much different from all I've discerned over my fifty-plus years.

On our first trip to the village we bumped into Lucy, Amelia, Steve and Maddie. Amelia was chatting to Lucy while pushing the buggy, with Jack, now nearly two, perched on the edge of his chair, surveying the scene as if he was looking for something of which he could register disapproval.

"I recognise that look," said Bob to me. "It's Paul at his most lordly."

A heavily pregnant Maddie and Steve were walking behind, talking to each other as if bosom pals. Lucy greeted us with a beaming smile.

She and Maddie are in their element in the chaotic world they've created for themselves and their acolytes. The casualties strewn along the path behind them are out of sight, one way and another. Lucy allows Bill Hardisty to take her out for dinner every Wednesday evening, his evening off from the pub, but still appears to be resting from further nocturnal activities. *Battle Bus to Bowness* is scheduled for broadcast in a couple of weeks. Kieron, James's friend, has successfully delivered both his boss to the project, and the project to completion. Not only that, but Lucy gushes as to how he's become such a big friend that he's coming over to listen to the broadcast with them. I took one look at radiant-faced Maddie and quickly could think of a reason why. If Amelia had the same thought, she didn't betray it. Steve still seems to be part of the team, but he told me in an aside that he knows his days are numbered, once the play has actually gone out. He clearly believes that his efforts have not been properly recognised by Lucy.

I asked her if she still had no plans to write something else. Maddie answered for her.

"I doubt it. She's soon going to have all her work cut out looking after Class 4, Jack and my baby. I'm taking Bob's advice. I'm going to do my education certificate at Manchester Met from next September, so I can become a teacher."

"Not at Sheffield?" I asked naughtily, suspecting immediately that the closeness of Manchester to St Chad's might be less of a factor than the proximity of the University to Salford Quays and Kieron. If Maddie suspects her own motives, she's well-rehearsed in fooling herself.

"No. Manchester is much easier for me to get back here to Amelia and the baby, at least most nights. The trains from Manchester to here aren't quick but they are regular."

I didn't want to ask where she'd be on the other nights. I had another side conversation with Steve, while Alice and Richie played with Jack. He became impatient with them and started to whinge. Lucy was called into action. Bob joined the tail-end of my conversation with Steve, Maddie now listening. Steve's mother isn't proving enough company and he's missing his old life in Cheltenham. I'm still not sure how much he's left behind there, as he's always kept his personal life to himself. He's started going back for weekends to join in archaeological digs, a love of which we share, staying in a hotel now that his house has been let. He asked Bob if he'd mind if I join him on a dig occasionally. Bob was fine with the idea, with Steve thanking him too profusely. His move to Keswick has been a mistake and he knows it. As John Ruskin said, it's almost too beautiful to live in. It's certainly too wet unless you're a duck.

Nor is the Fishwick madhouse he's linked himself to the answer for the Steve I used to know. I'm not sure if there is any answer though for later-life loneliness. Bob says that he's found it with me and the kids. I'm not sure he really has in full. He spends much of what spare time he has sitting in his chair, missing all that he's lost. I'm younger, I've still got my parents, and, with Bob and the children, this time is the best that life has had to offer me, with archaeology as a bonus. In company, he stays cheerful, playing with the kids and keeping in touch with where things are at for them, but he's seen so much before. His brain must be nearly full. I love him for the way he won't give in to that. Most seem to. He knows all the children well for what they are, and not just as names, which incredibly he never gets wrong. I sometimes do. But I know he pines after the warmth of the past, the people and pets that have gone, his grandparents and parents, his first dog Rover, Blackpool as the centre of the show-business universe, Lancashire the home both of the Industrial Revolution and his agricultural labourer ancestors, northern grammar schools as the envy of the nation, brass bands (and silver ones in the case of St Chad's, still to be heard in their full pomp at the Gala), workers' education, trade unionists who'd worked on the trade first. And most of all, in the background, a gentle Christendom to give meaning to all to which no meaning can be given. His first wife Jane loved him despite all this. I love him because of it. They are his identity, the individual part added to whatever it is that's created that's common to all humanity when sperm first meets egg. Charlotte can't yet see

225

how much she shares all this with him. As Jane told her too, I'm sure she will someday, maybe when she's suffered the personal pain of rejected love, or the death of a loved one. That will be the point where I hope she'll see there is sometimes a clash between liberal values and empirical nature. The personal has never been that political for me though. I guess it once was for Jane when she despaired of Bob as a husband. Not now, I think. She's learnt something. She's lost much and knows she still has something left to lose. The cow will not defend it with a moat of sickly syrup though!

*

Before we returned to Nether Piddle, we had a Budget. Theresa announced that austerity is over, Chancellor Hammond that we were on the way to ending it. They're still not quite on the same hymn sheet. I doubt if we've even started on it yet. Any expenditure increases are to keep us standing still at best. There's an event to take place that will decide if we can move on. Until we know what Brexit can be negotiated, if any, and then how it works, nobody can know which way we're heading. I suppose that, while I've been living, there has always been uncertainty, probably far worse than this on several occasions but the fact that this is happening so publicly makes it feel like the place we're heading is Armageddon.

CHAPTER TWENTY-FOUR
November 2018

Lucy has asked us to the party she's arranged to celebrate *Battle Bus,* which is on the Saturday following the broadcast. It's a long way to go for a party, but my parents are free to babysit, so Bob and I have decided to drive up.

On the day of the broadcast itself, she and Maddie were entertained by Kieran for a first hearing in his Salford Quays apartment. I hope Amelia is thinking of her contingency plans. We've managed to listen to the play at home on our DAB radio, which sadly is scarcely used in the evenings. We've lost the radio habit. The play is good fun and for someone not seeking any pregnant pauses the experience is no doubt rewarding. Lucy lives too much in the present for those. As the final credits rolled, I felt, though, that the whole thing had been somewhat derivative and oversold. I suspect Bob did too. We're far too polite to say so, even to each other. Why I seem to have no trouble writing it, I don't know. I suppose I'm assuming that only Bob will ever read this.

We couldn't get away until after lunch on the Saturday. I had to feed parents and children first. Then the M6 was a total mess, with roadworks all the way up, which meant that we weren't at Ruth's until half an hour before we were due at the party. Ruth had been invited too. We were still earlier than the fashionably late arrival of most guests. Punctuality is a characteristic Bob and I share, so both of us arrived feeling more than a little fraught. A glass of fizzy isn't the best thing to calm the nerves, but that was what was on offer.

People arrived that we didn't know: Lucy's childhood friends; colleagues from school, congregation members from the Catholic Church along with two priests; from Media City; from her dance class; and last but certainly not least in consumption terms, from the pub. Lucy had gone to town, with external caterers. Bob was disappointed that there were no pork pies to be had. The canapés were circulating freely though, and the gannets of St Chad's were none too subtle in ensuring they didn't miss any. Lucy wisely wasn't drinking; she was high on the atmosphere. She's often been the centre of attention, but I think that being the star of the show rather than the novelty act was new to her. Her dress was right too, short but stylish, and at least looking expensive, although I doubt it was. She sparkled with energy. This was her lovely day. Nobody could begrudge it her. Bill Hardisty's eyes never seemed to leave her, and he followed her round the room like a bull mastiff behind his mistress, on a lead and not a leash. Lisa and Dave had generously been invited. Lisa also looked pretty good in a very smart mid-length dress, and Dave had scrubbed up well. They were every inch a couple.

Lucy couldn't wait to introduce us to Kieron. He was, as expected, chatting to Maddie, who in her condition had chosen to sit down while smiling beatifically at all who passed her way. We could soon see why he and James were friends. Kieron was just above average height, and slim, looking more like an up-and-coming manager than a creative, but was urbane and witty, and had the compulsory floppy hair. For our benefit, he performed a Donald Trump impression, accompanied by a comedy riff that sounded suspiciously like one we'd heard on a late-night satire show. He then swept his hair back into place and said that working with Lucy had been the most enjoyable thing he'd done in his career to date. Lucy fluttered her eyelashes at him. I've never been able to do that.

"Crawler," said Maddie to him. He'd need more than flattery, I thought, to usurp Amelia in her affections. He'd need patience.

"He can recognise talent when he sees it," said Lucy, her face wreathed in smiles.

We were each given homework, a CD of the show, along with a booklet of the screen play, signed by Lucy Fishwick, with love. Even so, it was a good party. Ruth chatted to another BBC man for most of the evening, the budget officer. He was twenty years younger than her. She was the tipsiest of us as we left. It's hard being a middle-aged singleton. We said our thanks and farewells to Lucy, telling her that the party had been well worth the trip.

"Bill booked the caterers," she revealed. "They were good, weren't they?"

And with that, she ruffled the nape of Bill's neck. His eyes nearly popped out. Was his ship about to come in at last?

Back in Nether Piddle, we listened again with the children. They laughed, Alice at the right places, and Richie a second or so behind Alice. I'll just let you see the script for the start of the last scene, for you to get a feel of it.

ACT III
Scene 5
(Back on the bus)

The engine of the bus stutters into life and can be heard above the babble of conversation

DOREEN

Well, that was a day and a half, alright.

HILDA

No, it wasn't. It's only eight o'clock now. It's not gone dark yet.

DOREEN

Maybe we set off yesterday morning. It feels like we did. Then it would be.

HILDA

Don't be soft. The police were as quick as they could be. It's a good job they arrived when they did. I didn't like the look of that sawn-off shotgun at all.

DOREEN

Was it really sawn-off? It looked a very nice gun to me. They must have had a really sharp saw. It would go well on our sideboard next to that paper knife we won at bowls.

HILDA

That's what the police called it. It didn't look like it

had been sawn, so I think they were just saying that for effect. I think it was like the one the bank robber had on that nasty episode of *Endeavour* we didn't like for being so rough, when he and the girl were held hostage. Young Morse went deathly white when he saw the gun, if you remember.

DOREEN

He's a good actor, being able to do that, nearly as good as the real Morse. But we weren't in a bank. It was only a little post office. I'm surprised it hasn't been closed down. They all have been round our way. And if you don't like things so rough, why did you trip up that young man with your trolley? You could have hurt him. He very nearly fell on his knife. Is that what they call a …

HILDA

… Machete? You tripped the other one up with your stick. He could have shot himself if he'd had his finger on the trigger.

FRED

He could have shot us. Neither Morse is real either. They're both actors.

HILDA

He'd have only shot one of us, unless we were stood in a line and the bullet went through us all in turn.

FRED

Bullets can ricochet. It could have hit more than one of us even if we weren't standing in line. Athletic got a goal like that a couple of weeks ago.

HILDA

Not football again! Perhaps the shop will be closed down now as not safe. You know what these Health and Safety people are …

DOREEN

… like. It would be a pity if it had to close down. I mean, they're not likely to get robbed again like that in a hurry, are they? It's a long way to go from Manchester just to rob a post office. That machete thing only looked like a sheath knife to me. That's what our Tom had when he was in the Boy ….

HILDA

… Scouts. Not for long. I remember Ma took it off

him. She must have been worried he'd rob a post office too.

DOREEN

I wonder if we can get the driver to stop at the services to buy some sweets. With the postmaster having to talk to the police, we didn't get the Kendal Mint Cake for our Jason that we promised him. We could get him a box of *Heroes* instead. He likes those.

FRED

You could buy a box for yourselves too.

(Laughter)

It continued like this for a few more pages, before a final short scene whose principal source could only be Bob, possibly via Maddie. I'll show you that later on. Kieron did Lucy proud with the production. The acting was spot-on, I have to admit. And the writing's much better than mine. So well-done, Lucy, local hero.

*

Theresa claims to have a final deal, with an arrangement of smoke and mirrors for the 'Backstop' that's pleasing no-one, and which on straight arithmetic is not capable of getting a majority in parliament. The DUP and the European Research Group bloc of her own

MPs, Boris and Jacob included, will vote against it, as well as the Opposition. None of them is interested in finding a solution, but only in winning their little bit of the debate. And, in order to do that, truth has become unnecessary, the permanent legacy of Trump's presidency. I'm sure in the end they'll find their modest victories to be very hollow. Increasingly I think that true victory comes in defeat. The corollary to this is that true defeat comes with victory. That's the outcome of the wretched referendum.

Theresa's fudge has only just managed to squeeze through the Cabinet, such is the internal opposition. So little emphasis is being placed on the accompanying Political Declaration that the deal is little more than the Withdrawal Agreement. The next stage is for the European leaders to accept it, which they will, mainly out of sheer boredom. After that, it has to pass what's being called the 'meaningful' vote in the House of Commons. 'Meaningless' could equally well apply. If it had any chance of averting Armageddon, despite my misgivings, I'd be signed up, but nobody thinks it can. It only kicks the problem to the next stage of negotiation, by which time we'll have left the EU. But is staying in worth a Corbyn Government? As you've read, that would be Sophie's Choice.

I've just realised that I'm using 'Armageddon' where Bob was saying 'Apocalypse'. I've mentioned this to him, saying that mine is a place, and his is a time.

"I guess I see heaven as a place with no time," he said.

Do I see eternity as a time with no place? I think so. But surely existence needs both?

*

In mid-December, Maddie went into a long and painful labour.

We were kept updated by Ruth. With Amelia and not Lucy by her bedside, she gave birth to a little girl. She is to be called Bethany, a residual biblical gesture from Maddie. Swabs have been provided and the comparisons made. James is not the father. Carl is.

Back at her house on The Breck, Maddie rang Carl to tell him the news. He'd wished her well in a low voice, presumably with a wife not quite in earshot. Lucy called Ruth, who messaged Bob to ask that he tell the Shackletons. It was Helen who answered him, as I listened on.

"I've got the news," he said as she answered. "I think you'll be pleased. Not sure about Richard, and I guess James will be upset. It's the other guy's, Carl's."

"Thank God for that, Bob. She'd have wrecked his life," Helen replied, clearly relieved.

"Just make sure he doesn't wreck it for himself in his disappointment. He's a soulful bugger, like his father."

"I'll get him for you, Bob. He's back home early for Christmas. Richard's out and it will come better from you than from me. He sees you as a friend."

The next thing Bob knew was hearing James' voice on the phone. Bob's voice went even further to the back of his mouth as he spoke softly.

"Probably not the news you wanted to hear, lad," he said. "The tests have been done. It's Carl's."

There was a long silence. I was expecting the next voice to be Helen's. We could hear stifled sobs. But James didn't let go of the phone. Sounding shaky, he was still determined to speak.

"It's probably for the best, Bob. Maddie and Amelia have got a child with a father that doesn't want anything to do with her. That's what Maddie really wanted."

"He might do now. Fatherhood can change men for the better."

"I doubt it with Carl. What's her name going to be?" asked James, to show humanity hadn't deserted him.

"Bethany. Where Lazarus was raised."

"And my dreams killed," James sadly murmured.

"You'll have more of those," Bob said. "Someday, when you least expect it, a girl will come knocking with a bucket load. Are you enjoying Oxford? What period are you doing?"

"The Anglo-Saxons. Dad says that they're, or is that we're, history now and someone should give them a decent burial."

"In a Christian graveyard and not on a funeral pyre, I hope. Most folk seem to disclaim anything to do with them and claim a dubious Celtic past."

"Well, they did intermingle with the British when they came. Our DNA is only about one third from them."

"I guess it's the way of life we had here for more than a thousand years that I mourn. My grandparents were still living it. And I try to! I gather you're at Oriel, your Dad's old college. I did a summer school there once. It's a lovely place, so you enjoy yourself. All this will turn out for the best. As my Grannie said as we moved Granddad's corpse between rooms after he died, it all goes to mould the character. Good luck lad, you deserve some."

"Thank you, Bob. I'll do my best."

At least James was laughing as he passed the phone back to Helen. There's nothing Bob is better at than cheering people up with black humour. Helen was in no doubt that more suitable than Maddie would come along. The impression she gave was that nobody could be worse. Richard called us back a few minutes ago to say that James seemed resigned to his fate. His fear was that a resigned approach to life could become permanent with James. He speaks from experience.

Father and son have an innocence that sits uneasily in the present age. I've just been watching this very funny show, *Fleabag*, that everyone's talking about. It even started with consensual anal sex between man and woman when a fully-functioning, birth-controlled vagina was available. I couldn't help but wonder if that was what Carl had that James didn't. And I just laughed at that thought. While I watched, Bob preferred to do something else. He'll never watch sex scenes. He always says that you shouldn't let other people get your kicks for you, not that he's ever suggested me facing the other way, I'm very pleased to say.

CHAPTER TWENTY-FIVE
Christmas 2018

It doesn't look like the vote on whether or not to accept Theresa's deal is going to be meaningless after all. The outcome could be so disastrous that maybe a meaning can emerge. The EU is happy with Theresa's deal as we expected, perhaps a bit too happy. But, as well as the DUP not supporting it, the Conservatives are in total disarray. Two distinct groupings in her own party won't vote for it either. The European Research Group, most of whom want a No-Deal Brexit, have moved from fulmination into intractable opposition. Then there are the Remainers who think they might get a second referendum if they vote it down. On the other side of the House, Jeremy Corbyn hopes he can force a General Election out of the chaos, and so will also oppose the deal he would much prefer to vote for. Parliament has closed down for Christmas with everything up in the air. The vote will be in mid-January. I can't see how the hard Brexiteers can win the endgame now, with the Remainers across the whole of parliament a substantial majority. General election, or not, a second referendum looks possible. Oh Joy! Hideous as the prospect is, I think it would be the best outcome. We might get to stay in.

Although Bob gives the impression that he'd much prefer to be discussing Barthes' trinitarian formulation or Blackpool's back four, he's reading avidly the other pages of *The Times* as well as the crossword and the sport, cursing MP's for thinking they know better than the people while knowing only too well that they do. What with that and the comings and goings of the Fishwicks, he's walking with a new spring in his step. Last night in bed, enough neurons sparked for us to make pleasant love, flesh and spirit in harmony. At seventy-three, he still can manage without a chemical dildo.

This Christmas, Sophie's parents, finally cleared of family responsibilities, have come to England from Vancouver for a holiday. They're basing themselves in Lancashire after a spell in Richmond. This means that we are heading north, although it was by rotation meant to be a Nether Piddle year. Malcolm and Jackie Fry are the proud mixed-race parents of their brilliant daughter, and three other bright children who are fending for themselves back in Canada. Accompanying Malcolm and Jackie to the north-west are Sophie and Robert, along with Patrick, who's now eight, and little Susanna, who's still only five. Apart from whistle-stop visits for the two christenings, Jackie and Malcolm have not been to England. The few longer visits have involved the Brits going to Canada. Ten years ago, Jane promised to take them round Liverpool if ever they did get here. Not to be outdone, Bob offered them Blackpool. He'd also suggested a walk round Malham Cove. Thank goodness that winter, coupled with the wear and tear of the intervening ten years on Malcom's knees, have ruled that one out. Malcolm is massively overweight, and the walk could well have killed him even back then.

They're a little older than me and a decade and a half younger than Bob. As you know, Sophie gets on better with Bob than she does with Jane, so it's no surprise that she's made their Lancashire base nearer to us, in the comparative luxury of the best hotel in Lytham St Annes. It's a shame for their kids that Blackpool Pleasure Beach is closed, not that either of them is anything like old enough to go on the white-knuckle rides such as 'The Big One'. I've told our children that I'll never be old enough. Bob's still game. He's been going to

Pleasure Beach since he was five. He's promised Richie that next summer he can have a go at kicking a ball to try to knock down cut-out figures of famous footballers.

"They're probably now painted as Aguero, Rashford, Salah, Vardy and Harry Kane," he said. "It was Stanley Matthews, Stan Mortensen, Tommy Lawton, Nat Lofthouse and Tom Finney when I first went on. I think they repaint the old figures as the new heroes every few years. They waste nowt there if they can help it."

The party arrived in their Toyota Prius hybrid people carrier, Sophie and Robert both wishing to be environmentally friendly. We're not the ones to knock that. Even with a car that large, it must have been a squeeze to fit people, luggage and presents in.

Malcolm and Jackie are Methodist, as still is Maddie. When we bumped into her in the village on Saturday, her offer to take them to Chapel the next day was accepted. They preferred this to going to the big Anglican carol service that Bob was trying to sell.

"You've got no class," he told them with a grin.

"That's your culture, not ours," replied Jackie.

"I thought that's what you'd come over here for."

Lucy went with them. Kieron and Amelia trooped along too. Lucy insisted on crossing herself as she entered, to Maddie's chagrin. She'd said nothing but her looks could have killed. Jackie giggled with delight as she told us.

"Lucy thinks no-one but a Catholic has any class, Bob."

"She could be right there," he said.

*

Liverpool and Blackpool are two of the whiter places in the UK. Many children on the Lancashire coast are still blue-eyed and fair-haired. Even so, Jackie and Malcolm have felt immediately at home in multicultural, contemporary Britain. The mild winter of the area reminds them of home. The flat vowels of the residents are at one with the flat accents of Canada.

"What did you make of Maddie," Bob asked Sophie, after describing how she had broken the heart of his best friend's son.

"I think she's insecure more than anything. I don't suppose her erratic childhood with Lucy helped. There's no reason of course why lesbians can't be loyal to their partners too. I think that Kieron is smitten, and she's becoming interested. I'm not sure if that isn't because he represents a more glamorous future. I expect that she's on track for breaking everyone's heart but her own."

"I'm pretty sure she'll one day manage that too," he replied.

So, Sophie is more censorious about moral conduct than Bob would ever be. He never casts the first stone, failing safe with 'live and let live' as his default mode, despite her jibe about his Victorian attitudes last year. He knew the late Victorians in his family and liked them. But they were the ones who'd survived the Great War. He didn't know their parents' generation, who'd seen their offspring slaughtered, or the one before that who'd kicked the era off. I think he'd have found them harder to take in their sternness, despite their engineering prowess. It was a Lancastrian though, Robert Peel, who had the conscience to repeal the Corn Laws, as he's told me on more than one occasion. And wreck his party for a generation! Lancastrians don't make natural Tories.

Even so, Bob and Sophie really do get on well. We've mainly shown them arguing in our writing, but it's lovely to see two people of such different ages and backgrounds sharing the same life force. You don't need to agree with someone to like them. Their eyes light up when they meet. Robert is looking relaxed on this trip, which at his age probably means that he's given up on further career ambitions, even though he says he's overworked. He's already talking of retirement. He and Bob have several father-and-son chats about the important things in life: football and cricket. They might not be allowed to go to Bloomfield Road to watch Blackpool, but it doesn't stop them talking incessantly about it.

*

Blackpool has a very big sea. Massive waves crashed majestically into the sea wall yesterday, Christmas Eve, as we all walked along in the spray. The idea was to leave the car at the south end of Pleasure Beach and walk to North Pier. That would be enough of the fresh air and fun; we'd then take a tram ride back. Even this proved too much for Malcolm, and the tram was needed to take him northwards from South Pier as well. Robert accompanied him. Bob's the one with the officially bad heart, but he led the charge of the rest of us, including all the kids, along the prom and down North Pier as well. I know one day he'll just keel over. I don't know what I'll do without him. Will all his family stay around then or will visiting me be just another bi-annual chore for them?

All the warning signs are elsewhere. Malcolm should lose lots of weight. It's almost as if, having put on so much timber, he can no longer do anything about it.

We'd bought tickets months ago to go to the pantomime at the Grand Theatre. We occupied half a row at the front of the Dress Circle. We'd booked there on the basis that the cast can't quite reach you with their water pistols, at least without drenching everybody in the stalls. Blackpool's best show days may be well behind, but they still know how to make people of all ages laugh.

Surprisingly though, it was *Beauty and the Beast* and not a panto as old as time. Seemingly, no traditions can survive the age of Disney intact. This time, whereas I'm fine with corn oil and cinnamon, it seems like sacrilege to me.

I'm not going to list them by name, but with all Ruth's family and ours, plus the Canadian party, there were 15 people to feed for Christmas Lunch. We really needed a pterodactyl, an oven the size of a power station boiler and to hire the Church Hall filled with trestle tables. But somehow Ruth's dining room did fit everyone in, and with a bit of cheating on what was and wasn't turkey, everyone was fed. Jane and Geoffrey live in an apartment in Liverpool's Sefton Park and there is no way that all of us, or even the less syrupy part they'd want to see, could fit in there at once. They were to join us later in the afternoon and go home last thing in the evening.

It was already going dark by the time that lunch was disposed of. By the time the two Liverpudlians arrived, it was pitch black outside. I viewed Jane with my best icy stare. She didn't look at me at all.

When Robert married Sophie in Vancouver those ten years ago and this visit first mooted, Bob was in his second-time-around relationship with Jane, spending their time together either bonking or arguing from what I've been told, sometimes at the same time. They'd gone to the wedding as a couple. By her own admission, Jane had not behaved well even then and the two of them had a stinker of a row, Bob breaking up with her on arrival home. Jane though had already pencilled in Geoffrey as her next victim. Once home, Bob found out I was pregnant with our Alice, and we set up our home. These two relationships have worked well for the decade. There's something to be said for divorce. I wish I could have said that something to Frank before he was overtaken by dementia and couldn't have understood.

The new arrivals by convention had to talk to each available child before moving on to the adults. This didn't prove too difficult as they arrived laden with presents. A short reprise of yesterday's present giving took place. As ever, Jane had chosen well. The children were thrilled with their high quality, thoughtful gifts. Hell, I'd even got to like the woman a bit, before the sticky remark! I can't forget that though, nor how she sank her elegantly long nails into Bob metaphorically, and on occasion literally, I believe, to keep him from me, without really wanting him for herself.

*

Charlotte and Sophie have become firm friends, so much so that Charlotte is already talking about doing a law conversion after she's finished her Politics degree. It's pretty ironic that Bob has to see not only his daughter-in-law but also a granddaughter in an activity he's spent half a lifetime deriding. At least Tom is in engineering, working up in the north-east in the motor industry. For how much longer after Brexit, we can't be sure. I imagine Bob would have liked a nuclear physicist and a vicar amongst his children or grandchildren. Maybe Alice and Richie can oblige, although I doubt that he'll be around by then to see it.

*

On Boxing Day, Robert, Sophie, Patrick, Susanna, Jackie and Malcolm started their move to a less posh hotel on the outskirts of Liverpool, where they were to stay for a couple of days. They intended to book in and then drive to Jane and Geoff's flat in Sefton Park for lunch. Recognising Malcolm's walking difficulties, only a short afternoon stroll along the Albert Dock was planned for the afternoon. Bob warned Malcolm not to commit the faux pas of thinking the Billy Fury statue was of Elvis. We all waved off their eco-friendly van with a rug, laden as it also was with far more presents that they'd come with.

"You'll need a shoehorn to get out in Liverpool," Bob said.

Unfortunately, the shoehorn was needed much sooner than that. We received a phone call quarter of an hour later saying that they'd had a flat tyre before they'd even reached the motorway. Robert could see a big nail in the tread. He told us that he'd called for roadside assistance, which was going to be a couple of hours. His excuse for not changing the wheel himself was that getting to the space-saving spare wheel made for a Dinky car would be like moving house. Even then, the wheel nuts probably wouldn't turn with the Mickey Mouse wheel brace he assumed had been provided, currently buried under cases and presents. And there was a ditch on one side of the car and a busy road on the other. In other words, he wanted help from his Dad. Some structures are too engrained to be varied.

Operation Rescue was immediately commissioned by Bob. It involved commandeering Ruth's smaller, older Vauxhall Zafira people-carrier, where Bob was a named driver on the insurance, and which can just about take seven people. Bob was to drive to the incident in that. All but Robert would be decanted to that car, plus enough baggage so that the spare wheel and locking nut could be found for the Prius. Robert would remain for roadside assistance. Bob would drive the others to Liverpool in time for the lunch waiting for them, and immediately come back home to ours.

Bob arrived at the tyre scene to the great relief of the assembled. He'd taken a warning sign which he immediately put fifty yards behind. Even with that, the transfer including child car seat was perilous, so they didn't hang about. Malcolm jokily complained about his bad back as he rolled into the front passenger seat. Within a couple of minutes, they were waving goodbye to a forlorn Robert standing on the other side of the ditch for safety. They'd been driving about ten minutes and were a couple of miles short of where the M55 merges with the M6 when Bob noticed that Malcolm, sat alongside him, had slumped further into his chair. When asked if he was okay, he gasped that he had chest pains. Jackie immediately sensed that it was something serious from the back.

"Stop the car, Bob," she said.

Bob recognised the symptoms from first-hand experience. He said nothing at first. He slowed down and swung the car onto the A6, then turning right towards Preston.

"The hospital's just down here," he then replied. "Breathe slowly and steadily, if you can, Malcolm."

"Stop, Bob, stop," screamed Jackie, desperately trying to take her seat belt off.

"He knows what he's doing, Mum," Sophie snapped back, as she prevented Jackie from moving.

The kids had both turned pale but didn't cry. They were too shocked.

"Keep calm and hang in there, pal," Bob said to Malcolm. "We're there."

The others saw the Preston Royal Hospital signs. They all fell silent, Malcolm still clutching his chest.

As Bob parked in the ambulance bays in front of the Emergency Department door, he saw a couple of paramedics with a trolley. They'd just finished handing over a patient and were walking back to their vehicle.

"I think our passenger's having a heart attack," he yelled.

The paramedics rushed straight over. It didn't take them long to agree.

CHAPTER TWENTY-SIX
The Last Days of 2018

Malcolm was carefully laid on the trolley and taken straight into the department while the crash team were summoned. Jackie went with him. Sophie and the kids stayed in the car. Bob drove to the car park, while he and Sophie discussed what to do.

"The first minutes can be the vital ones," Bob told her. "If he pulls through those, he's in with a decent chance. Let's hang around in reception with the kids until we know more."

Fortunately, in these days of mobile phones, it's possible to keep in touch, provided all signs to switch them off are ignored. First, Bob rang Jane in Liverpool to tell her about the problem, while Sophie called Robert, still waiting by the roadside. The RAC arrived while they were on the line. A revised plan of campaign was agreed that Bob and Robert would take the kids to Liverpool in the Zafira once Robert arrived, leaving the Prius at the hospital for Sophie and Jackie to use if and when they could get away. A few minutes later, Jackie rang Sophie to tell her that Malcolm had been stabilised and would soon to be taken for angioplasty.

In the lull from this activity, Bob called me to tell me what was going on. Robert then did reach the scene, clutching health insurance policy details that Jackie and Malcolm had taken out, recovered from a suitcase in his car. Jackie emerged from behind closed doors to greet him. For the benefit of the children, she said out loud a quick prayer for Malcolm, to which they all added "Amen". The adults agreed that it was best the children didn't see Grandpa, as they called

Malcolm, until things were clearer. Jackie then returned inside with Sophie to await Malcolm's return from angioplasty, and to find out which ward he was going to next.

In the car park, Robert and Bob strapped the children into the Zafira, before transferring the rest of the luggage into the boot. They drove off to Liverpool, without checking into the hotel, so as still to be in time for lunch at Jane's.

*

Once the car was unloaded, Bob prepared to set off back to Ruth's.

"Where do you think you're going?" Jane asked. "You're this afternoon's chauffeur. The kids need distracting and the trip to Albert Dock will be the best way. We can't fit Robert and the kids, car seats and all, into our little Polo. You're joining us for lunch and for all that."

I got a nervous-sounding phone call from Bob at this stage, advising me of the necessity of the revised arrangements. Jane was listening.

"Ok, that's what you'll have to do," I agreed. "If she's steamed a syrup pudding, tell her you get all you need of that from me. More likely, it will be a lemon tart."

He not only chuckled but thought this was too good not to have an audience. He repeated it verbatim to Jane. She borrowed his phone.

"You should know me by now, Wendy. I'm bittersweet. There's both lemon and treacle tart," she told me.

"Why do I only see your lemon side then, Jane? Remember that we agreed to be sisters under the skin, when Bob had his heart attack."

"I remember. I think he said, 'In which case it's deeply subcutaneous', when we told him." She then turned to Bob, still holding the phone. "Your perfect wife has just given me fifty lines for insolent behaviour."

"She should have given you a ten-page essay as an imposition," I heard Bob growl. "Title: Are the peacemakers blessed or cursed?"

"Depends on who's going to win," she replied before passing the phone back to Bob and walking off.

I ignored that and asked Bob if he thought Malcolm was going to win his battle.

"I'm not sure, love," he said. "He was in a bad way before he had the attack. Maybe there was already some big damage."

We said our farewells, with him promising to come home the minute the excursion was finished.

At the table, to show no favour between husband, son and ex, Jane sat between the two grandchildren. They were understandably mardy. It didn't help that, with the delay followed by a speedy journey, the beef inevitably was over-cooked, and the vegetables underdone. Before the puddings, Robert had a call from Sophie. The angioplasty had taken place and Malcolm was sleeping reasonably peacefully. Sophie and Jackie were going to stay at the Ibis hotel near the hospital overnight. They asked if Bob could drop off some clothes and toiletries on his way back.

The puddings went down a treat with the slightly better news about Malcolm. The kids went for the treacle tart. So did Bob, as he was to tell me smugly when he eventually did get back. I guess he had to. Jane and Geoffrey had lemon tart. Robert had both.

A case was hastily packed for Bob to drop off in Preston later, before the afternoon excursion to the Albert Dock and the Mersey, plus the statue of Billy Fury. This had reached mythical status in Susanna's eyes following the big build-up by Bob in honour of his own youth.

There was of course no way that Jane was ceding her role as tourist guide to Bob. She and Geoffrey drove there separately from him, Robert and the kids. She greeted them in the car park like a holiday rep carrying a corporate umbrella aloft. Being Boxing Day, most of the attractions were shut, but this is a place best seen from the outside. They marched through the twee shops by the Dock to see Billy Fury. I've seen the sculpture a couple of times. It is good. The day was grey and dank, and so inevitably was the river

But nobody could get even halfway to paradise with the worry about Malcolm pervading the atmosphere. Late in the afternoon, Robert briefly couldn't reach Sophie at the hospital. They feared the worst. It was only that she'd popped down to the restaurant for some coffee. There were no more crises. Bob came home that evening having dropped Robert and kids at their hotel, and the suitcase for Sophie and Jackie at theirs in Preston.

"It was a bit like an out-of-body experience seeing someone else have a heart attack. I felt like I was having it," said Bob to me later that evening.

*

Bob and I visited Malcolm a couple of times while were still in the north-west, to take some of the weight off Jackie and Sophie. He has a jolly Consultant, named Ali, with an unfailing good humour; a splendid chap, with the mannerisms of the British officer class of a bygone era, confident in his own skin. He found more time to answer our questions than I've ever found before in the NHS. This is in stark contrast to a couple of hijab-wearing nurses who are punctilious in their duties but are much more reserved than all the other nurses, saying what seems to be the bare minimum. They appear to be no easier with Jackie and Malcolm than they are with us. Sophie thinks that, with their broad Lancashire accents, they're actually more outgoing than would be the case in Richmond. The word that springs to my mind is submissive, to their employers, to their family, to their God. Jane would no doubt say that I'm also too obedient to tradition and circumstance. That's the way I'm made. But I can't and won't see some of what happens in the world to be the will of God. I do need occasionally to kick against the traces. These Muslim girls live on separate tables living separate lives. They'll think that about me too, I'm sure. The two great religions have a barrier erected between them. Can that be God's will too? Whatever, it's not likely that any conversation between our faiths is going to happen any time soon. That debate between the God still in process and the infinite Almighty isn't on anyone's agenda, including God's apparently. You can't force it.

But, like Bob, I don't think we can ever claim to know the will of God, which certainly won't be found from any priest or in any creed. Any revelation, seen through a mirror darkly, only comes through that mix of history and story that we all use to make sense of our lives.

*

Malcolm took a lot longer than Bob had to recover and not only because he'd been carrying far too much weight. He has, as Bob suspected, substantially more wrong with him, with significant left ventricular damage, leading to an uncertain longer-term prognosis.

He was kept in fortnight and then taken by private ambulance to Richmond to continue his recuperation. It was another six weeks before they made it back to Vancouver. Their plane left Heathrow in a thunderstorm, with the tears from Sophie's eyes falling harder than the rain. She feels guilty that she couldn't go back with them. She's told Robert that she doesn't expect to see him again. She thinks that she could have stopped him from going to seed if she'd stayed in Canada. I doubt that's the case, but that's another thing she has in common with Bob. A conscience. Hers is a modern version.

I hope Malcolm will at least stick to his improved diet to give himself some sort of chance.

CHAPTER TWENTY-SEVEN
Early 2019

Theresa always stood no chance at all on the big parliamentary vote. She suffered a staggering defeat, the worst in the democratic era. She lost by 230 votes. With any luck it could signal the demise of the Tories forever, says Bob. He's always found them too snobby. I'm sure though that healthy politics require there to be respectable right-wing and left-wing parties, or else mad extremists will step into the breach. Many people crave for a centrist party to emerge out of this debacle, from moderate Labour and compassionate Tories. If it does, I don't think it will stick. They may share the same view as to the desirable outcome, but one side will favour the state taking the action, the other a private or charity-based solution. English politics is in a mess, as is our society. We need to stay in the European Union to save us from ourselves! But like Felix the Cat, Mrs May keeps on walking. She's now trying to reach out to other parties, and failing dismally, not altogether surprising as in Bob's phrase, she has the cloth ears of a mill girl, but without the nous. She's insufficiently charismatic and doesn't know how to be flexible.

Jeremy Corbyn refused to talk to her a couple of weeks ago, unless she took leaving without a deal off the table. That would remove her only bargaining chip with the EU, not that it's worth much. As Article 50 has already been enacted, it would also require fresh legislation, which would split her party in two. I doubt if he realised this, but I'm sure the people advising him had worked it out. Suddenly, they have him not only talking to Theresa, but actually making some suggestions that could allow Labour to support a deal. Yvette Cooper, wife of Bob's chum, Ed Balls, has started pulling the strings from the Labour back benches. These, of course, all involve a Customs Union, as well as staying a member of the Single Market, both of which Theresa is desperately trying to avoid, although the only solution which can ever work, if badly. The Tory manifesto for the last general election explicitly excluded the possibility. Jeremy's equally anxious to avoid a second referendum, one where his party could well want him to campaign to remain. But then after a series of votes that frustrated all sides in the Commons, and with a string of resignations in his party over his perceived anti-Semitism, he's been forced into acknowledging it as a last resort. Theresa hopes that her own Brexiteers will now back her, out of fear of that, and that she can get a second vote through, provided she can dress up as significant any meaningless concession she gets from the EU on the 'Backstop'. Then we'll be out, with no prince from Disneyland to ride to our rescue. That's more than unlikely though, as the European Research Group is even more intransigent than the DUP, being total nutters and not just religious ones. March 29 is rapidly approaching, and an extension to the timetable could well be the next development. We wait and see. As a nation, we've no shared purpose and aren't able to take back control. Bob's exasperation has finally got the better of him.

"I'm fed up of living with a lie occupying my brain," he says. "It's bloody stupid that we're leaving. It's always been obvious that remaining is the best answer. We're ending up half-in, half-out without any ability to change a thing. I guess I hoped something else would turn up to honour the vote. It hasn't. Let's have a second referendum. I'll again vote to stay in."

"Alleluia," I reply.

"Mind you, the one thing I'm not going to do is pretend I'm on still with the working class. They want out and I've joined the elite."

"I think you joined that many years ago," I said with a smile.

"Yep, I was enlisted when I went to grammar school, if not before," he laughed.

"You were born to be in charge," I said. "Just as well you were born too intelligent to want to be."

Of course, this change of mind from Bob will probably mean one thing. He and I are not allowed to be on the winning side. Out of all this mess, we will leave, with or without a deal. Theresa is keeping on walking, hearing no other voice than the one in her head. Some cross-party discussions are happening, with neither leader showing any enthusiasm. With resignations in both main parties, desultory attempts to form a centrist party have started. They claim to be Remainers, but this could yet prove to be a mortal blow to Remain, as the elders and priests heading up the main parties will now have to find an answer that protects their position. For the Labour leadership, that's crashing out without a deal and blaming the Tories for it. For the Tories, that means terrifying their maniacs with the prospect of staying in. Their plummy Attorney-General, Geoffrey Cox, is working on a form of words to make it sound as if the Backstop isn't for real. Unfortunately, it is.

All this is happening at a time when there are no new developments in the Fishwick world. Perhaps even the Councils of Heaven can't manage these two things at once. Our politicians do have something in common with the characters I've been writing about. They look after their own interests first. And only Maddie admits to it. But can she always stay ahead of the game, or will the elders catch up with her and make her conform? I doubt if they'll succeed in giving her the lobotomy that so many parliamentarians seem to have suffered.

*

I was wrong. The omnipotent can do two things at once, even without a woman in the Godhead. We've arrived yesterday in St Chad's for the Spring half-term to hot news of yet more Fishwick follies, breathlessly told us by Lucy, who actually pushed Jack round so she could tell us personally. Carl has showed up. I really did think we'd seen the last of him. But, in an event worthy of Rudolf Hess landing in Scotland to sue for peace in the middle of the war, he knocked without warning at the door of Maddie's house. Amelia, who was vacuuming the living room at the time, opened it. Maddie was feeding Bethany upstairs. Invited in by Amelia, Carl plonked himself on the couch.

"That's when I arrived with Jack in the buggy," Lucy told us with a giggle. "It was perfect timing." She described the scene with great glee. Again, Amelia the cleaning lady had opened the door.

"On entry, I did a double-take, saying WTF in its unreduced form," Lucy continued. She'd clearly been rehearsing telling this story, as if it was a chapter in her next book, a more contemporary work. "There was a hint of an LOL in response from Amelia. But I'm not one to be speech struck for long."

I'm not sure if Lucy is showing self-awareness there, or the absence of it.

"Just visiting? It's about bloody time," she'd next said, to Carl.

"No, I've come to stay, if they'll have me," he'd replied.

Carrying Bethany, Maddie then emerged to see who and what it was that had halted the noisy vacuum cleaner. Without a word, she

257

sat on the couch next to Carl and resumed breast-feeding. Carl was suitably tearful as he held Bethany for the first time. He'd had a row with his wife, a terminal one, he claimed. He needed to see Bethany grow up, he declared. Nothing else could or should matter. He'd happily sleep in the spare bedroom, expecting nothing else. Is this his equivalent of being locked up for the rest of his life in Spandau? Or, with these two girls for company, should I say Spandex? Whatever, I have hoped that he will re-discover his gentler side, but this does sound somewhat out of character. It sounds more like some sort of mental breakdown to me. Who knew that he'd be the first in the madhouse to lose it? Possibly you all did. It's often the most outwardly confident who crack.

When he'd finished speaking, Amelia re-started the vacuum cleaner. "With her pretty, upturned nose higher in the air than ever in a pantomime pose while grinning like a Cheshire cat," Lucy said. "Carl lifted up his legs as she ran the vacuum over the carpet in front of him, and then hurriedly thrust them back under the table as soon as she'd done that bit."

"We might take you back on that basis," said Maddie, as usual speaking for Amelia too. "You are Bethany's father after all. But only if you've got a job to come to. We could do with the money while I'm on my course."

"I'll get one. I'll see if I can get the last one I had back."

"You can stop two weeks, and if you haven't got it by then, it's no-go. But I warn you, it's no sex. Amelia and I give each other all we want."

"I couldn't stop myself from pulling a face at that," Lucy explained. "Amelia didn't seem to be worried about the competition from Carl staying. She said nothing. The deal was done."

Lucy has never been a big one on Catholic guilt, honouring as she did most of the tenets of her Church more in the breach than in the observance. Indeed, this combination of circumstances as presented provided no fresh challenge to traditional moral teaching. She was uneasy though, without being able to put her finger on exactly why. She asked us what we thought about it.

"It all sounds too glib," she said.

"It does that," said Bob.

Ruth had a glimmer of an idea, but not one she wanted to share with Lucy without evidence. She tested it on Bob and me only after she'd left.

Ruth reckons that Amelia is more cunning than she looks, and also that she has form. On Ruth's theory, Amelia rang Carl up a few days ago to tell him that she wanted a baby of her own. She knew that he'd started to crack. She'd be happy that he moves back in, provided he acted as her stud. Carl detests his wife and wants Maddie again, but Amelia is probably fanciable enough to him for those duties to be performable. He'd manufactured a row with his wife, not difficult given his previous conduct, and turned up with Amelia's full knowledge. She knows that finances are too tight and rightly reckoned that Maddie would accept him back as a paying tenant.

We don't know at this stage whether to accept Ruth's theory or not. It sounds too far-fetched, and also a high-risk strategy for Amelia as it's possible that Carl and Maddie could get it together again. That's clearly what he must want. We're also not sure if either verification or falsification can or will ever be made available. No wreckage from a Messerschmitt landing will be found.

Lucy was delighted with what followed. The next weekend, she'd happily reported to Ruth, each bedroom at the house in the Breck had two differently-gendered occupants. Kieron was in with

Maddie. Carl was covering Amelia. Perhaps Amelia really had planned all this. What a star!

When Lucy visited on Monday, with Carl at his job in advertising and Kieron at BBC, Salford Quays, to her chagrin she'd found Maddie and Amelia in bed together. By the time we were back at Easter, a working arrangement at weekends of lesbian days and heterosexual nights had become settled practice and established fact. Even the Shackletons knew the routine in Hertfordshire without us needing to tell them, from information readily available on the internet. Helen's even now brazen enough to be using Instagram, where the electronic action seems to be moving to and for which she's far too old, I'm sure.

I can't help but compare the fickleness of their affections with the behaviour of the scheming MP's in the house over Brexit. Out of fear, they mainly stay in their party, but they're not loyal to it. Is that because they don't have an identity that they're confident about? Don't they wish to show loyalty as a sign of their affection? But, then again, in the Fylde Frolics, only James and Paul stayed loyal. And look where that's got them.

*

Carl and Amelia, chalk and cheese, are playing at being happy with each other. She's confided to Charlotte that at least he doesn't boss her about as much as Maddie does. He's accepted being displaced from Maddie's bed, although Lucy says that he seems shell-shocked, consistent with a nervous breakdown theory. Maddie is constantly tired with Bethany's demands and is more than happy to limit her heterosexual activities. She sees Kieron, her weekend sleeping companion, as a route to self-improvement, a view Lucy encourages. Maddie is reading in record time every book he recommends, only breaking off after lunch midweek for a romp with Amelia if Bethany is asleep. When confronted by Lucy about her cross-gender promiscuity, she's said that she sees it as her religious duty to give Amelia this daily pleasure. She is, she claimed, getting the best of both worlds, with Kieron's demands not too great, and Amelia brilliant to make love to. Lucy, in a strange mix of prude and prophetess, expects it all to come crashing down in divine judgement.

*

Lancashire's cricket ignominy is one way or another again being replicated in the football teams supported by Bob and Richard. Blackpool have finally got rid of their dreadful owner at the cost of being put into receivership, without knowing what that will entail. To commemorate this possible good news required a suitable celebration. We drove up to St Chad's for the weekend and the first permissible match for several years that true supporters such as Bob and Ben could attend. It was also the rite of passage of Alice and Richie's first-ever game, Bob having sent off for four tickets. The game ended in a draw against the none-too-mighty Southend, with a last-minute equaliser by Blackpool. The old town may no longer be able to win, but it can still break even. The points deduction they would normally suffer from having gone bust could mean the difference between promotion and relegation. The authorities haven't decided to impose it yet, which hopefully means they won't, provided a solvent business plan can be hatched up. It will be a total fiction of course, as all business plans are. Richie has explained it all to me in great detail. Bob, as always in these matters, fears the worst, something he and Robert have just discussed for the last half-hour on the phone.

As they walked away from the ground to the car after the match, in a line of four down the middle of the road re-establishing tribal territorial rights, they were overtaken by a gang of three, clad in assorted tangerine scarves and bobble hats. Maddie was in the middle, with one arm round Kieron and the other Amelia.

"Are you going to come to every match?" Bob asked.

"I'm a City fan," said Kieron. "Maddie kitted us out in this stuff from an old cupboard. She's kept it from Blackpool's better days. She's been glory-hunting with me to the Etihad a few times recently."

"I don't really like football," said Amelia. "I only came for the party."

"Anything to escape the clusterfuck of Brexit. Sorry, kids, I didn't say that," said Maddie. "Well, maybe I did. I've always supported Blackpool. City are something else, though."

"Blackpool are my team," Richie said proudly. "Dad's told me how his Dad used to bring him to see Matthews and Mortensen. We could still be promoted this season."

"Sure thing," said Maddie.

Fortunately, Richie is too young to realise that this isn't an encouraging remark, nor that the Receiver may yet not be kind. Bob and Richard also discuss football financial matters more than they do Brexit when they ring each other up. It seems like the owner of Bolton Wanderers, who hasn't got the money to keep his club out of some sort of bankruptcy for much longer, has been trying to sell the club all season, with about as much success as Theresa has had in her much less important negotiation. The players and staff are not always paid. They are languishing near the bottom of the division above Blackpool, with relegation looking inevitable. A deal for their sale to a new owner is in the balance. Traditionally, they've been a stronger team than Blackpool. On the other hand, Blackpool's greatest moment happened when they beat Bolton four-three in the 1953 Cup Final, the most famous of all time. Bob and Richard behave as if honours are even.

"No wonder both towns voted for Brexit," Bob tells me. "We've had our heritage ripped from us by spivs and City slickers."

There's been a book knocking around for a year or two now by David Goodhardt which breaks down Britain and its people into 'somewheres' and 'anywheres'. I've always thought it a bit of nonsense as we're all 'somewheres' in having a hinterland which is reflected in our personality and which is but a small part of humanity's experience. Closing down on new experiences though is to ignore what life offers us. People are trying to say that Remainers are 'anywheres' and Brexiteers are 'somewheres'. That's not helpful. The heritage Bob and Richard, both Remainers, talk about is of many decades ago. It was going before the cowboys moved in on the game, taken away from them by a much greater power than those guys, who are more the symptom than the cause. Richard and Bob both accept that that to be the case, and can hear tomorrow calling, yet neither of them can come on in and support one of the Manchester clubs or Liverpool, and nor should they. They've too many memories to lose, rich memories of what made them, but sadly from a time now buried deep in the sealed coffin, well beyond retrieval. Yes, they're 'somewheres', but not professional northerners.

*

Geoffrey Cox, Attorney-General, has helped Theresa negotiate some minor legal concessions to the 'Backstop' agreement, and then been asked to mark his own work in an opinion delivered before the second big Brexit vote. He's given himself bottom marks. "The legal risk is unchanged," he's opined. Nobody can understand why he didn't say: "Although now much less likely, there remains a small residual risk in law that the UK could be kept in the 'Backstop' without any further legal recourse." That was what he was expected to say and would have covered his backside, while giving Theresa a prayer. He should have asked Amelia to write his script. He loves being centre-stage and sounding off though, like an old-time actor-manager hamming up every scene. He is also an ardent Brexiteer. If there is some Machiavellian scheming going on, perhaps he still thinks that a no-deal Brexit can be achieved. I can't see how the politics will permit that though. Unless the European Research Group support this deal at the very last minute, it will need some Labour support to get it over the line. Cox is just another sad guy trying to make out he's in control when he isn't. He's not even managing what his name implies by steering the boat. I'm sure our politicians have always been as inept and as under-principled as this bunch are, but, in the past, we didn't have to see so much of them. They don't make a pretty sight.

And so, Theresa has lost in the House again, this time by 149 votes. The DUP of course had to vote against the deal, given Cox's advice. They are increasingly in favour of remaining in the EU, as no way round their problem can be found; 75 Tories also voted against, including Boris and Jacob. I still think they must be mad, not banking what they've won. They're too male-dominated. They needed a 'Maddie' as leader and well as an 'Amelia' as strategist. They'd have known when to cut their losses. If all her party had voted for her deal, Theresa would have sneaked home by one vote. She could have won more Labour support too if it had been close and if she'd asked nicely. That would have seen us out, if without any agreed basis for negotiating the most important thing, the commercial deal. It would have been better to have rolled all the negotiations up into one in the first place. But the Government wasn't ready; it wasn't expecting the referendum result it got. Jeremy Corbyn is of course again doing his best not to call for a second referendum when most of his MPs want just that, along with his young supporters.

We even had a third vote on the deal. That failed by 58 votes. Theresa, with encouragement from a cross-party pincer movement of weak Brexiteers and Remainers who seized control of the parliamentary agenda, has finally decided to stop banging her head against a brick wall. She's seeking a joint approach with Jeremy Corbyn, while obtaining a 'flextension', a flexible extension, with the EU for a further six months, until the end of September.

The Speaker, the very epitome of pomposity, John Bercow, has now encouraged Members to take over the role of the Executive; I hope this doesn't set a precedent. The separation of duties is the biggest safeguard we have in avoiding autocracy. When somebody makes the claim that they are acting in the interests of democracy, you know they're not.

What's the betting that this will produce nothing either and we still won't be ready when that time's up? The only thing that will change is Theresa being thrown out for somebody else who won't be able to turn a square into a circle. We'll all be dead by the time we leave.

"Sounds a bit like my last few months of marriage with Jane," said Bob. "That did more harm than good."

*

It's a late Easter. Blackpool Football Club have got away without a points penalty, but are playing badly, Richie tells me. They won't be promoted, and it's the same division for them next year, still seeking a new owner. Bolton Wanderers have been relegated and will be joining them there. Their players even came out on strike over unpaid wages. They haven't got a new owner yet either and have been placed in Administration. They'll have a big points penalty to start next season. "At least we might survive to fight another day. Losing Bolton Wanderers would be the ultimate sign from above that my day is done," Richard has just told Bob on the phone. The ownership uncertainty around both teams isn't bothering Richie, who is already talking excitedly about the matches between them this coming season.

*

The news from Canada is of Malcom making a painfully slow recovery. Jackie rings us once a week, concerned that too much damage may have done. Because I remember Bob bouncing back from his heart attack, I'd hoped the same for Malcolm. Sophie and Robert are going out there this Easter with their children.

The updates from Ruth at St Chad's change quicker than a rolling News broadcast. The efforts of Amelia and Carl in bed have been rewarded. A baby is on its way. Maddie hasn't even pretended to be pleased with this news. The prospect of another mewling brat in the house, with Bethany still not crawling and with Jack fully into the terrible twos at her mother's, has been enough to send her into the bosom of papal orthodoxy. She's proposed marriage to Kieron, convinced by Lucy that he really should be the one for her. No, that can't be right; this is Maddie. She'll have convinced herself that he's the one who'll get her up the ladder. The besotted poor chap has accepted. He can't realise how much better than her he could get. I'll have to put him in the same category as James, only unluckier. He's got what he craved for, James didn't. They're marrying in the Catholic Church in a fortnight. Kieron's given up his flat and moved into Maddie's house already, driving to Manchester each day. They're not going to sell until they know where Maddie will be teaching, and that is sixteen months away. Ruth's getting to know them a bit, and says she thinks that Maddie still enjoys living in St Chad's. She expects that Maddie will then wangle a teaching post nearby. The only decision that Kieron is allowed to make is whether he should go into Salford Quays down the M602 or along the East Lancashire Road. And either way leads to the same traffic trouble.

I imagine Amelia likes St Chad's too. If Maddie has a conscience, she keeps it well hidden, to be referred to in her own time and on her own terms. She's asked Carl and Amelia to find their own place within a month, before her return from honeymoon. I'm not sure how well she's thought that through. Amelia was planning to work mainly nights so that she could look after Bethany once Maddie restarted at college.

Maddie's decision has also placed too great a strain on a relationship that was manufactured from the start. Carl had come back to St Chad's for the beguiling Maddie, and not the gentle Amelia. He's been spurred into finding himself and his mojo again, by a new woman who has found him. She's a dancer in a Blackpool nightclub, with two children and a house of her own. I'm not sure if this is a descent into hell or ascent into heaven from where we first met him as a married man with a mission on a Mission. Probably it's the latter; he'll always fall on his feet, that one. And, with any luck, he'll only have to dance to her tune on the dance floor.

So, poor Amelia's contrived domestic bliss has come crashing down. She shouldn't be surprised. What is schemed for won't usually survive exposure to reality. The empirical trumps the logical. Maddie cheerfully has left her on her own with the prospect of nowhere to live, or at least she would have done without the emergence of Lucy as fairy godmother. She's offered Amelia a room in her house until she's found somewhere better. She and Jack often stay at the pub with Bill anyway, leaving Amelia with the big house all to herself.

I don't think that any of these partners loves each other in the way I do Bob. I wonder if he loves me the same way. He tells me he does. I ask if he loved Jane like that too.

"I first loved an idea of her that she wasn't. It's only the last few years that I've really understood her for what she is, and that's someone very separate from me. I've always felt connected to you. We're meant to walk hand-in-hand," he said, picking each word carefully and honestly.

He then added: "I don't think these girls ever loved each other in any deep way, nor the guys they went with. Too much of it's been in public. It's been a play they're putting on for themselves. It'll run a lot longer yet, with a few more changes of cast."

"As long as both of them manage to keep some sort of show on the road," I said.

CHAPTER TWENTY-EIGHT
Spring 2019

Lucy didn't know whether to be pleased with Maddie's upcoming nuptials or angry about Amelia's treatment. Her response has been instant. After welcoming Amelia to live in her house while she finds something else, she's bought herself a silly hat to wear at the wedding. And, as usual, she's asked Landlord Bill to be her 'plus one' as per the invitation. Amelia is a big-hearted girl and is still going to act as Maid of Honour. James has turned down the chance to be Best Man, or even to attend the wedding. Another friend of Kieron has had to be approached. Maddie says James is being churlish. The rest of us think he's made his first good decision as concerns her.

*

Lucy and Bill have spent long hours together planning the reception, which to save money will take place in Bill's pub. Why it has taken so long when the sandwiches and pork pies will be identical to those at Paul's funeral, when there will be no table decorations, and when the wedding cake is coming from Darlington's on the Breck, requires no explanation.

We have been invited. Bob obviously has made some sort of impression on Maddie. I think she's needed to make him into a father figure and then to ignore what he says, as she never had the chance to run rings round her own father like that. We're going to have to go up to St Chad's again. There's also an invitation for Ruth and Charlotte, without 'plus-ones'. Ruth wouldn't have had one, and Maddie wasn't going to give Charlotte the chance to parade her new beau.

Tom's away in Wales with his mates. This leaves the dilemma of who is going to look after the younger children, our Alice and Richie, and Ruth's Ben. Fifteen-year old Rachel volunteers. Although, thankfully, she's much less serious than Charlotte, she's still full of common sense. Elderly Ethel Metcalfe next door says she'll keep a watchful eye on proceedings, which is kind of her, though makes me more worried in case one of them knocks her over!

While the four of us walked down the Breck to the Catholic Church, I asked Bob who would be giving Maddie away, if anybody. He remembered that Catholics don't have anyone do that. Ruth actually did know that Lucy was walking her up the aisle. Lucy had told her that she wasn't giving Maddie away but, as they reached the end of the aisle, she might give her a hefty kick up the bum and say, "Good riddance." It may be a while before that reaches the formal liturgy.

Amelia isn't showing any signs yet. She dressed in a shortish, lemon outfit, remarkably suitable for a sensible Yorkshire miss on a Lancashire spring day. But Maddie has been co-ordinating things. She'd been to the nursing home the night before to find the right clothes for her Gran, who had on her best yellow top and a cream blazer. Lisa, accompanied by Dave, was dressed in lemon too. Kieron's sister, a couple of years younger than him, was also very similarly attired. He's from an Irish Catholic family. His parents gave the outward appearance of being pleased by it all. They were justly proud of their son and his career at the BBC. We spoke to them briefly at the reception, upstairs at the pub. They made some mention of Maddie's bisexuality. Good Christians that they are, they were sufficiently confused by modern mores to shrug their shoulders.

Maddie wore white. Not all devils have been cast out of her though. When we were on our own, she came over to us, cheekily saying to Charlotte, "It could have been you if you'd played your cards right."

"Apart from one reason, Maddie," Charlotte replied. "I didn't fancy either of you enough. That James was maybe more my type, but stupidly he only had eyes for you."

That's Bob's granddaughter, giving as good as she gets, if ruder than he would be while drinking his host's wine. Maybe she acquired that side of her personality from Jane. Whatever, Charlotte has survived her night of doubt and sorrow. She's found herself. I expect that means she's also frequently finding herself in bed with Seb, in the privacy of his Reading hall of residence.

"You're welcome to James," Maddie replied. "The two of you would stay permanently moonstruck, waiting for life to begin. And I only asked you so I could gloat."

"Congratulations even so, Maddie," Charlotte said, turning into a version of her mother, Ruth the Peacemaker, who was keenly listening. "I hope you'll be happy together. I think you will be."

"I doubt if many others are thinking that, my own mother included. I'll do my best."

Bob and I wished Maddie good luck too. She thanked us for coming, speaking to Bob directly.

"I'm sorry I've given you such a run-around, old man. It was my idea that Mum asked you, because you've been good for me. Please tell your friend Richard that I'm sorry too."

"And Helen?" Bob asked.

"No way," she replied. "I'm carrying on sticking the pins into her effigy."

With a coarse cackle, she moved on to the next group.

271

Lucy was the next to move in our direction, Bill Hardisty alongside, pushing her mother in her wheelchair. His tie was round his earhole. He'd enjoyed more than his fair share of the Prosecco acquired at wholesale price. That wasn't the sole reason for the smile on his face though, furnished by Lucy.

"It's been a great day, hasn't it?" Lucy said. "And you can live through it all over again. Bill and I are getting married too."

"At least as far as I can tell, with this one his previous wife's dead," said Freda. "Doesn't our Maddie look gorgeous? I wish I could have had clothes like that when I was her age."

"I bet you were a heartbreaker, Freda, just like your daughter and granddaughter," Bob said.

"Well, I had my moments, I suppose," she replied.

We said our heartfelt congratulations to Lucy and Bill. When they'd left us, I asked Bob if he thought Lucy had just run out of options.

"Perhaps she thinks she has, but she could still pull. No, I think they've always liked each other, and she's realised that's the sort of guy she needs. I hope her liver's strong enough."

He then snorted with laughter.

"What's so funny?" I asked him.

"Do you realise that the story we've both been busy writing up could have finished in the first chapter if Paul and I hadn't been in the pub when Lucy came barging in. They could have got it together then."

"If that had been the main story," I said, "there wouldn't have been much of a plot."

"There always will be one," he replied. "You just have to search for it."

"I'm still looking for one in what's actually happened,"

I answered.

"So am I. Like Brexit, it's not finished yet."

"There'll never be a meaning to be found in that."

We both felt flat as the reception continued after the happy couple left for Manchester Airport. Things wouldn't have turned out any different if we hadn't existed but would have happened faster. Apart from young Jack, that is, who would have been someone else altogether if Bill had fathered him. And apart also from Paul, who wouldn't have been a father. Perhaps he wouldn't have been dead either.

Charlotte was looking thoroughly miserable by this point, without a plus-one to whom she could make a mocking commentary on the proceedings. We stoically put in another half-hour before saying out thanks to Lucy and leaving. The children we'd left with Ethel made a good excuse. Back home, we were greeted by happy, smiling faces, the broadest of which was hers. She'd had a lovely afternoon.

In the summer half-term, we didn't go north again. We'd decided to have another holiday of our own and had a glorious few days in Vienna, just Bob, me and the two children.

*

Will Brexit ever be over? The 'flextension' has meant that the UK has just had to take part in the Euro elections, allowing voters a free shot at the main parties, a chance they weren't going to miss. Nigel Farage's hastily formed Brexit Party topped the polls, picking up large numbers of Tories and many Labour blue-collar voters as well as nearly all previous UKIP votes. Many Labour Remainers, seeking a second referendum, voted for the Liberal Democrats, who finished second. With no prospect of ever being able to deliver a deal, Theresa has resigned, while staying on as caretaker while the Tories elect a new leader. Boris Johnson is odds-on favourite, despite all his personal and political baggage, being seen as the only man who can avoid them being wiped off the political map. They could well face annihilation at the next election, whenever it may be, unless they've delivered Brexit. Nobody knows how Johnson can possibly do it though.

Even Jacob Rees-Mogg is supporting him. But there are nine other contenders, including: Michael Gove, unloved by Leavers for shafting Johnson last time, and for supporting Theresa's deal; the Foreign Secretary Jeremy Hunt, presenting himself as the grown-up candidate yet to me who looks like a little boy still in short pants, walking like Zebedee as if on springs; and a particularly hard line leaver called Dominic Raab, who if elected plans to prorogue, that is suspend, parliament so that he can take us out without a parliamentary vote. In a sense, he's the only one who has a plan that in theory could work, but with such an enormous affront to parliamentary democracy that nobody sensible would consider it. Or would they? Is Boris sensible to anything but his own desires? I'd have thought that by-passing the mother of parliaments should seem more than a step too far to anybody calling themselves a conservative.

But why we should think it to be the mother of parliaments when we didn't get universal suffrage until 1928 is a mystery to me. Simon de Montfort and his robber barons must have had good PR. John Bercow is a worthy successor to them.

Anyway, this last week there has been an apparently interminable process involving Tory MPs which has whittled down the number of candidates to two, who are to be presented to the constituencies for them to choose: Jeremy Hunt and Boris Johnson. Hunt was initially a Remainer, who now 'respects' the referendum result. He beat Michael Gove to second place by two votes, perhaps after some tactical voting by Johnson supporters, eager for revenge on Gove. At least, the undignified squabble that would have been inevitable in a Johnson-Gove scrap won't take place. I'll stick up for Hunt, but then I'd probably support Beelzebub against Boris, upper-class and with no class, not fit to lick the boots of nature's gentlefolk that I've described here, or even Maddie. Decent folk are not that hard to find outside politics.

The Johnson campaign has got off to a bad start straight away. An argument he's had with his girlfriend in her flat has been overheard. The first cause seems to be that he spilt a glass of wine on her sofa and then was insufficiently concerned about it. The post-incident analysis was conducted as a bawling match. I hope this might be the start his campaign train's derailment. The strong expectation though is that he will become Leader sometime in July. He then won't either be able to deliver a new deal from the EU or get a vote in Parliament to leave without a deal by the end of October. He's not yet said that he won't prorogue parliament in those circumstances, but it is not thought likely. There may then have to be a General Election, in which he would, in order to recover the Brexit Party vote, need to campaign on a no-deal ticket, thus splitting his Party. In a General Election, the sensible majority in the country wouldn't have an obvious candidate, so there is a strong chance that, with four parties splitting the vote, Labour would win with a 30% share. I just hope in that scenario they'd need LibDem support, we'd get a referendum and we'd agree to stay in. But party politics is bust; reality has changed too fast for politicians to keep up. The demise of the Tories doesn't bother me. It's the opposite of me, the manual working-class, I feel most sorry for. By the end of this process, their Labour Party will have been totally stolen from them by the metropolitan tendency who of course,

275

will still try to pretend they're on the workers' side. Risibly to the rest of us, their self-image has a need to believe this to be the case.

There are many other potential outcomes which will be equally grotesque to behold. Whatever happens, I can't stomach the idea of having to listen to yet more politicking involving people who should have died with shame for causing the mess that we're in. These wretches who go into politics, surely of itself an admission of egomania, are not capable of the calm and rational discussion I like, which is never a bawling match and usually too polite even to be called a debate. I crave for a long period of time without hearing the voice of any politician. They'll certainly not be up for that this next few months. It's what I'm going to do though. I've had my fill. I can take no more. I've lost the will to live. I'm going to spare you the rest of the Brexit tale. If ever we do reach a decision, Bob can take over the writing again. Until then, it's total silence from me on the subject. I'm going to be resigned enough to say the outcome must be the will of God. In which case, resistance is futile. We'll all be dead soon enough.

If love affairs, however tangled, didn't end up quicker than this, nobody would ever read a romance.

*

A few weeks after we returned from Vienna, there was a major crisis in St Chad's. Lucy's and Maddie's domestic arrangements can only work provided that, when one of them has something else, they can rope the other one in. Amelia still generously is prepared to help out, but still works mainly on the day shifts at her nursing home. Neither of their men folk are much use if something goes wrong on a working weekday. In truth, Bill wouldn't be much use if he was called upon at any time, nor will he be until Jack is ready to drink out of a pint glass.

Freda fell badly at her nursing home in Penwortham while she was being taken back to her room after lunch. Breakages and concussion were suspected, and a stroke was considered a likely cause. She wasn't properly conscious. Paramedics took her by ambulance to Royal Preston Hospital. Maddie received the first call from the nursing home, as Lucy was teaching in her classroom without her phone. Jack, still not quite old enough for pre-school, was at the child minder's, not due to be picked up by Lucy until four o'clock. Maddie wanted to be at the hospital as soon as she could be but was looking after Bethany. The school secretary at Wheat Street School, presumably grabbing a late lunch, didn't answer the phone.

It didn't take Maddie long to work out the sort of person she needed in this sort of crisis, one who fortunately lived only round the corner. Ms Dependability did answer the call. Ten minutes later, Bethany in her carrycot was dropped off at Ruth's front door with a bottle of feed already made up, along with a tin of formula milk and some nappies plus sacks, on the assumption that it could be a long night at the hospital. Maddie was crying her eyes out as she drove off furiously to Preston. She did really love somebody after all. Ruth realised that it was to her Grandmother that Maddie had turned for comfort in her tomboy years.

Ruth was deputed to ring the school to tell Lucy. Twenty minutes after having succeeded in that, Lucy dropped Jack off at Ruth's before rushing off to Preston. He wasn't too impressed at the haste of his mother's departure, so howled. This of course set Bethany off. Ruth had faced this sort of thing before, although her children hadn't been quite so insistent. She ignored Bethany while parking Jack in front of the television tuned to CBeebies, giving him a biscuit and a glass of juice. She then picked up Bethany, cuddled her and settled her into a feed. She was still doing this when Rachel and Ben came home from school.

Maddie was sitting by her Gran's trolley in A and E when Lucy arrived. They'd tidied Freda up a bit, but she did look a mess. She was awake, and greeted Lucy with, "Hello, love. You didn't need have come. I'm alright. Our Maddie's doing a smashing job."

With the need to see a doctor, then blood tests, then X rays, it was a long haul. There was no sign of any breakages, nor evidence of a stroke, but her blood pressure was moving about alarmingly. She would have to stop in while this was stabilised and while her injuries healed. There seemed to be little prospect of finding a ward until the morning. It had reached mid-evening and it was well past the time that they should have relieved Ruth. Maddie didn't want to leave her Gran, but she was the one with a very young baby. She had to say goodbye, leaving Lucy to spend another hour there before kissing Freda goodnight.

When Maddie reached Ruth's, Rachel came to open the door from the front room, where she and Ben were watching Netflix. In the living room, Bethany was in Ruth's arms, on her third feed. Jack was curled up on the couch fast asleep. Ruth and Maddie spoke in whispers to avoid waking him. Maddie took her jacket off and gently took Bethany in her arms, continuing to feed her once she had sat down opposite Ruth. When Bethany had settled again, Maddie gave all the news about Freda.

"You're obviously very fond of her. We're seeing a side of you we haven't seen before," Ruth said

"I hope it's a side I can show you a bit more of in the future," Maddie replied. "I know I've not been nice to your Charlotte. It didn't help that I quite fancied her."

"It was James, Carl and Amelia I was thinking you could have been kinder to. And your own mother with Dave. Charlotte's strong enough to look after herself."

"I know that's true, but apart from James, they've all enjoyed the ride, I think. Maybe he did too."

Ruth smiled. "I think he enjoyed that part of the ride more than the ending. When you kicked him out, I'm told you didn't even look at him to say goodbye."

"I deliberately kept my eyes from doing it. That was the only way I knew to prevent a soppy farewell, which would have made things worse. Really, we hardly knew each other. It's not like with Gran who I've known all my life. I'll maybe at least say goodbye if it ends up that way with Kieron."

"On the courtroom steps isn't the place to say it. Divorce is the bitterest thing I know. Do your best to avoid that."

"I'd better get this little madam home," Maddie said. "Thank you for everything tonight. You and your father have been brilliant, when I haven't deserved it."

It was another half an hour after she left that Lucy came for Jack. After she'd left, Ruth rang us up to tell us what had happened. Freda was back to her Nursing Home four days later.

During this kerfuffle, both Bob was delighted to hear that his football club had a new owner. I hoped that would be an augury. Perhaps its isn't. Richard was hoping for similar for his beloved Wanderers, but their potential deal is proving far more problematic. I'm no football fan, but even I can't imagine the football scores being read out without hearing the Bolton Wanderers name. It's what's meant by an institution. The world should be stopped dead in its tracks while that's sorted out.

CHAPTER TWENTY-NINE
July 2019

We still haven't got a new prime minister, and I'm sticking to my promise of no more politics. The whole atmosphere in the country is of resignation to whatever fate has in store. But other things have been slowly moving onwards. Lucy's wedding is set for later this month. We'll be going up to St Chad's for that. The news from Vancouver about Malcom is worrying. It seems like he may need a second operation. And things are bad in Totnes too. The tamoxifen hasn't done the trick. Joan's been taking an aromatase inhibitor too, but all to no avail. Her cancer is back with a vengeance. Care can now only be palliative. Bob drove down there for a quick visit before we start the holidays. She's resigned to her fate. They'd remembered together their parents, their grandparents, and forgotten names from the past. That's what people talk about when closing in on death. It must be in the hope that you might meet them again, or even that you can feel their presence at the door.

Not all is so dismal. It's summer, the sun is shining in Nether Piddle, and I've a nice weekend planned. The apocalypse facing the nation has been put on hold. It's just a pity it can't stay like this permanently. Tomorrow, Saturday, I'm going to a dig with Steve, who's driving down tonight from Keswick. He says that the view looking over the site at first light is to die for, and that we have to be there early to see it. Bob is looking after the children for the day.

Something strange happened this evening. We all went for a walk around the woods. As we were ambling along, an absolutely naked young man marched past us, pausing briefly to say, "Good Morning." Bob and I sniggered at each other. Alice looked dumbfounded. Richie asked if the man was Jesus.

"I expect he thinks so," answered Bob.

*

On Sunday, my parents are coming over. There's a large piece of lamb in the fridge ready for their visit, along with the fruit for a summer pudding. I'll have to be back from the dig tomorrow evening in time to make that. I'll delete this sentence, a reminder to myself, when I pick up on this again next week, and I'll tell you about the strange thing Bob just said to me.

Book Three

CHAPTER THIRTY
Christmas 2019

I've not been able to write this last few months. This will be the last chapter, and it has to be written by me, Bob. The Lord giveth, and the Lord taketh away. The Day of the Lord so cometh as a thief in the night. Wendy did set off with Steve before dawn cracked. Steve proceeded to drive straight into an unlit skip just around the corner from our house. He must have had to squeeze his car through the same, narrow gap the previous day too. I heard the crash. He was killed instantaneously. I was the first to get there. Unconscious, Wendy breathed her last as I cradled her in my arms. I hope she could feel that I was there.

It was Steve's fault as much as that of the unknown prankster who'd moved the lamp intended to light up the skip. He usually did drive too fast for his abilities. God knows why, but he'd been edgy in the house the previous evening. I imagine Judas Iscariot was a bit that way too before he got called out at the Last Supper. Several times during the evening, Steve told us how his life had stalled. Pity his bloody car didn't that morning.

I'm still totally bereft. If God is the judge, and Christ the redeemer, in my life, Jane only sometimes succeeded in being the judge, but Wendy definitely was my redeemer. She's gone and she didn't deserve it. She wasn't without sin, but a second thought would always put right any small mistake she made. She's been the paschal lamb, the sacrifice demanded by the story for our years of happiness. She's paid for my life.

No angels tried to save her. We'd broken the Commandment about adultery but not the rules surrounding entering into a sacrament. Why the flying fuck should any of that matter anyway? Is this the way the wild God of the Old Testament behaves? Or has he subjugated his will to the orthodox and become a priest? I'll plump for the primitive God. Christ then came to fulfil the law, to make priestly rules irrelevant, providing a life to imitate in their place. The virtues behind his life can be seen in the shadows for those who don't know about him. He could bring light only through his death. Wendy's had to do that too. Even though she was such a fine person, a righteous person, the God of Job has either allowed the devil to see her off in order to watch us suffer or done the job himself as her punishment for not seeing it through with Frank. Or is this something that couldn't be changed? Was this always in the plan? And I'm not meant to feel bitter about it? I'm afraid I do.

Frank died a week after Wendy. In the heavens above, she must have asked for that. We could and I'm sure would have been married by now if she'd lived after he'd died. She and our children would have changed their surname. Alice would no longer have carried my Grannie's name of Alice Smith.

On a whim, I'd asked Wendy on the day before the crash that, if we all did enter those pearly gates, would she prefer grumpy old me to the handsome, dashing, young guy she'd been engaged to before Frank, who'd broken things off with her? She'd looked puzzled and asked if I'd been thinking about my break-up with Jane again. I hadn't been; it was a transient but genuine moment of insecurity. She then told me not to be so soft; it would always be me. I miss her so much.

So, instead of Lucy's wedding, we had a funeral a hundred miles south. Swarbricks and Smiths were unrepresented at the nuptials. We presented a sad sight, Wendy's parents, the children and me. The service was held at St Andrew's Parish Church in our home village of Nether Piddle, followed by a cremation, so that her ashes could be placed with my coffin in St Chad's cemetery when that hole is dug.

You won't manage to be walking beside someone when the great call comes, even if you're one of the few who can remember Josef Locke singing the words. As a distraction, the children and I trudged through the woods as the sun set this afternoon, toward a hauntingly bare canopy of trees, past the point where we'd seen the naked Jesus. The memory caused me a smile. But then, once we reached the path through the woods, looking down to focus on not tripping over the roots in the twilight, my depression was back.

This book is just a snippet of a few years we've spent in today's mixed-up confusion. I can't make sense of the events either. I've reached old age, and it's their world, that of the next couple of generations, now. Do they have to chuck out so much of what I hold dear? Or at least they would do if they were ever capable of actually doing anything. We didn't disown the past, however much we rebelled.

It would have been better not to walk through the trees, but to look at the woods from the outside: to try to view the whole and not the parts; to integrate, and not to differentiate, my new-found motto. I'll try to see the field that I'm walking through as the mind of the Almighty, a field made and eternally existing as a result of him collapsing a myriad of waveforms into the firm ground under my feet, while allowing me to think of the past in whatever way I choose. He'll also allow me to decide when I want to turn and go back home. I've preferred to bring everything from the past with me. I hope it's all in my eternal soul, nothing forgotten but everything I've done wrong forgiven. I'll walk until I'm knackered.

Richard and Helen had stayed with us the night before the funeral, with him then giving the eulogy, a thoughtful piece about how Wendy made most of the decisions without ever needing to claim the credit. He and I probably both feel guilt from our false claims of past glories. Ruth read the lesson, crying only as she walked past the coffin on her way back from the lectern. Neither Walter nor Audrey felt up to doing it. My first family had all come to give support, from Richmond, St Chad's and even Liverpool, Jane and Geoffrey returning from holiday early to be here. Quite a few of Wendy's friends and students came too. Our grief was too deep for us to be able to share it fully with them. The heart-ending sight of Alice sobbing her heart out at the crematorium, with little Richie doing his best to comfort her, will stay with me forever. A curtain drawn, a veil drawn across a life, and that's it.

I'd hired the village hall, and to there we repaired while the fire did its work. The next time I met up with Wendy was when I collected a 'tasteful' mahogany ashes casket with my favourite photograph of her in the lid. All courtesy of a funeral director I'd never met before and never will do again. Still, he did a good job and the box was a piece of brown furniture. It's a box of only the good memories, 'made manifest' and 'revealed by fire' as the good book has it. With Wendy, all the memories are good, apart from the last one. It's my Ark of the Covenant, the promise that I'll see her again. With young children about though, I've had to keep it in a locked cupboard and not on the sideboard.

I also went to Steve's funeral less than a week later, on my own. It soon became obvious from the male mourners that he hadn't been quite as celibate as Wendy believed. I tried to look and sound dignified. If he's conned his way through those pearly gates, I hope he was full of remorse, at least until Wendy forgave him, which she will have done. She can do that on my behalf too, because I'm nowhere near ready to. My rock, I've given to her the keys to heaven. I hope she'll get me in.

I can't help but feel that my actual biggest sin has been in moving to the middle-class. That's where Wendy started and finished, something she never felt the need to apologise for. I suppose I should feel no need either, but I mourn what I left behind. I do hope that Paradise resembles St Chad's in the fifties more than her Cheltenham of the seventies, and is a world without telephones, fridges and central heating. I want to riddle the ashes and make a fresh coal fire each morning. After all, there will be no global warming in heaven.

On August Bank Holiday, Ruth reported a tremendous bang and the house shaking in St Chad's. That was the sound of my career ending in a bang and not a whimper. 2.9 on the Richter scale, was recorded, which although classified as minor, we still a hundred times the permitted amount. It was heard and felt by everybody for miles around. Cuadrilla were soon having to pack their bags. In a sense, I was pleased. Maybe it will stop that bit of pratting around without anything being achieved. I wonder if Wendy was behind that as well as Frank's death.

In late September, I had a phone call from Margy. I'd not been in touch. She'd only just found out about Wendy's death.

"Why didn't you tell me," she asked straightaway, before expressing what sounded less than heartfelt commiserations.

"I was too upset to do any of the ringing round. Ruth did that for me. I didn't know who she'd told until after the funeral, and then it was too late."

I know that last bit sounds weak, because it is. I don't want any possibility of anything new or even a re-tread in my life, not even with Jane. It will always be Wendy. I asked Margy how life was going with her daughter in Northumberland. She was full of her folk club, and village life, both of which she'd thrown herself into. I wasn't too successful in entering into her enthusiasm.

"That was always the problem with you, Bob. You'd never quite fully join anything. We could still spend some great times together."

"It's too late for that now, Margy. It's best left where it is. I'm not a joiner, nor a leaver."

"You joined with Jane; you joined with Wendy. Why never with me?"

"I can't answer that. I guess it just wasn't meant to be. I'll grieve for times past, but you can't re-invent them."

"You mean you won't. You could if you wanted," she said.

"No, you can't go back all the way," I replied.

"You could if you wanted. Well, that's it until the Christmas card. Fare thee well, Big Man."

"Fare the well too, Margy."

And that's that, I think. For Margy, my biggest sin, along with Bob Dylan, was not staying with the project. I'll offer my sincere apologies to the Pete Seeger/Joan Baez crew that I didn't, but I couldn't. Just sometimes, I wish I could have. But the world is bound to be a messy place as, collectively, humans don't usually make things better when they try to. Too ordered a society would be no good for what I still see as the purpose of life, making unique souls and not carbon copies. No project planned by humans will ever make things perfect. It won't often make them better.

Malcolm didn't improve. He passed away late in October, before he'd had the chance of a second operation. All that drama of the shuffling of the cars didn't lead to any happier ending. Sophie is still beating herself up at not being in Canada for the final act. It seems there's always a price to be paid for 'bettering' yourself. With her family just about all left home, Jackie's lonely but still needed as matriarch in Vancouver, her life gone from noisy to quietish. I pick up her family photos on Facebook, where two sad people half a world apart can send messages to each other. She's putting on a brave face.

Lucy and Bill, Maddie and Kieron, look to be well settled. Dave and Lisa are marrying next Spring, and she's not even pregnant. Lucy still wonders if he's firing blanks, particularly as he didn't get either Fishwick into the club either. I don't need to form an opinion on that. Time will tell.

Amelia has at last moved out of Lucy's house. She's found a new woman to love, which is what she wants. The new and old orders of the world have been honoured. And she had a surprise for us when she had her baby. It was a little girl, one who must have a very black father by the colour of her skin. Amelia always was a surprise package to me. Ruth and Wendy had it wrong. Perhaps she hadn't schemed to have Carl back and was glad when he was gone again. Or if she did, she'd hedged her bets. Inadvertently or nor, we may well have given you fake news. Honest, we didn't intend to mislead you. Real fake news isn't meant to be believed, but to stop you believing in anything. There's too much of that around. It would be a crying shame if we've done the same. Whatever, I have to admire Amelia for taking everything in her stride. She's been well worth knowing, even though we didn't have much to say to each other.

Maddie is already pregnant again. What I hope for her and Kieron is that, once they have the children they want, they show some ambition for themselves. It would be nice for that to be in the north-west, but I know they may need to go to London. If they don't, my betting is that they won't last together for too long. Even if they do both find outlets for their gifts, they'll then probably outgrow each other. It will be a race to see if Kieron's infatuation expires first, or

291

Maddie's restlessness beats him to it. It's too long to the menopause and beyond to think she'll succeed in being faithful. But just maybe she will, and they'll stay together. She's for once taken my advice and written a novel, full of quirky black humour, while doing her education course. She's a bright girl. She's seeking a publisher. And as we have learnt, what Maddie wants, Maddie gets. Look out for it in Waterstone's.

She's sent me a PDF copy as I was the one that suggested she wrote. It is, how should we say, interesting, and it is exquisitely written. There's beauty in her soul somewhere amid the atavistic memory of a brutal past. Two lesbian women live in a suburban house, which has been given the unlikely name of Gaza. They kidnap an Adonis of a man, chain and gag him, cut his hair and gouge his eyes out. They use him as a sex slave until they've both successfully given birth. They then open the door to permit his escape. Unable to see, he dances with the two girls until they lead him to the edge of the swimming pool. He falls in and drowns. The dance continues around his body until he comes back to life. He tells them how he was swimming underwater with a little boy who wasn't big enough to climb out of the pool. One of the girls jumps into the pool never to be seen again.

I recalled how Amy saw the machines taking over from humans. A dystopian view of the future now seems to be standard for their generation. Yet they're not without hope for their own lives. Personal optimism still trumps collective pessimism, which is perhaps as well. James was sent a PDF of Maddie's book too and found it intriguing. He's now able to be her friend without asking for more. This is how exactly she likes it. "A metaphor for our age," is how he described the book, before saying, "It's as well I escaped before I fell in the pool. She would have pushed me in and held me down." Whether

Carl has seen his experiences of these years as no more than a figure of speech, I don't know. He's still only occasionally managing to visit Bethany despite living close, and Maddie giving him every opportunity. The one mystery I can't explain is why he came back, unless it was stage-managed by Amelia. I guess he really must have had some sort of mental crisis he's still not fully through. Wendy wrote how she couldn't pin him down. There are some people in life who don't want something once they've got it, until they've lost it. Maybe that's how he is. He'll need a few more dancing partners if so.

Lucy asked me what Paul would have thought of Maddie's book. It's difficult to imagine the horror in his Leavisite reaction to its absence of morality, and its extended use of metaphor. At least I hope metaphor is what it is, or otherwise we've all nearly been down the cellar with Fred and Rosemary West. But, even so, I do think Paul would have liked it, and I said so. In a funny sort of way, it describes two lives without precedent as well as morality. Maddie is Lucy's daughter, and Lucy loved Paul. Meeting them all has been a challenge I do feel grateful for. They didn't kill Wendy. They didn't bore Wendy. They amused her.

I didn't care for the book or its message of course. Story for me needs more than metaphor; it needs the flesh and bone of history. People don't pick their identity; it picks them. But my world view is seemingly over. Maddie is the future; a future that could well dispense with men altogether, and then with all humanity as the cyborgs take over. She's tried my view of life from many angles and can't quite get it. If my religion is aimed at any one group, it is for those who feel lost. If a revival is going to happen anywhere, in these times you'd expect it to be from the charismatic end, and not traditional Catholics nor Conservative Evangelicals. Maddie hasn't found any message to her comfort though, preferring to live without an answer. For the time being, my faith will have to get by without her and most others. I won't be around long enough to see if anybody else picks up the baton, perhaps from Africa, maybe even China. I can only hope that the light will still be flickering enough in the West for Alice and Richie to see it. May they be full of grace and truth. Much fuller than I have been.

If the story had been different, maybe Maddie could have embraced the message. And Charlotte too. Luther would in this revised version have persuaded the Catholic Church to come to its senses over indulgences. James would have banged the heads of Peter, Paul and John together, so they didn't contradict each other quite so much, thereby laying the structures for two millennia of dispute. Adam would have said to Eve: "Of course we can eat that bloody apple unless it gives us tummy ache. That's what we're meant to do." The real challenge to the faith doesn't come from science or philosophy. It doesn't even come from those who propound the faith, although we invariably sound like losers. It comes from the story itself, and that's the one we've been given. You can't change that now, even when modern understanding reveals something unworthy. When I read, for instance, the tale of Saul and David in the Old Testament, I can see how it was re-spun centuries later in the interests of the Jerusalem temple functionaries, just as nowadays Fox News can re-spin the US Presidential Race, to rather quicker timescales. But that's what we're stuck with. Overall, some sort of sense can be made of it all. However profanely, I do feel confident that Maddie will be teaching the Holy Allegory in her RE classes. That's something. She's an eternal winner, not loser.

Ethel Metcalfe fell ill last month and died within the week. I've had good value recently out of my dark grey suit, white shirt and black tie. Ruth has suggested that I sell up in Nether Piddle and buy

Ethel's house, next door to hers as it is. We would be company for each other and could share childcare duties when the other wanted to go out. I was in a dilemma between letting my daughter down if I didn't, or Wendy's parents if I did, I asked them if they'd like to move in with us in St Chad's. They live for their grandchildren and so it's perhaps not surprising that they've jumped at the chance. So, there are two houses to be sold, and one to be bought. That should keep us all busy. Ethel's son has promised us first refusal once probate has been obtained

We all want to flee from the scene of our previous happiness, our ever-present tragedy. Maybe Wendy has arranged all this with the courts of heaven. It means I'll be able get the odd evening down the pub with Audrey and Walter at home too. And with the landlord's wife seeing herself as the principal entertainment there, I expect them to be very odd evenings. The move means leaving Hattie's and Sheba's ashes behind, but they'll never leave my heart. That's where to bury them, in the profound hope we'll meet up again.

My sister Joan breathed her last early this month in a hospice, surrounded by her children. I made the long trek to Devon for the funeral. It only hit me on the drive home that I am now a complete orphan. There's nobody left here who remembers the Victorian Britain that occupied the whole twentieth century. No longer can the mournful sound of a brass band be heard playing in the distance as a eulogy for those two forgotten generations who hoped for our future. So, other than to die, I've no choice but to look forward. I haven't made a good start though. Carefully positioned in the back of the car is one milking stool, previous owner Grannie.

I've decided to get a new dog; one we can share with the family next door once we get to St Chad's. It's time our kids had a new one, with all the joy and heartache it brings. We're going to get him once we're back at Nether Piddle for the New Year, after Christmas at Ruth's. He's two years old, a rescue dog, big and hairy, called Marmaduke. That's too good a name to change. There's still happiness to be had. Maybe he'll help me see the difference between the wood and the trees on our tats. Armageddon and the apocalypse that Wendy and I expected to happen as we wrote this wasn't to be Brexit. It won't even be the increasingly likely world-wide climate disaster however many billions are killed. It wasn't to be the loss of my football club, or Richard's. Yes, poor old Bolton did finally manage to get a new owner in the week this season started but were left without any players. Their inevitable decline makes only the faintest whimper of a noise. No, the big crunch in my life was to Steve's sports car. That disaster was personal to Wendy and me. That's in the end what apocalypses are, the sum of many personal disasters.

But it does feel like a hard rain will come soon. When you first become politically conscious, to quote the young Dylan at the feet of Woody Guthrie, the world seems sick and hungry, tired and torn, looking like it's dying when it's hardly been born. It still does when you're old too. It is one degree Celsius hotter now too. Without engineers, it wouldn't have been. It's amazing how much damage you can do when you're trying to help. Maybe I should have been a lawyer. Hot air doesn't warm the planet that much.

We now have Christmas, post-apocalyptic and therefore misplaced in time in my frame of reference, which is really the only one I can know. Why am I still left here? I lived in the past for too long before I met Wendy, and it's a lonely place. I think I must have used it all up then. No, there can only be one reason. I'm to make this Christmas as good a one as I can for Alice and Richie. That's still the something I've to do with the time I've got left, to give these two as much as I can of what Wendy would have given them. The purpose of life can't only be to perpetuate it, but it's a necessary part, including passing down my preciously polished Y Chromosome to Robert and Richie. That will have mutated and shortened in a few thousand years in the unlikely event it survives the hard rain that's soon going to fall. It's passing down the way of life that I most want to do.

So, I'll tell them all about Wendy as if she's still here, trying not to rake mournfully over the ashes. The carved crib scene is again taking pride of place on the sideboard, in this week before Christmas in the hope that God will be with us. We won't move to St Chad's until next July, so that the kids start their new schools in September.

Wendy assumed that at some stage I'd pick up the Brexit tale she was describing so well. Her telling of that story was interrupted at the point where she could stomach it no longer. I don't really want to, but I suppose I'll have to, for completeness sake. Our new prime minister, Boris Johnson, really did try to prorogue parliament in an attempt to leave the EU on October 31 without a deal. This was in response to the Speaker, John Bercow, effectively allowing parliament take control of executive matters. The Supreme Court then judged this prorogation move to be illegal. All hell broke loose in parliament, with Johnson claiming that parliament and the elite were frustrating the will of the people. He wanted to hold an election on precisely those terms. By this point, the Tories had no semblance of a majority, not even one to call an election by means of losing a vote of no confidence in themselves, an election from which the Labour Party was running scared for fear of losing out badly in their leaver heartlands. We had total deadlock. Defections and expulsions in both parties were daily occurrences, with a rising number of Independent MPs who'd either left the two main parties in despair or had been kicked out. Jo Swinson, the leader of the Liberal Democrats, chose to say that when the election did happen, she would fight it on the basis of staying in the EU without a referendum. Almost out of the blue, with ten days before the deadline, Johnson produced a deal with the EU which avoided a backstop agreement, but which was less firm on Northern Ireland having identical customs arrangements to the rest of the UK. The residual Conservative Party, now cleansed of all Remainers, and the Brexit party, both endorsed the deal. It still couldn't clear Parliament, and so the EU gave us a further extension until the end of January. With that, resistance to a General Election weakened, and one took place just over a week ago.

Boris Johnson fought a simple campaign with great gusto, using as few facts as possible, and those he did use lacked veracity. His motto was, "Get Brexit done." Jeremy Corbyn went for a renationalising manifesto with even higher spending than in 2017, claimed to be fully costed. Perhaps it was, but it certainly didn't look any too affordable. Jacob Rees-Mogg was kept locked away for the duration after thoughtless comments resulted in his reputation self-combusting. The Tories now have a majority of 80 in the house. The good folk of the towns in the North and Midlands, 13 in the north-west alone, including Blackpool and a Bolton seat, and many more in the north-east and Yorkshire, have turned blue. I suppose they took the view that if you can't beat the bastards then you might as well join them, if only for a while. All the independent MPs have lost their seats, as has Jo Swinson. So, Boris has his Brexit. He now has to negotiate trade deals with the EU, the USA and many others while fixing the economic decline of towns like Richard's and mine that nobody else has managed to do this last half-century. I wish him well in mission impossible. Jeremy Corbyn is to be replaced. I'm backing the Labour MP for Wigan, Lisa Nandy, who more than any other MP has analysed the problems thrown up for the towns by modern living. The national party's membership though is not only well to the left but is city based. The Momentum party within a party is no doubt scheming to stitch things up, and the only realistic challenge to them will come from the stolidly stodgy Keir Starmer, who, God forbid, is both a Londoner and a barrister. The thought of him following Corbyn makes me think my life must have been in vain!

Before Wendy died, I'd told her I'd become a fully-signed up Remainer again. After her death, as the debate progressed, I couldn't see any other way out of the mess but this one. Working class folk aren't stupid; they saw that too. I spoilt my ballot paper but have more than enjoyed the resulting discomfiture of the bien pensant. Phoney or real, pride in being northern is what I felt at the result. They've done something, even if it was only to spit. It's a decision, if not the best one, perhaps even a stupid one. Time will now tell if Boris Johnson can rise up and have done with lesser things. I more than doubt it.

To most of the country, on either side of the debate, the last three years have looked like a failure of our unwritten constitution. But a type of vindication has followed. My view of MPs collectively has never been high, recruited as they mainly are from the ranks of the self-important, but as you know from my ethical views, I'm not keen on a rule-based approach to life, so I did hope that good sense could emerge from the random chaos, without any need for an authoritarian leader either. Heaven won't be a place on earth. The world will always be messy, with free will accompanied by animal needs and desires. If humans built a new Jerusalem, just like in the old one, we would crucify Christ. And it would still be subject to earthquake, famine and pestilence.

While all this was happening, most people continued to live their lives as if none of it really mattered. They joked about the apocalypse just round the corner but didn't expect one. And that's what I did too, with a weak smile on my face. The only apocalypse that mattered to me had happened. She's gone.

I'm dreading New Year's Eve. I can remember how badly I cracked up the years my parents died, and this will be ten times worse. The BBC will have a concert by someone who I have vaguely heard of but too young for me to know their music, while too old for the kids in our family. There will be that wretched fireworks display in the middle of the concert, the most witless entertainment known to humanity at any time of history, but mind-bogglingly gormless when all focus elsewhere is on climate change. New Year's Eve used to be better when the jocks held the stage, and the only Donald then in focus was looking for his troosers. I'd find a Watchnight service to go to, if I wasn't looking after the children. No-one can see you crying when you're praying.

Once the kids are back to school in January, I'll be spending my days doing *The Times* Crossword and Killer Sudoku. To solve the crossword, I seem to need all my brain, all the dirty tricks and pseudo-knowledge acquired through life. The Sudoku is focused on the left-hand, where I've spent too much time. Both sides are ingredients of the real me, with the whole greater than the sum of the parts. I won't be reading much fiction though. There seems to be a disconnect between the literary novels I've read and the way the world now is. They didn't manage to capture the universal when I thought they had done. And Wendy and I haven't managed to in these writings either. This Godless age has new writers, ones I just can't get. It's not only that the old certainty has gone. No longer do we know what it is we're meant to be uncertain about. And with the means to annihilate stalking the planet and people just as evil as they've always been, it really does look odds-on they'll be a major wipe-out of humankind this century, probably before the hard rain from climate change has drowned us all. I pray that the children survive it. I've always assumed that the human story coming so far means that God has blessed it, and it will turn out fine. I wonder if I've only kidded myself. An optimist sees God in control, a pessimist the devil.

When I've finished with the newspaper and puzzles, I'll go for a short walk. Out of breath, I'll stand in the field facing those trees, like the naked walker stripped of all identity, either waiting in vain to be filled up with the Spirit or thinking I'm about to pass out. I know I'll never again feel the peace that passeth all understanding in this life, if I ever did. Sometimes I've found hope, but not much peace. That's not the point of my life.

I'll be pleased when the children are back home. Richard tells me, now that his kids have grown, he finds himself waiting for *Pointless* to come on the telly. Pleasant programme that it is, it tells you all you need to know about getting old. And he's got a vocation, a wife, dogs and cats to keep him company. The problem with retirement is that you don't have a job to keep you distractedly bored.

I just have one outstanding promise of Wendy's to deliver and need to place two more people before this story ends. Neither are from the madhouse that the modern world has become to me. Both are of my generation, people who know what it's all felt like to us, when we could rebel against the status quo without abandoning it. One is my great friend Richard. The other is my ex-wife, Jane. I hope that at least in the next life she'll be Jane the Just and not the Hanging Judge.

After the move, on her visits to see Ruth, I'll see her more often than I have done since we last broke up. She'd said back then that we were only breaking up in this life: in the next Wendy would have to share me with her. You might remember that Wendy's written something similar. And I thought paradise was a place of eternal rest! Well, at least it shouldn't be boring up there. Jane reminded me of her intention while we were sitting in one corner of Ruth's living room today, Boxing Day, drinking a glass of red wine together. Geoffrey was watching us with his usual benign smile and glass of port.

"Only if you promise to like me," I said, trying to keep things light.

"I can't promise that even in paradise," she'd said. "I've two others I've loved too. And you're the only one I've found impossible. But I've loved you, and that won't stop."

She pulled my hand to her lips and kissed it.

"One more toast to the ill-starred couple," she said.

We clinked our glasses. You can't choose who you love, but you can choose to stop. She was once so easy to love, and then it became damn near impossible. It must be that, despite our differences, we chose not to stop.

"The ill-starred couple," we said together.

"Not ill-starred at all," said Geoff. "Just think of the dynasty you've produced. And not a snowflake among them."

He's been a good guy. It's been well worth knowing him too. I'm pleased that Jane is living her last years in his peace. I did say though that I was a real snowflake, wanting a safe space from the horrors yet to come. Jane asked if we could all hide in there together. I suppose I could honestly say that my contribution to writing this is both a great thank you to Wendy for saving me from despair, and also to Jane for putting me into it. When push comes to shove, I can't forget that. I should have realised when Jane and I were courting all those year ago that she would need to play those games I first found amusing, but which became so distressing, with more than just me. It will always be Wendy first, up above and down below. She saved me. She offered me unconditional love. I hope she felt that I loved her the same way.

I met Richard in London last week, the day before the election, after a little bit of business I had to tie up. We met in the steak restaurant in Smithfield we'd last been in in 2006, just before the business deal we did that brought me together with Wendy. In the distance was a glorious ring of Church bells, pealing out the good news to nobody but us and we'd already heard it. The present is a foreign country. They do things differently here. There's no need for salvation if all you think you need is a boost to your self-esteem. The message of the cross is foolishness unless you see defeat as the only real victory.

The restaurant was gloomy when Richard and I first met there, and it still is. That's not changed. We ordered our steaks, both hoping our ancient teeth would be up to the task. Richard used to be teetotal after a health scare, but in old age permits himself the odd glass. We ordered a bottle of Merlot, billed to have subtle tannins. Tasting them at all is difficult enough nowadays. Age even takes your taste buds from you. Richard soon saw how badly I was still mourning Wendy.

"I remember you lecturing me about how you have to take everything with you when I tried to dismiss a sad part of my past," he said. "If you look at your time with Wendy, it was wonderful. Your life has been great, one you'd have volunteered for but not one you could have started or even thought of. It's had its own meaning. Be grateful, not bitter."

He's right. We both sat there saying nothing. The story we tell ourselves, the pattern we impose on events, is the meaning of our lives, however illusory the narrative appears to others. Eventually, I smiled wanly.

"Not that there's much great going on at the moment," I said. "Do you know that Elvis Costello song? 'I should be drinking a toast to absent friends, Instead of these comedians.' The Big O did a great version. Wendy and I both liked it. It sums up Trump, Putin and all our useless lot well. Comedians, all. I'm not sure that, with Wendy gone, it doesn't apply to most of my friends too. We're not often with who we want to be with. If it wasn't for the kids, I'd wish I was somewhere else, though God knows where, if not dead. Quite probably it's what others have thought about us two all our lives, just two time-wasters."

"I know the song well. We'd both make lousy comedians, but we've seen life as more a comedy than a tragedy. We've not wasted our time. It reminds me of the speech I once heard Frankie Worthington give in corporate hospitality before a Bolton game. 'I spent all my money on women and booze. It could have been worse. I could have wasted it,' he said. I think he'd nicked if from George Raft via Georgie Best. A life lived is never a life wasted though, Bob. Yours certainly hasn't been. I sometimes think I should have achieved more and that I've been a disappointment to people."

"You haven't to me, pal. I've never even thought that I've been a disappointment to folk, other of course than to Jane. Maybe I should have. Life doesn't seem like a comedy while I toss and turn in bed at night. What worries me is how bitter I am as my mind races round. Not just about the crash, but at how much the world has changed. I have thought dreams that are homicidal, not suicidal. Christendom's gone, and I bloody well miss it."

We both left it there. There's not much point deciding that you buggered up your life when it's too late to do anything about it. I often think that my life has only meant something because I wanted to believe it did. I'll never know the grim, self-confident smugness of the non-believer. But even if I have kidded myself, I still think I was right to believe.

Richard and I both know we're nearing the end of our days. That's why we picked a place to eat where good things came from. We know we'll both die in the hope that there will be a purpose for our souls, as well as our stories having had a meaning, as we carry nothing in our hand but a cross we could bear, but with a heart bursting for more to come. Despite all the pain and suffering that religious observance has caused the world, we can't not believe the old, old story. It was the right one for us. I doubt that any more is going to be revealed to us in the years between today and our deaths. I can't see how humankind's existence has a physical benefit. All we've done is harm the planet we're on. So, if there is a purpose to our existence, it must be the making of our souls. This is who I am.

I'll probably die suddenly having a heart attack. Richard reckons he'll go with cancer occupying his body, including his brain, by the time the last trumpet sounds for him. Either way, the golden evening brightening in the west can only be summoned with a death rattle, if at all. Imagery isn't going to save us. Nor is there a biological mechanism that can. We need that God of the Old Testament to be real and to have the compassion to do that. Richard claims to have received messages from his mother and father from beyond the grave. They sound convincing, but that was personal to him. Such messages don't work as well second-hand. Nobody has been in touch with me from the other side as far as I know. Maybe I'm too blind to see. I did have those two muntjacs mooching like dogs at the bottom of the garden.

Yet in a funny sort of way, I have fewer doubts than Richard. My confident exterior that's probably irritated you throughout this tale is no front. It's me. I might be just a speck in the spacetime of an enormous cosmos, yet part of the noise you hear isn't bluster.

A God may have viewed our entire lives before they started, but for us there has been no precedent. The beginning of wisdom is to realise first that, whoever is in control, you're not. 'I am not my own' says on old catechism that Richard's preached about. Maybe we only do exist in the mind of God. That way, we could survive death. Even so, the lesson of life and of writing this book is that you don't have to accept everything that's in the original script. Most, yes, but not all. If you don't sometimes kick back, then you don't exist. A fictional character would serve the same purpose. And then, a story can be thrown away without hurting anybody.

Later in the meal, over pudding, I told him about this book, and asked whether or not I should leave a copy to pass on to Alice and Richie for when they're grown up. He asked me to send him one.

Wendy never did get round to putting the final scene of Lucy's play into this story. It would be a shame for you to miss it. I think it shows that Lucy does sometimes listen.

ACT III
Scene 6 (Return to Lower Shuttlebottom)

*There's the sound of a coach pulling up, followed
by the wakening buzz of conversation*

DOREEN

Wakey, wakey. Here we are. Home, sweet home at last. Back where we started.

HILDA

I was awake. I didn't need the Billy Cotton. We're not right back where we started. We're on the other side of the road and facing the other way.

FRED

And if time had stood still while we're gone, we'd be meeting ourselves coming back. That sounds like our lives in a nutshell.

HILDA

It won't be sweet at home either. The driver didn't stop at the services, did he? We'll get some *Heroes* at the shop tomorrow and tell Jason they came from Bowness.

DOREEN

He's clever. I bet he'll be able to tell. Hurry up, I'm dying for a wee.

HILDA

We've all had too much excitement for one day. So
am I. It were a reet good day out though, weren't
it, as our Dad would have said. Can we get those
robbers back up there again for next year's trip?

FRED

They'll still be inside. There might not be a next
year for us. This is probably our swansong. Next
stop the graveyard.

DOREEN

It's being so miserable that keeps him happy.

HILDA

No, it's being so miserable that keeps him miserable.
And the rest of us.

Cue Closing Music.

So, apologies from me, Bob Swarbrick if I've made you miserable
without any good reason. Somehow, what eclipsed my region, my
social class, my religion won't let their death throes be told, the
future having no use for them. The cleft in the Rock of Ages has
been filled with Polyfilla. So, when the apologetics have been written
by real novelists, when the false distinctions have been analysed by
sociologists, when the spurious equations have been formulated by

scientists, I doubt if they'll have managed to say any more.

Richard rang me up yesterday to wish us a Merry Christmas and he gave me his views on this book.

"It's spot-on the way I feel, Bob. It's not a young person's book, though. Don't let anyone see it before they're seventy, and on borrowed time. There's no need to know before then. Let our kids remember us as good fathers and bad comedians."

Life is a comedy That should have been the mood of this book. Richard doesn't seem to think Wendy and I have achieved that. But all will be clear, and we'll all be laughing when God is all in all.

As Martin said to Mrs Luther on a crowded Worms tram on his way to the Diet: "Here I stand. I can do no other."

I'll more than take Richard's advice. I'll finish it off tonight and then throw it away in the morning. That's if I can bear to. It would be easy to chuck my stuff. But Wendy's? I'm not so sure about that.

Postscript

2036

I can't call this addendum to the manuscript a Book, because it's not part of the story and it won't last long. This is Helen Shackleton writing. A plague did indeed come almost immediately, the coronavirus, making Brexit superfluous, but fortunately none of the characters from this tale were taken. Bob didn't feel the need to return to the text to tell this tale. I imagine that, with his young family, he was trying not to notice the four horsemen on his back lawn. The Last Judgement is still to come, though Richard and Bob have since both gone to meet their maker. Bob popped his clogs suddenly on Christmas Day 2025, and my Richard (I think that, even as a southerner, I'm allowed the personal pronoun for the man I loved) died a couple of years ago. It was the cancer that got him, the pain of which he bore with equanimity. He seemed at peace with himself in his very last moments.

In his indecision, after he'd tidied it up, Bob sent this manuscript to Richard and me, specifically asking me, as the one most likely to live the longest, to decide if there was a right time to pass it on to his family. Personally, I think the ears of youth were well capable of hearing this and laughing when it was written. It wasn't closing time for their generation. But I've held back until now just to be sure.

Bob's family and my family are now the same thing. At Richard's funeral, James and Alice as a young woman met again after these many years. They've tied the knot, marrying at St Chad's church. Alice is expecting. I can't begin to imagine how the present day and the past combine in both their memories, particularly Alice's as she perhaps went through childhood and University years both knowing and not knowing the future. She'll have to tell you herself. But it seemed right and proper that on the day before the wedding ceremony they walked me round the graveyard where this story started.

It's like, as a Shackleton, I'm also co-opted into the Swarbrick clan. Bob and Richard have grafted a story on to their family history which I'm part of, like it or not. I mustn't be the reason for that circle to be broken.

Kieron and Maddie, still together and living in London, were among the guests at the wedding. They'd had a son, Daniel, only a year after they'd married and before they'd moved south. Bethany and Daniel are now well into their teens, making good educational progress at independent schools. I learnt all this from Maddie, talking loudly to James, though mainly for my benefit, about her world of North London media parties. I was in conversation in a neighbouring group and affecting not to be listening to her. She's become almost the archetype of North London middle-class, even speaking with little trace of her Fylde accent. I would have expected for her to be partnered with a woman again by now, so clearly what appeared to be her physical preference in times past, but the move south and the company she keeps seem to have served as an effective vaginectomy for both types of partner. I suppose that, after such a chaotic start to her life and having explored most options already, the only act of free will open to her is to be conventional. Although, in the sort of paradox Richard would have found amusing, if that's the reason, then there's no free will attaching to it.

She and Kieron have had no further children after Daniel. She displayed no fresh bile towards me, indeed, although guarded, she was friendly. Maybe the move to London has also worked as the lobotomy that Wendy thought it would take to civilise her. She did say to me in an aside later that life would have been more soulful if she'd picked James, presumably aware of how she'd come across. She's still teaching philosophy and religion, at Bethany's school, not finding anything further that she wanted to write after her successful first novel. I got the impression from her hardened face that there aren't many illusions in the story of her life that she's telling herself. She's no longer in the market for imagery, if she ever really was. It feels more like she knows what it's all meant and that the only way out is to raise a resigned, white flag against her own nature. She hasn't broken her own heart, as Sophie expected her to do, nor Kieron's. So, perhaps Bob is still acting as her guardian angel or, more fancifully, maybe it's the unborn brother she once nearly had who is protecting her.

Lucy hasn't changed much. Old habits die hard. Bill died not long after Bob, an inevitable consequence of food and alcohol intake beyond his substantial capacity. All credit to her, she did give him a cheerful and eventful last episode in his life. She's been foot free and fancy loose since but formed no further strong attachment. She flirted outrageously with anything in trousers at the wedding, young and old alike, but it felt like she was just going through the motions. She knows that she too has had her day. Her son, John-Paul, is taking a year's break before University, at a meditation centre in Kerala. I imagine that his heritage and his upbringing have given him much to think about.

I was even invited to Ruth's wedding a couple of months ago, for a second foray to the north. If anyone deserves late life happiness, it's her. She seems to have found a very pleasant and erudite, if somewhat elderly, gentleman.

Alice's younger brother, Richie, has written a family history of all that happened before he was born, in the form of a novel, which he has called *Where's Sailor Jack?* That title is in honour of his paternal grandfather. The events described in this manuscript were only touched on lightly in that book, as his sources were of the years prior to this period. He gave me a copy of his book at the wedding. I have to say that he's done an amazing job in understanding how things were back then. I remember them as if they happened yesterday. I told him all about this book by Wendy and Bob which I'm now going to send to all family members. I hope he and Alice will love such a poignant reminder of their childhood. I think the two books make a pair. Sadly, *No Precedent* also makes it only too clear how alienating old age can be. Richard was right about that. That's what I'm about to face. It's the old, not the young, who most need protecting from this book's contents.

If the four horsemen haven't come back again, Richie will perhaps want to write a new history in another fifty years when he's nearer the end than the beginning. It's a shame that I won't be around to read it. I'd like to know how they'll all get on. I'm the outsider of the family no more. There's no precedence in an unbroken circle.

Printed in Poland
by Amazon Fulfillment
Poland Sp. z o.o., Wrocław

58882842R00188